A Lady of

Spirit

A steampunk adventure novel
Magnificent Devices Book Six

Shelley Adina

Moonshell
Books

Moonshell Books, Inc.
www.moonshellbooks.com

This is a work of fiction. Names, characters, places, and incidents are a product of the author's imagination. Locales and public names are sometimes used for atmospheric purposes. Any resemblance to actual people, living or dead, or to businesses, companies, events, institutions, or locales is completely coincidental.

Book Layout ©2013 BookDesignTemplates.com
Art by Claudia McKinney at phatpuppyart.com
Images from Shutterstock.com, used under license
Design by Kalen O'Donnell
Author font by Anthony Piraino at OneButtonMouse.com
"Neptune's Maid" lyrics ©2014 Shelley Adina Bates, music ©2014 JR Shanty Co. All rights reserved.

A Lady of Spirit / Shelley Adina—1st ed.
ISBN 978-1-939087-15-7

For Aleta Pardalis
a lady of spirit—and exquisite taste

Grateful thanks to Julianne and Richard of
JR Shanty Co for bringing "Neptune's Maid"
to life in music

and to

Julie H. Ferguson,
Beacon Literary Services, and
James S. Ferguson, 3rd Hand Inc., for their
knowledge of undersea zeppelins

1

This business of names—carrying one, marrying one, burying one—was a puzzle, and no mistake.

From her seat in the transept of St. Mary's Church, hard by Cadogan Square and the edifice in which the bride had been christened, Maggie watched as Emilie Fragonard paced up the aisle on the arm of her father. Though she was swathed in a veil that stretched away behind her for twenty feet, it was sheer enough that one could take in the splendor of her Worth gown, said to have been sent from Paris at enough expense to feed and house an English village for a year.

Maggie rather doubted that. Emilie was not that sort of girl, and while her wedding dress of cream Duch-

esse satin was indeed a marvel of embroidery and tucking and lace, it was more likely the work of loving
hands—and an extremely close eye on the latest fashion
plates from Monsieur Worth's studio.

Behind the bride, carrying a basket of salmon-
colored roses and maidenhair fern, came her chief
bridesmaid, Lady Claire Trevelyan, upon whose inclu-
sion the former had insisted. Following her were eleven
girls of appropriate age and social standing, upon whom
the bride's mother had insisted.

"Doesn't the Lady look fine!" Maggie whispered to
Lizzie seated next to her, whom she still—stubbornly,
against all evidence to the contrary—called *sister*.

Lizzie nodded, her keen green eyes alight with admiration. "Emilie kept her promise. No pink. That
Wedgewood blue sets off the Lady's auburn hair perfectly."

Mr. Andrew Malvern, on Lizzie's other side, turned
from his rapt contemplation of the chief bridesmaid to
lift an eyebrow at the girls—an indication that they
should stop whispering and show their respect for both
the occasion and the aforesaid edifice.

Maggie stifled the urge to apologize. He would have
the rest of the service and the entirety of the wedding
breakfast to make calf's eyes at Claire, whereas comments upon one's impressions of pretty dresses were
only appropriate during that first ephemeral moment.

*Oh, stop it. You're only making a nuisance of your-
self so you don't have to think about what happens tomorrow.*

Tomorrow, when this business of names might actually have to be wrestled with.

A LADY OF SPIRIT

"Dearly beloved, we are gathered together here in the sight of God, and in the face of this congregation, to join together this man and this woman in holy matrimony ..."

Because it was a simple fact that the Lady had a name, on the occasions—like the present one—when she chose to use it. Lizzie had a name to which she was entitled. Even Snouts and Jake had a name, though the occasions on which she'd ever heard it could be counted upon the fingers of one hand. Maggie alone bore a name to which she was *not* entitled, a discovery that she and Lizzie had made only a few weeks ago.

Upon their graduation from the lycee in Munich that they had been attending while Lady Claire completed her engineering degree, Lizzie had met a man called Charles Seacombe, a gentleman of affairs who had become her patron, and who was ultimately revealed as her father. Lizzie had been happy to learn she had a half-brother, Claude, by Charles's first wife. Her happiness had been crushed when their father had been unmasked as Charles de Maupassant—traitor, anarchist, and would-be murderer of two members of the royal family, including the heir to the throne ... and Maggie and Lizzie themselves.

"If any man present knows of an impediment to the union of Emilie Fragonard and Peter Livingston, Lord Selwyn, I charge you to declare it now."

As street sparrows years ago, when they bothered to think about names at all, the girls had remembered theirs to be de Maupassant—which on the tongues of the five-year-old ragamuffins they had been, had become "Mopsie." The Mopsies they were and the Mopsies they had remained until they had come under the care of the Lady and had had to be registered in a proper school.

But neither of them cared now to take the name of a traitor. Claude, who along with his father, had changed his name to Seacombe in order for there to be a male heir for the shipping company belonging to his late stepmother's family, saw no reason why they should not change theirs, too. Lizzie quite agreed. But when the girls returned to Munich and changed their registrations at school in the fall, Maggie still did not know what name she would write on the form.

"Wilt thou have this woman to thy wedded wife, to live together after God's ordinance in the holy estate of matrimony? Wilt thou love her, comfort her, honor, and keep her in sickness and in health; and, forsaking all other, keep thee only unto her, so long as ye both shall live?"

Which was worse—keeping a traitor's name or one you weren't entitled to in the eyes of the law? For the ugly truth was that Maggie didn't know who her father was. At least Lizzie knew, though as she'd tell you herself, she'd rather not, thank you very much. All Maggie knew was that Lizzie's mother Elaine and her own mother Catherine had been sisters.

Something had happened to Catherine that resulted in Maggie's birth during the same week as Lizzie's. Something that no one knew ... or was willing to speak of. Something that Maggie was determined to find out on their trip down to Cornwall tomorrow.

"I, Emilie, take thee, Peter, to my wedded husband, to have and to hold from this day forward, for better for worse, for richer for poorer, in sickness and in health, to love, cherish, and to obey, till death us do part, according to God's holy ordinance; and thereto I give thee my troth."

Standing at Emilie's left, the basket of roses at her feet so that she could hold Emilie's enormous bouquet with both hands, the Lady combed the crowd until she located Lizzie and Maggie in the transept. Her expression softened with love and Maggie put both love and encouragement into her return smile. *Buck up—only a little while longer.*

Mr. Malvern's shoulders rose and fell in what looked suspiciously like a sigh.

"Forasmuch as Peter and Emilie have consented together in holy wedlock, and have witnessed the same before God and this company, and thereto have given and pledged their troth either to other, and have declared the same by giving and receiving of a ring, and by joining of hands; I pronounce that they be man and wife together, in the name of the Father, and of the Son, and of the Holy Ghost."

"Thank heaven," Maggie distinctly heard from the bride's side of the church.

The Lady compressed her lips in an effort to maintain the gravity the occasion warranted, but when the groom bent his lanky form and bestowed a tender kiss upon the new Lady Selwyn, her eyes took on the quiet satisfaction and happiness of a woman who was truly glad for her friend's good fortune.

The fact that the title of Lady Selwyn had once nearly been Claire's had not escaped the attention of many in the church. But Maggie knew all too well that the Lady was well rid of it—and of the man who would have bestowed it upon her.

The bride and groom practically floated into the vestibule to sign the parish register. When they reappeared, Lady Selwyn was proudly wearing the small but ancient tiara that was now hers by right. Claire shepherded the rest of the bridesmaids down the length of the aisle after the couple, and was decanted onto the church steps where the carriages waited.

Maggie drew a deep breath. "Well, that's done, and I hope they will be very happy."

She and Lizzie took Mr. Malvern's proffered arms and were escorted in style out the side doors for the short walk across the square to the Fragonard house.

"I am sure they will," Mr. Malvern said. "From what Claire says, I understand they have waited patiently for this day, and under Mr. Liv—I mean, Lord Selwyn's good management, they even have a home to go to in the country."

"With all this happiness and patience in the air," Lizzie said innocently, "it would not surprise me to see more than one engagement blossom while it is still summer."

But if she had hoped that Mr. Malvern might smile at such a joke, she was gravely disappointed. His pleasant expression never faded, but some of its animation did, and the corners of his eyes pinched in a way that struck Maggie's heart.

"She meant to cheer you, Mr. Malvern," Maggie said softly. "Please don't think any more of it."

Too late, Lizzie realized that teasing could hurt a person just as effectively as a direct assault. "Oh, Mr. Malvern, I didn't mean—I hope you won't—"

"It's all right, girls," he said gently. "It's perfectly obvious to everyone but Claire that my feelings have not changed since our adventures in the Canadas five years ago. But I say, does she not look glorious in that blue dress?"

The carriage bearing the bride and groom clattered past, drawn by two gray horses, and followed by several more containing Lady Claire and the bevy of bridesmaids. "Why do they insist on horse-drawn carriages?" Lizzie wondered aloud. "Only Bloods drive them any more. Do they *want* to look hopelessly behind the times?"

"They want to look as though they are above the times—as though the times do not matter," Mr. Malvern observed. "However, I suspect that, despite the family carriage, Lord and Lady Selwyn do not harbor such old-fashioned views. I have it on good authority that they will be taking their wedding tour of the Lakes in a spanking new six-piston Obermeister steam landau."

But Maggie was not to be distracted by talk of vehicles. She could not bear that her sister might have hurt his feelings a moment ago, after all he had done for them, and if it lay in her power, she would make it right.

"Do not despair about the Lady, Mr. Malvern," she said, squeezing his arm. "Captain Hollys asked her three times, you know. You still have a chance."

"Yes, but the answer the third time was just the same as the first, from what I understand," he replied with a hint of gloom. "At least, it must have been, since I have observed in the society pages lately that he is cutting quite a swath."

"I'd say your chances were even better, then," Lizzie told him. "Why would she turn down such a brave man—and a baronet to boot—unless her heart were already engaged elsewhere?"

"What, with Zeppelin airships?"

"No," Lizzie said in a tone that implied he was being a poultice when she was trying to be serious and grown-up. "With a gentleman who has backed her up from the first, and who she has said herself is her intellectual equal in every way."

Maggie felt the jolt of his surprise as though the Lady had fired her lightning rifle past his ear. "She said that?"

"She did," Maggie confirmed. "It's none of our business, sir, but really, you ought to try again."

He patted her gloved hand lying upon the sleeve of his morning jacket. "I know your intentions are good, Maggie, but if a man proposes once and the lady declines to reply, then he ought to be satisfied that she knows her mind. Particularly the lady we are discussing behind her back."

But that had been five years ago. Had he really not tried again since? Then again, anyone observing Captain Hollys's courtship would have done the proper thing and stood back, once he knew how the land lay.

Maggie exchanged a glance with Lizzie. How lucky for him that they had not so much practice as he had in doing the proper thing.

2

The Fragonards, having realized that with only one daughter they would have only a single chance to pay off a decade of social debts, had laid on a spread of mammoth proportions.

"Ices," said Maggie on a long sigh of satisfaction after demolishing a raspberry one and following it with lemon coconut. "I adore ices—particularly for breakfast."

"That leaves all the profiteroles for me, then," Lizzie told her, measuring the succulent pyramid in the middle of the dessert table with a calculating eye. "No wonder we get on so well."

"Don't even think of pulling one out of the bottom," Maggie warned her. "I think they're all stuck to one another. Imagine the mess."

"Imagine the people who wouldn't see me filling my pockets."

"Your pretty suit has no pockets."

"More's the pity," Lizzie said with regret. "You did remind Claude that he's to be at Wilton Crescent tomorrow morning at eight, didn't you?"

"I sent a note, and I'm sure you did, too. Don't fret, Liz. He'll come. He might forget his hat, his cane, and his own name, but if there is breakfast involved before a journey, he won't miss it. Besides, Lewis is at the club tonight."

Which settled it. Whilst he was in Town, Claude was staying at the Gaius Club, which unbeknownst to the raffish young Blood gentlemen who gambled there, was owned and operated by their fellow former alley mouse, Lewis Protheroe, who also acted as the Lady's secretary. No one had told Claude that the unprepossessing young man who managed the Lady's correspondence was the same person as the one who cleared away dishes at the club and served the gentlemen their Caledonian whiskey.

No one noticed Lewis. Hardly anyone spoke to him. Which was why he was quietly building an empire on the house winnings, to say nothing of the information flowing as freely as the liquor in its smoky rooms.

The bride and groom cut the cake, and plates were handed round to all the guests. Then Emilie retired with her bridesmaids to change into her traveling costume.

When she emerged in a practical brown suit with beautiful velvet and crocheted lace trim adorning the jacket, and a saucy hat of roses, tulle, and feathers that did not clash with her spectacles in the least, Claire joined the girls.

> *"The ring for marriage within a year;*
> *The penny is for wealth, my dear;*
> *The thimble for old maid or bachelor born;*
> *The button for sweethearts all forlorn. "*

She opened her hand. "Look what was in my piece of the bride's cake."

It was a small tin ring.

"Lady," Maggie breathed. "Do you think the rhyme will come true?"

The Lady laughed. "I hardly think so, darling. I am as yet unspoken for and one needs at least a year to plan what Alice calls a *shindig* like this."

"If you'd stop refusing proposals, Lady, it might have a chance to come true," Lizzie said rather peevishly. Maggie chalked it up to the profiteroles and a corset that was too snug as a consequence.

But the Lady only gazed at her, as if wondering where that had come from. "I do not refuse them willynilly, Lizzie. Would you have wanted me to be Princess Frog-Face?"

Even Maggie could not stifle a giggle at the thought of the Kaiser's nephew, whose unfortunate looks and inability to believe himself refused had earned him Lizzie's undying scorn.

"No," Lizzie admitted. "But there would be nothing wrong with being Lady Hollys."

But at this, Claire's face paled and turned so bleak that Lizzie touched the hand that still held the little ring. "I'm sorry, Lady. I didn't mean it. Or I did, but I shouldn't have said so."

"You know my feelings on that subject," Claire whispered. "Ian is a good man and does not deserve to have his perfectly honorable name bandied about in this manner."

Which did absolutely nothing to explain why she had declined the privilege of bearing it. Maggie had overheard his first proposal herself, and she still didn't understand why the Lady had refused him.

But then, she didn't understand why poor Mr. Malvern didn't try again, either.

In fact, despite having reached the age of sixteen, there were simply too many things in this world that Maggie could not decipher. It was enough to make a girl want to go home to the back garden and find one of Rosie the chicken's many progeny to cuddle.

"Claire, how perfectly lovely to see you."

The Lady turned and Maggie was surprised to see her smile at the young woman dressed in the next best thing to a ballgown when it was barely one o'clock in the afternoon. The other woman laid a languid hand upon her lacy breast so that both of them could take in the splendor of the enormous diamond and thick gold wedding band upon it.

"Why, Catherine," Claire said. "It has been an age. I see you are married—how wonderful. Belated felicitations. This is my ward, Margaret Seacombe. Maggie, this is an old schoolmate of mine. Lady Catherine Montrose, now …?"

"Mrs. David Haliburton." The woman's overbite gave her a lisp. "But Claire, I see no rings upon your hands save that peculiar metal one. Twenty-five is the first corner, you know. You'd better hurry up."

Maggie resisted the urge to stamp on the nasty mort's pink slipper, but the Lady appeared unperturbed. Instead, she examined the steel ring upon the smallest finger of her right hand with pride.

"This is an engineer's ring. I received my degree from the University of Bavaria, you know, and will be joining the Zeppelin Airship Works next month as a developer of new airship technologies."

Mrs. Haliburton's rather bland features took on an expression of horror. "You will be working for your living?"

Maggie could keep silent no longer. "Lady Claire chooses to advance human knowledge in that field—as her close friend the Empress of Prussia can attest."

"Really."

"Maggie, darling, you mustn't take the Empress's name in vain. You know how she hates that."

"Well, she would. And did, that day you sailed in the prototype together."

"That is very true, but—"

"Come, Claire, engineer or not, we must have you introduced," Mrs. Haliburton said impatiently, as if talk of the Empress made her wish to change the subject. "Mr. Haliburton has several friends here among the company who would be delighted to meet you, despite your, er, education."

"How very kind of you. Do you see much of Julia Wellesley—I mean, Lady Mount-Batting?"

"Oh, yes. We are still very close, you know. There she is, over there."

She waved a hand in the direction of another young woman, who was so fashionably dressed and corseted it was a wonder she could breathe. Her brown curls were piled upon her head under an afterthought of a hat, and the ruffled train of her skirt seemed to engulf the feet of the young man with whom she was conversing.

Conversing in a rather more intimate manner than one typically did with a man who was not one's husband.

"Is that her brother?" Lady Claire inquired.

"Oh, no, that's Justin Knight, one of her intimate circle. The Duke of Warrington's heir, you know. Julia has many admirers. It's the fashion these days to have beaux. It makes parties such fun."

"But she's married," Maggie blurted.

Catherine gave her the kind of look that said *children should be seen and not heard.* "You cannot be expected to understand, dear. You are very young, and have been traveling in foreign parts."

The Lady laid a cool hand upon Maggie's sleeve. "It was lovely to see you, Catherine. Do give my greetings to Mr. Haliburton."

And they strolled away before Maggie could do something that would put a proper bend in the woman's snooty snout. Oh, she would not actually have done anything to embarrass her guardian, but my goodness, surely some small gesture—a tiny accident with a glass of punch, say—would be appropriate under the circumstances?

She and Lizzie had not had much practice in being condescended to. How did the Lady bear being spoken to in that way? Did she simply not care? Was she above such things, or did she feel them as keenly as Maggie did and was simply better at hiding it?

When she found Lizzie several minutes later and got these questions off her chest, Lizzie gazed thoughtfully into the distance, where Mr. Malvern was doing his best to converse with a young lady. He had rather an air of *once more into the breach* about him, as though he had assigned himself a task and was going to perform it though it killed him.

"We must get them alone in a room, Mags," Lizzie finally said. "It's a wedding, innit, and Mr. Malvern already has courtship on his mind. We must simply give him an opportunity to court the Lady instead of who-ever that is."

"How are we going to do that? We can't just collar them and push them into a closet. And most of these rooms have people in them."

"You're going to find an empty room and keep people out of it until I can get both Mr. Malvern and the Lady in. I was just in the powder room, and there is no one in Mr. Fragonard's study next door. You go hold the fort, and I'll tell Mr. Malvern the Lady wants to speak with him privately. We'll have no trouble with him—and I'll think of something to tell her."

It was a pretty straightforward plan despite having been concocted in two seconds. "Right. And while you fetch the Lady, I'll keep him occupied."

"Done."

Maggie found the study with no trouble. It was at the back of the house and smelled of wax and paper and leather furniture. She closed the door, then arranged herself upon the leather sofa with a wrist over her eyes, in case anyone should look in.

When the door opened and closed a moment later and she heard the lock turn, she lowered her arm. "Mr. Malvern, I'm afraid I—" She stopped. "I beg your pardon, I was expecting someone else."

"Clearly," said the dashing young man who was the son of the Duke of Something-or-other. "And I was expecting Julia. What an interesting situation."

"I'm sorry, but my guardian will be here at any moment, and I do not feel well," Maggie said in her best plaintive tones. "Perhaps you might fetch me a glass of water?"

"In a moment. You don't look ill to me. Sure you weren't waiting for someone?"

"My guardian."

"No, you weren't. Come on, you can tell me. A pretty little thing like you? Well, whoever he is, he'll have to get past me first." He advanced upon the sofa, and Maggie sat up, the first stirrings of alarm fluttering in her breast.

"I'm Justin. What's your name?"

"Margaret."

"Who's your guardian?"

"Lady Claire Trevelyan."

But instead of backing off like any sensible cove at the Lady's name, he laughed. "Oh, I've heard of you lot. Julia's told me. Terribly entertaining, dashing about the world with the Dunsmuirs and getting up a *fascinating* reputation. I daresay once you've kissed an Injun or two you'd be glad to have a kiss from a gentleman, wouldn't you?"

Maggie hardly knew which outrageous statement to take on first. Or maybe it didn't matter. The most urgent concern was getting up off this sofa before he trapped her on it.

She slid under his arm and made sure her shoulder caught him right in the solar plexus as she pushed to her feet. He sat down upon the sofa with a suddenness that would have caused any other man to think more carefully about his next actions.

But apparently careful thought was not Justin Knight's forte.

He rose, straightening his wine-colored brocade waistcoat. "A young lady of spirit, are you? Providential, what? I like 'em with a bit of spunk. Come here, darling. Just one kiss, that's all I want. When was the last time you were kissed by the son of a duke?"

"Tuesday," Maggie lied breathlessly. She'd never been kissed, and there was no way on God's green that this idiot was going to be her first.

"At Lady Weatherley's ball, hmm? So you've got some experience, then. All right, I'll play the game—you be the mouse, and I'll be the cat."

He advanced once more, and Maggie spread her feet slightly, her weight evenly balanced and slightly forward. With both hands, she gathered her skirts as though preparing to run again, and feinted with a glance to the right.

He lunged to intercept her, and when his weight was all on one leg, she kicked the load-bearing knee as hard as she could.

With an incoherent howl, he fell to the other knee. She brought one elbow down on the back of his neck with all the force she had, and he sprawled on the

Turkish carpet, his chin bouncing off it hard enough to make his teeth clack.

A knock sounded on the door. "Maggie?" Mr. Malvern said. "It's Andrew Malvern. Lizzie says you're not feeling well."

Justin Knight groaned and attempted to get up. Maggie stepped on his back and flattened him once more as all the breath was pushed out of his lungs. She dropped her skirts decorously, crossed the room, and unlocked the door to let Mr. Malvern in.

He took in the scene in an instant. "Good heavens. What happened here?"

"Tripped on the bloody rug," the gentleman mumbled, attempting to rise. Blood trickled from the corner of his mouth. Ah. Apparently he had bitten his tongue.

What a pity he hadn't done so in a metaphorical sense before he told such a bold-faced lie. He obviously expected her to go along with it to save them both face, but she had no interest in allowing him to get away with such behavior for the sake of … what? His standing in society? Hers?

"He attempted to assault me," Maggie said. "I dissuaded him as Mr. Yau taught us on *Lady Lucy*."

"I see that you have. Well done, Maggie. And now I shall do my part to clear away this situation by taking out the rubbish."

He opened the French doors and stalked back to Justin Knight, who had managed to stand. "If I catch you laying a finger on a young lady—*any* young lady— again, this is the least you can expect, you ruffian."

He grasped the back of the young man's coat and the waistband of his trousers, and tossed him bodily through the window. The heir of the Duke of Whatsis landed flat on his face in the flowerbed, mowing down a bank of phlox and frightening two doves up into the trees.

The gardeners had just watered the gardens so that the flowers would be at their freshest for the wedding reception. When Justin Knight rose, his face, hands, chest, and trousers were covered in sticky wet soil.

"You damnable wretch!" he shouted. "You'll be sorry for this! You'll—"

Mr. Malvern closed the doors in his face and locked them, leaving the other man with no choice except to return to the house via either the servants' entrance or the front door, both of which would ensure his complete mortification.

Maggie smiled as he took the third option. He vaulted over the garden wall and took himself off, and good riddance, too.

"Are you sure you're all right, Maggie?" Mr. Malvern said, laying his hands on her shoulders and examining her for damage. "He didn't hurt you, did he?"

"No. He wanted a kiss, but I was not prepared to give him one."

"I am glad to hear it. His reputation is not one I'd be prepared to have associated with you."

"Maggie? Andrew?" The Lady stepped into the study and glanced from one to the other, then to the rug, which was rucked up, and a small occasional table, which had been knocked over. "What has happened?"

"It's all right, Claire," Andrew told her, releasing Maggie after a brief hug. "Justin Knight made a poor assumption about our girl here, and she corrected him as Mr. Yau taught her."

"Did she?" The Lady's face cleared and a sunny smile dawned upon it. "Well done. Has he gone?"

"He needed to change his clothes and get some medical attention, so yes."

"Even better." She hugged Maggie in her turn, and Maggie wrapped her arms around her waist, pressing her nose into the crook of the Lady's shoulder. The lace of her high collar felt scratchy upon her cheek. Claire's perfume warmed her gently, that mix of roses and cinnamon that had come to mean safety. Security. Approval and love.

"What were you doing in here in the first place, my darling?" the Lady asked softly. "Lizzie said you didn't feel well?"

The moment for courtship had passed, and to be honest, Maggie felt a little queasy now that the danger had been ejected from the room. So she nodded.

The Lady wasted no time. "Emilie and Peter have gone, so there is no reason for us to stay, either. Andrew, if you would be so kind as to begin the landau's ignition sequence, I will collect our party and meet you outside."

So their plans had come to nothing. But despite that, Maggie took heart. For Mr. Malvern had come to her aid, and the Lady had treated him as though he was one of the family. That had to count for something.

3

"Up ship!" the Lady called out of the open hatch, and the ground crew—including Lewis and Snouts, who had come to see them off—released the ropes that tethered *Athena* and *Victory* to the airfield in Vauxhall Gardens.

The property had once been their home before Toll Cottage had burned to the ground. But now there was a cluster of snug little homes that housed the families of the men who ran the airfield for the Lady. Since it was the only airfield on the south bank, tolls for airships had become much more lucrative than tolls for boats had once been. And upriver, their nearest neighbor, the Morton Glass Works, ran efficiently under the owner-ship of Snouts—beg his pardon, Mr. Stephen

McTavish—using modern steam and automaton technologies that did not spew chemicals into the river and spoil the swimming for the children.

In *Victory*'s fanciful gondola, with its baroque trim painted gold, Lieutenant Thomas Terwilliger manned the engines, since unlike *Athena*, the airship had to be manually controlled and required a crew. And assisting him was Lizzie, the reason for which Maggie was quite sure the Lady did not know. Lizzie had not as yet confided in either of them, but Maggie had eyes in her head. From her post at the map table, she had observed Lizzie's gaze wander to their former squat-mate more than once that morning, to say nothing of the way he had squeezed her hands in greeting with rather more than brotherly enthusiasm.

Lizzie and Tigg were sweet on each other. Who'd have thought?

Though Maggie could hardly discount the truth— Tigg had grown into a handsome young man, his coffee-colored skin smooth and unblemished, his khaki uniform setting it off in a way that a girl might find most attractive. His brown eyes saw much more than a person often wanted them to, and the mind behind them was so sharp that when Tigg was in port, Mr. Malvern appreciated his help and advice in the laboratory he maintained in Orpington Close.

However, he was not in port very much. Tigg served aboard *Lady Lucy*, the personal flagship of the Dunsmuir family, and as often as not was in the air on his way to the Canadas, or the Antipodes, or some secret location on Lady Dunsmuir's business for the Queen. Aeronauts on private ships were all serving members of the Royal Aeronautic Corps, and should the country declare war, were all required to report to the Admiralty for duty and deployment. But in their glorious Queen's lengthy reign, there had only been minor skirmishes in the Balkans and the subcontinent of Hind, in protection of Her Majesty's economic interests there. In Maggie's lifetime, the closest they had come to war was the annual day of remembrance for fallen airships in November.

The only reason Tigg was with their party now and not aboard *Lady Lucy* was because the Dunsmuirs were enjoying a shooting holiday in Scotland with the Prince of Wales. Tigg had two weeks of ground leave, and instead of the myriad things he might have done or enjoyed on a lieutenant's pay, he had chosen to come with them to Penzance.

Maggie had not made up her mind whether it was for their protection or simply for friendship. But either way, this would be interesting.

When Windsor Castle had floated away beneath the two ships and they were officially out of London air space, Maggie saw *Athena* pull away slightly. "Full speed ahead, *Victory*," she called back to Tigg.

She turned her attention to the charts on the navigation table. Assisting her was Holly, a reddish-gold hen who took after her mother Rosie in both looks and temperament. She said to Claude, who was manning the helm, "Bear west southwest until we pass the airfield at Dartmoor, and then two points south to Penzance."

Tigg called, "Aren't Lady Claire and Mr. Malvern going to put down at Gwynn Place beforehand?"

"No, she seems to be as anxious to meet our grandparents as we are. They are to be guests at Seacombe House with us for three days." She removed Holly from the map, where the bird was pecking at the Channel Islands, and lifted her up to roost comfortably upon a bit of pipe. "Is that your understanding, too, Claude?"

Lizzie's half-brother was gently trying to convince Ivy, Holly's sister, who clearly hoped he might have a biscuit about his person, that he in fact did not.

He swept out an arm in an encompassing gesture much too extravagant for this time of the morning, and Ivy scuttled out of range. "They'll be ready and waiting with open arms, I'm sure. It feels like a perfect age since I was there—I'll be glad to see the old dears myself. I'm not related to them by blood, but they're still my stepmother's parents—and the only grandparents I've got." He peered out of the viewing port. "I say, that shabby vessel has quite the spring in her step. Best lay on the steam, old man."

Indeed, *Athena* was definitely increasing her lead. The Lady was always meaning to have *Athena* refurbished so it looked more like *Lady Lucy* or any other pleasure craft. But somehow *Athena* seemed to resist being made up like a society belle and remained exactly what she was—a lethal ship of war that looked deceptively plain in order to hide both her speed and her maneuverability, to say nothing of her capacity to carry and conceal weapons.

Sometimes Maggie suspected that the Lady felt such a kinship with her vessel that they were of one mind on the subject of a lady's capabilities.

The engines' pitch settled into a businesslike thrumming under Tigg's capable management, and Maggie bent her knees a little as the airship gained headway.

"The pigeons say the weather will be clear until noon, but there is a storm expected off the Channel late in the day," Tigg said, escorting Lizzie into the gondola. "We'll be there before it hits, I presume?"

"Yes indeed." Claude joined them at the table in front of the large viewing port. "It's a four-hour flight, so we'll be comfortably drinking tea before a raindrop hits the ground. I say, how do you read this lot, anyhow?"

Tigg looked rather amused. "It's a map, Claude. You just compare the lines—this river for instance. See it down there?"

Claude looked from one to the other and back again. "How do you know it's the same river?"

"Because there aren't any other rivers that big hereabouts," Lizzie told him. "It's the Thames, silly."

Claude passed an arm about her waist with easy affection. "You see why I needed a tutor in geography—and why I prevail upon my friends to fly with me," he said without a drop of compunction. "I'm no better on the ground. In Paris, if the Eiffel Tower wasn't there I'd be hopelessly lost all the time."

The giant iron structure was the largest mooring mast in France. Maggie fancied that most of the population used it to navigate, both on the ground and in the air.

"You're not going back right away, are you?" Lizzie gave him a squeeze in return. "I've barely got to know you. Please say you aren't."

"Not for a bit, old girl." He released her to stand at the viewing port, then started as he realized Holly was balanced upon the pipe over his head. "Deuced disconcerting, poultry popping up all about the place. No, classes don't begin at the Sorbonne until the second week in September, don't you know. Before I decamp for more fashionable climes and join Dolly and Cynthia and the others in Venice for one last romp, I count upon a good long visit." He glanced back at them. "As will you?"

Maggie nodded, wishing he would hug her with the same easy familiarity. But what was she to him? Only a step-cousin. And one he didn't know nearly as well as he knew Lizzie, who had spent more time in his company.

Maggie had grown up calling Lizzie *sister*. And now this young man, all arms and legs and slang and humor, was the only one who had the right to do so. It just didn't sit well—and Maggie was ashamed of herself for feeling that way.

"So that will be our plan, then," Claude said heartily. "Camp with the grands for a week or two and go clamming on the beach. Do a little velosurfing. Take a run up to Newquay to see how the undersea train is getting on—truly, Maggie, you'll love that."

"If you say so."

"Certainly we'll go," Lizzie told him. "Now that my memories have returned and I know why I had such a fear of both air and water, I believe I could face an undersea train with equanimity."

"But do you remember our grandparents, Lizzie?" Maggie asked curiously. For despite what they both knew of that dreadful afternoon eleven years ago when Lizzie's mother had died at her husband's hands, Maggie still had no memories of her own of that day, or of anything before that. It was an enormous blank that imagination had to fill in from the dream plates their cousin Evan Douglas had shown them at Colliford Castle, and from Lizzie's recounting of the tale.

Lizzie shook her head. "I'm sure we will when we see them, won't we? There will be something familiar, even though we were only five the last time we were all together."

It would be lovely to have something pleasant from her past come back to her. Maggie picked up Ivy and gave her a cuddle. Then maybe she could look forward, into the future.

4

The harbor serving the Cornish town of Penzance was third only to Southampton and Falmouth for importance in the steam shipping trade—and, as Claude said, "there are those who would dispute that second to the point of fisticuffs."

Athena and *Victory* floated over St. Michael's Mount, where an ancient castle hosted a contingent of aeronauts on permanent guard duty of the south coast. They had sent pigeons announcing their intent to land, and as they passed, the flag dipped in acknowledgement. The Mount could only be accessed on foot twice a day during the ebb tide. On a wide stone causeway, people far below walked to and from the village nestled around the castle. Maggie hoped that they would leave plenty of time to return—being caught in the middle of the channel when the tide came in was not a very appealing prospect.

At the airfield, a large multi-passenger conveyance was waiting, bearing the emblem of the Seacombe Steamship Company. The driver tipped his cap and he and a boy proceeded to load their luggage onto the roof of the vehicle. When Andrew and Tigg offered to help, he demurred.

"Mrs. Seacombe 'ud have my head, sirs, if I were to treat her guests in such a manner. You have a seat and we'll be on our way shortly."

Maggie secured the hens in their cage and took it into her lap for the journey. The driver pointed out the offices of the company down on the harbor, and as they circled to the opposite side, he pointed out the sights— the mayor's home, the high street, the market. Higher they climbed, and at last, where large homes and terraced town houses overlooked the sea without the inconvenience of commerce cluttering the view, they crested the hill. After passing through a park that set apart this property even from its peers, the conveyance hissed and huffed to a stop on the circular drive outside a stone mansion whose mullioned windows commanded a prospect of nearly the entire harbor and the Mount as well.

Clearly the Seacombes were persons of influence in Penzance. Maggie smoothed her skirts and wished she had done as Claude suggested, and taken a moment to re-pin her hair and change her jacket to the one that matched the skirt.

But it was too late now.

She took Lizzie's hand as they were ushered into the large, bright room that possessed the mullioned windows. And standing in front of the fireplace, in which a fire had been lit though the day was not cold, stood two people.

"Grandpere, Grandmere, it is so good to see you." Claude bounded across the thick Aubusson rug to shake hands, and then gave his grandmother a hug. "It is my great joy to present your granddaughters at last—my half-sister Elizabeth and her cousin Margaret."

Still holding hands, as they might have done when they were small, Maggie and Lizzie approached the older couple. He looked as though he might have been a sailor once, with ruddy skin and a fringe of beard that encircled his face like a paper frill around a ham. He was expensively dressed in a rich waistcoat and wool trousers, and a ruby pin adorned his cravat.

Maggie curtsied, tugging surreptitiously on Lizzie's hand so that she did, too.

"Nonsense, my dears. We are family." Mrs. Seacombe—Grandmother—came forward and hugged first Lizzie, then Maggie. She was barely taller than both of them, and so slender that she did not need a corset— though Maggie felt its stiffness in her rigid posture. Her gray hair was arranged in a way that had been fashionable several years before, with a Psyche knot high on the head and curls framing the face. Her gown was fine lavender watered silk, with a cascade of Brussels lace down the breast held in place by a brooch winking with tawny diamonds.

Lady Davina Dunsmuir possessed a parure and tiara made of very similar diamonds, dug from the ground in the far north of the Canadas. Could these have come from the Firstwater Mine as well?

Their grandmother stepped back, still holding Lizzie's hands. "You have Elaine's eyes. Her father's eyes."

Maggie ventured a glance at her grandfather to see that he did indeed have green eyes, though they were faded now, perhaps from many years of looking out to sea.

"Welcome, my dear," Grandmother went on. "I cannot tell you what it meant to us to know that you had survived the crash—or how devastated we have been at what we believed to be your loss. When I think of the years we could have had together …"

"Now, now, Demelza," Grandfather said gruffly. "That's water under the keel. Welcome, my dear. I hope you will make Seacombe House your home."

"Thank you, Grandfather. Your welcome means so much to us. But what of Maggie?" Lizzie asked eagerly. "Does she resemble her mother—my aunt Catherine? We know so little of her."

At last Grandmother's gaze made its reluctant way to Maggie. "Perhaps, about the mouth and chin. But her eyes, I am afraid, resemble those of no one in the family. Since we do not know—"

Who her father was, nor the color of his eyes.

Her lips closed with the finality dictated by propriety and she looked over Lizzie's shoulder, releasing her hands at last. "Will you introduce us to your friends?"

Claude introduced Lady Claire, Mr. Malvern, and Tigg.

"Trevelyan," Grandfather said, dragging his gaze from Tigg, who, after shaking hands, was standing at ease with his hands clasped behind his back. Since he had acted as engineer this morning, he was still in his flight uniform and polished boots—and a fine sight it was, Maggie thought with pride. "You are St. Ives's daughter, from Gwynn Place?"

"I am," the Lady said. "The present viscount is my brother, and my lady mother is now married to Sir Richard Jermyn, whose lands march with ours. I have been acting as guardian to Maggie and Lizzie for the past five years."

"So we understand," he said. "You have our gratitude—and sometime during your visit we hope to hear all that has passed in those five years, and before that."

"We will tell you as much as we can," the Lady said, smiling. "Though Mr. Malvern and I will not be trespassing upon your hospitality for more than a few days—I am most anxious to see my mother and little brothers, so we will be sure to conclude our tale before we lift on Wednesday."

"Come, won't you have some tea?" Grandmother waved toward the table set between the two sofas in front of the fire. "Howel, do put another log on the fire. I grow chilled when the flames are low." The tea service was silver, the cups of porcelain so thin and delicate that Maggie could practically see the firelight through it.

"What a pretty pattern," she said as Grandmother poured and she took it upon herself to hand the cups around. "What flower is this?"

"It is called a dogwood," Grandmother said a little stiffly. "A tree that grows in the Fifteen Colonies, I understand."

"Ah, that explains why it is unfamiliar." Maggie picked up the plate of sandwiches and offered the Lady one. "We have been in the Texican Territories and in the Canadas, but flowering trees were not a noticeable part of the landscape in either place."

"Elizabeth, what are your plans once your visit here is concluded?" Grandmother asked her.

Maggie handed the plate to Tigg to hide her chagrin at the snub. What was wrong with talking about flowering plants? She would have thought that their travels would have been of keen interest to her grandparents, after what Grandfather had just said. Or that horticulture might be, at the very least, considering the glory of the gardens around the house. But what did she know of the conversational habits of older people in society? Other than the Dunsmuirs and Count von Zeppelin, and her teachers at the *lycee*, she had not been exposed to it much at all.

Tigg took a sandwich and twinkled at her, as if to say, *Cheer up. None of us belongs in a room sipping tea, do we?*

No, they certainly did not. In fact, she'd rather be exploring about this house, or down on the strand crossing the causeway to the Mount. Or better yet, going to Gwynn Place with the Lady to visit Polgarth and the chickens.

She had been corresponding with Lewis over the last year or two on the subject of genetics in connection with their hen Rosie, of dearly beloved memory. It was Lewis's opinion that temperament and intelligence could be emphasized in a breeding program just as much as feathering and laying capacity, and if Holly and Ivy were any indication, Rosie's chicks seemed to bear this out. She wanted to discuss it with Polgarth, whose scientific breeding of the Buff Orpingtons at Gwynn Place was said to be legendary in this part of the country.

Perhaps that was what she ought to do—leave Lizzie here with Claude and Tigg and the grands, and go with the Lady.

A woman in a housekeeper's navy dress appeared in the doorway. "Excuse me, ma'am, but the footman wishes to know what is to be done with the poultry in the hall. It seems to have come in with the young ladies instead of going round to the kitchen." A squawk of alarm sounded from the front of the house. "I was not aware that you had changed the menus since this morning, ma'am. Did you order chicken for dinner?"

"No!" Maggie shot off the sofa, upending her teacup onto the carpet and staining the front of her skirt. "Holly and Ivy are not to be dinner! They are our companions."

Lizzie put down her cup and vanished out the door past the housekeeper, and presently her voice joined the indignant tones of Holly and Ivy, dressing down the unfortunate footman.

Slowly, Grandmother raised the quizzing glass on its chain about her neck to survey the chaos.

"Margaret, pick up your cup. Mrs. Penny, would you send in the maid to clean up this mess?"

"I am sorry for the misunderstanding," the Lady said to Grandmother as, scarlet with shame, Maggie obeyed. "I ought to have told someone that the birds were with us—I simply assumed they would go up to our rooms with the luggage. If it is more convenient, I can return them to *Athena*, where they will be quite comfortable."

"We're not in the habit of considering the comfort of farm animals," Grandfather said. His eyebrows were having trouble settling down with all the excitement. A maid scuttled in with cloths and a bucket, and began to sop up the spilled tea in the priceless carpet.

Who could have guessed that such a small cup could have held such a deluge? Maggie wished she could sink into the floor and disappear.

"Oh, but we are," Mr. Malvern told him, smiling. "Holly and Ivy are the progeny of a most extraordinary bird who shared our adventures across the ocean. You haven't lived, sir, until you have seen a hen sailing through the air in a hatbox attached to a dirigible, having narrowly escaped being eaten by sky pirates."

"A hen concealing twenty thousand pounds worth of diamonds beneath her feathers, to boot," added the Lady. "All thanks to the quick thinking of Lizzie and Maggie, who did not allow themselves to be captured, either."

His powers of speech deserted Grandfather entirely, and the eyebrows appeared frozen in the high position.

Grandmother, however, was made of sterner stuff. "Diamonds notwithstanding, chickens are meant to be eaten, not carried about as though they were Persian cats." The quizzing glass rose again as Lizzie came in bearing the cage, with both Holly and Ivy standing in some agitation not within it, but upon her shoulders. "Remove those birds at once, Elizabeth. I will not have them soiling the floors."

The maid looked alarmed, and slipped out, presumably before she was called upon to clean that up, too.

"Of course, Grandmother. They needed a moment's soothing, that's all." Lizzie slipped a gentle hand under each bird's feet in turn, returned them to the cage, and set it upon the window seat, so that Holly and Ivy might look out upon the scenery.

"I meant remove them from the room."

Lizzie looked up in surprise. "They will not harm anything. The clasp is quite secure."

"Elizabeth, I do not argue, with you or anyone else. Obey me at once."

"But—"

"Come along, old thing, and I'll show you, Maggie, and the chickens to your rooms." Claude picked up the cage.

"Those birds are not to remain in this house."

Maggie dug in her heels. "But they're our companions. They go where we go."

"They may have done heretofore," Grandfather said with a glance at his wife. "I do not know what the custom is up at Gwynn Place, but here at Seacombe House, poultry belongs in the kitchen, cats belong in the warehouse, and dogs belong to other people. Please respect your grandmother's wishes."

Maggie was beginning to get the faintest glimmer of understanding as to why Lizzie's mother had been so eager to marry the first man who asked her. Had her own mother had the same experience? Had she run away? But what had happened to her that had resulted in Maggie's birth nine months later?

Or, as the Lady believed, had she fallen in love and it had ended unhappily?

"Don't worry about Holly and Ivy," the Lady said gently. "We do not wish to cause the household more work than six guests already do. Mr. Malvern and I will take them back to *Athena* this afternoon, where I will make sure they have the best cracked corn the larder has to offer—and possibly a bit of cheese as well."

Maggie's gaze met Lizzie's and they communicated in that silent way they had practically since birth. *We cannot fight this battle and win, but we may yet win the war. Patience and humor, as the Lady says. And courage.*

"Thank you, Lady Claire," Lizzie said at last. "That would be for the best."

Grandmother resumed her seat and poured another cup of tea, then sipped it and made a moue of distaste. "The pot has gone cold. Howel, would you ring for another? Lady Claire, gentlemen, girls ... we have invited several guests for dinner this evening to meet you. Once you have rested and changed, we dine at seven. We keep town hours here. When you hear the gong, please be prompt."

Town hours in London and Munich meant eight, or even nine. But perhaps in Penzance the sun set earlier.

While Mr. Malvern escorted the Lady and the hens out to hail a hansom cab to take them to the airfield, Claude showed the girls and Tigg upstairs. "I'm on this landing, and Tigg, you're here, in the bedroom overlooking the rose garden. I'm afraid the grands are a bit stuffy about ladies and gentlemen occupying the same wing, so Lizzie and Maggie, if you'll follow me along here?"

Their house on Wilton Crescent was posh, and heaven knew Gwynn Place was like a fairyland of wealth. But Seacombe House could hold its own in the grandeur department. It was not overly large, but it had dignity in the smooth polish of the balustrade under Maggie's hand, and when she looked down into the hall below, she saw the portraits of family members that she had not really noticed before.

Her family.

She would need to get back on the right foot with her grandparents, and learn about the people in these pictures. Elaine had had her portrait painted, and it now hung over the fireplace in the drawing room at Wilton Crescent—and would, Maggie imagined, until Lizzie someday married.

Perhaps there would be a picture of Catherine here at her childhood home. Perhaps she would finally see her mother's face, and learn something of her story.

And in doing so, learn something of her own.

5

"I have no intention of resting," Maggie said briskly after the maid—whose name was Tamsen—had unpacked their valises and shaken out and hung the dresses they were to wear to dinner. "I want to explore the house."

"I do, too ... but do you suppose we'll upset our grandmother?"

"She can hardly be more upset with me than she is already," Maggie said on a sigh. "I shall endeavor to be particularly silent at dinner."

"Then the Lady will think you're coming down with something. Just be yourself, Mags, and they can't help but love you."

But Maggie was not so sure. There had been a definite difference in the way the Seacombes had received her and the way they had treated Lizzie. She was quite sure that if Lizzie had spilled her tea, they would have asked if she had burned herself and offered napkins.

But perhaps she was being too sensitive—or too self-centered.

Maggie tapped on Claude's door, Lizzie on Tigg's.

"Didn't I tell you this was forbidden territory?" Claude whispered when he opened it. "The grands are just down at the end of this hall, in the big bedroom overlooking the sea. They're taking their naps."

"Come and explore with us," Maggie whispered back. "We want to see the house."

"All right, but you must be quiet until we get out of this wing. Let me get my jacket and we'll begin downstairs."

Along with the big drawing room, there was a morning room, a study, and a library. At the back of the house, as one might expect, were the kitchens, where the staff looked up, startled, from their preparations for dinner. Claude made the introductions, and Maggie flushed a little at being curtsied to for the first time in her life.

"That felt very strange," she whispered to Tigg as they climbed the stairs to the second floor.

"Best get used to it," he said. "The Seacombes seem to be persons of importance here, if the size of this place is any indication. That makes you important, too."

"Nonsense," Lizzie said. "It's not our names that make us important, it's what we do to bring honor to them, as you should know better than anyone."

Names again. Time to change the subject.

"Who sleeps in the other rooms in your wing?" she asked Claude when he turned along the gallery.

"No one. I don't think they're used."

"I want to see the rooms our mothers had when they were young," Lizzie told him. "Are those the empty ones?"

"Let's find out," Maggie suggested.

"Remember, walk softly and on no account must you giggle."

Maggie rather doubted that seeing her mother's old room was a laughing matter, but she took his point. It would not make the grands like her any better if she were caught snooping about without permission—she hadn't missed the fact that only Lizzie had been invited to treat Seacombe House as her own home.

The first room was decorated in a soft green with white trim. The bed had no old-fashioned hangings, but rather a gauzy canopy that was held up by wide grosgrain ribbons in a darker green. Combs and brushes had been laid out upon the dressing-table as if their owner would step in to use them at any moment. On the nightstand lay a book, as if put aside the evening before.

"Maggie, look. It's a copy of *Aesop's Fables*—the book that Mama used to read to us when we were small."

On the flyleaf was written in a girlish hand:

Elaine Seacombe, her book,
in hopes that it may strengthen her character

"I would say it worked," Maggie remarked. "Your mother had no shortage of character, from all accounts."

"So this was her room." Lizzie closed the book and laid it down as she had found it. She opened the wardrobe, but if she had hoped to find dresses from decades ago, and hats and ribbons that might have told her something of her mother's tastes, she was disappointed. The shelves contained nothing but linens and the winter spread for the bed. Its cubbyholes were empty, but in the drawers of the dresser, a faint scent rose from the paper that still lined them.

Lavender, with a hint of lemon.

Instantly, Maggie felt as though she were being enfolded in loving arms, pressing her nose to warm skin and breathing it in. A pang of loss rippled through her at the memory.

"She wore that scent," Maggie said. "I remember."

Lizzie nodded. "I do, too. Fancy it still being in the drawers when everything else has been cleared away. I don't suppose we'll find anything of her, will we?"

"I wonder why not? She was the good one."

At the door, Tigg stirred, as if someone had poked him in the ribs. Claude was standing guard outside, empty rooms having no interest for him, but Tigg had risked the impropriety of being in a bedroom with two young ladies to offer them his silent support.

"Don't say that, Mags," he said softly.

"Well, she was. She was the one who married well, who became stepmother to the only boy who could be heir to the shipping empire, who did everything right."

"Who was killed for it," Lizzie pointed out, her voice hollow.

"That was not her fault." She slipped an arm around Lizzie's waist. "If what you remember is the truth, she died protecting us. Which proves my point. Come, let's see if anything remains of *my* mother in this house."

The other bedroom was painted in a rose pink so soft that it was nearly cream, and the medallions on the ceiling and the wainscoting had likewise been painted white. Again, there was no indication that a young lady had grown up in this room, or dressed for a ball or giggled with her sister or daydreamed in the window seat, which looked out toward the east and would have caught the morning sun over the distant rooftops of their less important neighbors.

After one comprehensive glance, Maggie went straight to the top bureau drawer and bent to breathe in whatever scent might be left there.

Cedar.

No paper. What a disappointment.

A quick search of the closet—no wardrobe here—and the other drawers produced nothing but linen and a quantity of writing paper bearing the Seacombe crest of a stone arch with a wave coming through it.

A murmur down the hall made Maggie glance up at the door. *Billy Bolt*, Tigg mouthed, and Lizzie swept around the end of the bed to join him at the door, beckoning to Maggie.

"I'll just close up and meet you in the gallery," she whispered. "I want to see the top floor, too." Maybe paintings of disgraced daughters would be relegated to the servants' rooms.

Tigg and Lizzie vanished, the polished floors creaking a little as they beat a hasty retreat down the corridor.

A board creaked under Maggie's foot, too, as she stepped on it—a board between the closet and the bed with its cheerful flowered spread. It actually gave beneath her slipper. In her experience, only one kind of board did that: the kind that hid things a girl didn't want other people to see.

She knelt next to it and with quick fingers, she pressed and pried—and there it was. A pinhole. Clever Catherine. A board that tilted up could be discovered by anyone who stepped upon it the right way. But to discover a pinhole required powers of observation, and also a hairpin. She removed one of hers and bent up the tip, then inserted it in the tiny hole. With one quick tug, the board came up.

Empty.

Bother.

Maggie leaned down, patting the dimensions of the dusty compartment, then reached further in. Still nothing. She changed position and tried in the other direction. At the very end of the compartment, her fingers met something.

Paper.

It was all she could do to stretch that far, her nose practically on the floorboards. She pinched the paper between her forefinger and third finger, and pulled it out.

A letter, fragile with age and folded tightly to create its own envelope, as though paper were precious and not to be wasted. Upon the front was the direction, a single word in a masculine script: *Catherine.*

Maggie held it to her nose. Dust. Ink.

And fainter than memory, a scent, as if the paper had been clasped to a girlish bosom and had retained something of its owner's essence.

Maggie recognized it at once. No wonder it had always been one of her favorites.

Lilac.

She had become very familiar with the language of flowers during Emilie's consultations with Claire on the composition of the wedding bouquet.

Lilac, for first love.

6

May Day 1877

My dearest C—

It has been two nights since we met at the sawan *and I believe you must have bewitched me, for I cannot leave off thinking about you.*

I do not wish any harm or trouble to come to you on my account, so my head in all prudence advises me to go home to G.P. and take up my father's work, which would delight him. But my heart cannot see its way to such a sensible view. It cannot see anything at all but your lovely face in the moonlight, and your eyes full of stars.

Boscawen Trevithick tells me he can offer me employment as a stoker on the great steam engine at

Wheal Porth. As long as I do not have to be a tin miner, I will accept anything in order to stay in the parish.

Dare I hope you will be glad of this news? And if I should wander upon the strand, might a chance meeting occur again?

I believe I am—

Yours,

K.

"I cannot see that this course is a wise one."

Maggie jumped at the disembodied voice and came back to herself, the letter fluttering from her hand. She knelt to pick it up, and as she did, slipped the board that had concealed it all these years back into place.

Who had spoken?

"Have you had no sleep at all, Demelza? I cannot see that you have a choice in the matter," Grandfather said on the other side of the wall. His voice was querulous, as though he had just awakened. "If you have agreed the visit is to be two weeks, then two weeks it shall be."

Goodness. The head of her grandparents' bed must be right up against the adjoining wall. Had their whispers and creaking about awakened them?

Maggie slipped the letter into her pocket to ponder later, and pressed her ear to the wall beside the dresser. The Lady always said that eavesdroppers never heard any good of themselves, and perhaps that was true. But they heard any number of other useful things that more than made up for it.

"In any case, it is not likely we shall see much of them," Grandmother said. "Claude will show them about the country, I expect."

"Yes, more rattling about with picnics and frolics and other such nonsense. I was never more exhausted than when the last lot left. I wish Claude would leave off being a flibbertigibbet and settle down to business."

"He has a year of university yet, dear. Would you have him abandon his education?"

"I'd have him take up a proper education at the Seacombe Steamship Company. If he's going to inherit it, he should know it from the bottom up. Though I expect he will not make a very good cabin boy, or even a midshipman. Perhaps I shall start him as a lieutenant."

"Is he going to inherit?"

The bed creaked as, presumably, Grandfather rolled to one elbow to gaze at his wife. "What on earth do you mean? Of course he's going to bloody inherit. Who else have I got now that his father has crushed our hopes and betrayed the family in every possible way?"

"There are three now, Howel, as you very well know."

"There may be three grandchildren—two we may introduce into society—but only one will inherit. Girls cannot run a business."

Maggie's knees turned the consistency of apple jelly and she laid a steadying hand upon the picture rail.

Two …?

Society …?

Business …?

"Of course not. But though they cannot run the company, in all fairness, the shares must be divided equally among them."

"*Between* them. Surely you do not mean that *she* will inherit? She has no claim to what I have built all these years. Only the legitimate ones do."

"She is Catherine's daughter."

Coolness settled in Maggie's cheeks as the blood drained from her head. She should not have pulled her corset ribbons so tightly. She needed to take deep breaths now, and she could not.

"She is the by-blow of a nameless man to whom that girl gave her virtue and all hope of a claim to our wealth or our name."

"De Maupassant adopted the child, and then became Seacombe—at your request, if you recall. She has as good a claim to that name as Elizabeth does."

"Do not speak of that blackguard to me. I can only bear to think of him bearing my father's name for Claude's sake. Two hundred years of impeccable conduct are barely enough to counterbalance the shame he has brought upon it."

"This, too, shall pass. In the meantime, I must consider what to do about the other matter. I do not wish to offend Gwynn Place. Flora Trevelyan may have come down in the world, but her son is still the viscount and the St. Ives title is still one to be reckoned with in this part of the world."

"They can mind their own da—excuse me, dear— deuced business."

"If Lady Claire is their guardian, the girl is their business."

"She is received there?"

"Apparently."

"Well, they may do as they like. I am master here, and I say she is not."

"It's a little late for that, since she came in through the front door."

"You know what I mean, Demelza. You do not expect to present her to our friends and associates this evening, surely? A nameless bastard?"

"I do, and you will listen while I tell you why. You will bring more shame upon us by sending her upstairs with her dinner on a tray than you will by presenting her as Charles de Maupassant's adopted daughter."

"*What?*"

"Elizabeth is set on becoming a Seacombe, and so she will be, with my blessing and yours. Despite her unfortunate choice, at least Elaine's marriage was legitimate. But there is no getting around the fact that the other girl's parentage is in doubt. She will be no catch on the marriage mart, memory being what it is in Penzance. We will present her with charity and forbearance, as is only right for an adopted daughter, and then society will do what it does best—winnow the wheat from the chaff."

Her back against the wall, Maggie's knees failed altogether and she slid down soundlessly until she sat upon the floor, her head tilted against the wainscoting.

She should get up and leave. She should run, screaming, from this house, find the Lady, and fly away on the wind as fast as *Athena*'s engines could take her.

But still she did not move.

The bed creaked again, and then the floor. "You are sure, my dear? For the brunt of such 'charity' will fall upon you. Girls are not my concern."

"Completely sure. You may leave it to me, Howel. Now, do put on a different shirt. That one has a gravy stain upon the cuff."

Get up. Flee while they are moving about and the creaking will disguise the sound of your own steps.

When she made it out to the gallery, no one was there. Perhaps Lizzie and the boys had got tired of waiting, and continued their adventures without her.

She barely reached her room in time before the tea and biscuits came up, and she was violently sick into the washbasin.

෨෬

Her eyes bright and her cheeks flushed with exercise, Lizzie stepped into their room and halted as she saw Maggie laid down upon the bed.

"Mags? Are you not feeling well?"

"No. A little faint, that's all. Nothing to worry about." She swung her legs off the coverlet and sat up.

Lizzie sat beside her and passed an arm about her waist. "What is it? It smells like you've been sick. Did you try one of those odd fish sandwiches? I thought they smelled a little off, but what do I know about fish in this part of the world?"

"Perhaps it was the fish. I shall remember not to have it again. I'm much better now."

Not for worlds would Maggie reveal to Lizzie what she had overheard. This was her own battle to fight, and as soon as she could think of a way to fight it, she would do so. But in the meantime, Lizzie should not be deprived of her grandparents, her family, her future.

Lizzie, erstwhile alley mouse and daughter of a traitor, to become part owner of the Seacombe Steamship Company! There was no way on this earth that Maggie would prevent that from coming to pass—because if she confided what she had heard, Lizzie would cause the scene to end all scenes, and her bright prospects would go up like an explosion of Canton rockets.

So, instead of unburdening her heart to heal the grief of her grandparents' true opinion of her, instead of allowing Lizzie to comfort her and plan what they ought to do together, Maggie thanked heaven that she had a subterfuge ready to hand that might account for her lack of spirits.

She pulled the worn old letter from her pocket. "Look what I found under the floorboard in Mother's old room."

Lizzie read it swiftly, let out a long breath, then read it again with care.

"Do you think—could it be that *C* is Catherine?"

"I think it must be. Why else would this be concealed in her room?"

"Were there any more?"

"No, only this one, tucked away at the back of the compartment, as though it had been left behind when others were removed. If she and *K* began corresponding, it seems this might have been the first one. Smell it."

Lizzie did so, an inhalation touched with reverence. "Lilac. Your mother's scent?"

"It means 'first love,' remember? I wonder if she began to wear that scent then."

"How romantic." Lizzie smiled and turned her attention back to the letter. "I wonder who he was?"

"So do I. Liz—I think I must find out. What if he was … my father?"

Her cousin's green eyes were solemn as she thought this through. "May 1877. We were born in March of the following year."

"So he could have been."

"It's a leap, Mags. But leaving that aside, let us apply ourselves to what we can see. What can we glean of his character from what he has written?"

She should have thought of that herself, but eavesdropping had completely wiped all sensible thought from her mind. She focused on the ink, the letters, the meaning of the faded words.

"Well ... his writing is confident, the letters formed with the ease of long practice. His language is that of an educated man, wouldn't you say? He could not have been a crofter, or a tin miner. '*My head in all prudence advises me.*' Those are not the words of a fisherman. Or the spelling, either."

"On that subject you would know more than I. But look at this—'*It cannot see anything at all but your lovely face in the moonlight, and your eyes full of stars.*' Do you suppose he had been reading Byron? You know the poem—the one the Lady likes."

> *"She walks in beauty like the night*
> *Of cloudless climes and starry skies."*

"Yes, that one."

"That's even more of a leap, Liz. But it is lovely to contemplate, isn't it? That, if he was my father, he might have been an educated man who read poetry. And that my mother would be the kind of woman who appreciated such a man."

"Unlike our grandfather," Lizzie said, "who would appreciate a man of business, or an admiral, or something. No wonder they were not allowed to be together.

Poetry isn't going to run the Seacombe Steamship Company, is it?"

"Now you are really leaping. Who says they weren't allowed to be together?"

Lizzie turned to her, taking one cold hand in both her warm ones. "Think of what we know. Your mother was not married when she died in childbirth. I cannot believe that the man who wrote this letter would not have moved heaven and earth to marry her once he knew that you were coming into the world. Therefore, probability dictates that they were not permitted to marry."

"Or that something happened to him before they could."

"Or that," Lizzie agreed slowly.

"I must find out, Lizzie. I must know. Even if *K* turns out to be a mere May Day flirtation and not my father at all, I must know the truth." She paused. "And I do not think that I can simply ask our grandparents."

"Why not? I have no doubt that they know."

"I—I do not think they like me."

It took a lot to shock Lizzie, but Maggie had done it now.

"How can you say such a thing? They were perfectly civil in the drawing room—or were, until Holly and Ivy joined the party."

"They did get a little cranky after that—but not toward you."

"Oh, I felt it, all right. Depend upon it, they feel the same way toward you as they do toward me—which is to say, the polite interest of strangers. We may be blood, but we are not family yet, Mags, because they've only just met us. Give them time to warm to us. To become used to young folk around the place. Blood will out, you'll see, despite what the Lady says about intellect trumping all."

But Maggie was not so sure.

For whose blood, exactly, was running in her veins? And how did she propose to find out?

7

The Lady came into their room as they were putting the finishing touches on their toilettes before dinner.

"You have both put your hair up," she said with approval. "You look lovely. Though I must say, it makes me feel terribly old that my Mopsies are going about in society as young ladies."

"Would you rather we went as pickpockets?" Lizzie asked, eyes sparkling. "Because we could certainly oblige, couldn't we, Maggie?"

"Look what happened the last time you did that," Maggie pointed out. "You got blown up by a pocket watch."

"True." Lizzie's face held the memory of that night. "Thank goodness for Tigg. If he had not held off my attackers for those few seconds, I might have been killed."

"Yes, thank goodness for Tigg," the Lady agreed, her face as innocent and open as a flower. "How well he looks in his uniform—and I hear nothing but good things of him from Lord Dunsmuir. Our young engineer will be first officer within five years or I'm a stumpy gumpus."

Lizzie blushed and Maggie made the mistake of catching the Lady's eye.

One eyebrow rose in inquiry. The jig was up.

Or it would be, if she didn't do something. It wasn't that Lizzie would not want to talk about Tigg with the Lady. But if there was nothing yet to talk about, it could be embarrassing if others made assumptions that were not yet true.

Besides, Lizzie had hardly even confided in her yet. If anyone were to be the first to know, it should be Maggie.

"Lady, may I have your opinion?" she said, turning to the dressing table. "Should I wear something about my neck?"

Their jewel cases did not hold much—mostly because the Lady held strong opinions about what was suitable for young ladies, and Firstwater diamonds belonged about the throats of the engaged or married. So those were safely locked up at Wilton Crescent. And Lizzie was already wearing her mother's pearls.

"What about a bit of velvet ribbon to match your dress?" Claire asked. "Here. Put this little brooch on it and wear it choker style, as Princess Alexandra does. You know that personal adornment is not among my priorities, but there are some occasions that call for heavy artillery, and this is one of them."

The Lady tied the ribbon and Maggie had to admit that it was just what was needed to fill the modest neckline of her cream silk dinner dress with its tawny sash and puffed sleeves. And just what she needed to screw up her confidence to the sticking point. Even the Lady cast a puzzled eye upon her as they trooped down the staircase, but she said nothing. Maggie allowed her to think that she was still recovering from the fish.

She would not carry her sorry tale to Claire and expect her to go to battle on her account—because that was certainly what would happen. No, she would muster her own artillery and engage as best she could, and only when her own resources had been exhausted would she ask for help. She had not survived the alleys of Whitechapel, the desert wastes of the Texican Territory, or the excellent aim of a villain on the roof of his castle to be defeated in the drawing rooms of Penzance, for heaven's sake.

The Lady sailed into said drawing room as though she owned it, so Maggie, being the excellent mimic she was, did the same. With Tigg, who had been waiting by the door with Mr. Malvern, they joined their grandparents and began the introductions without delay. Mr. So-and-so. Mrs. Such-and-such. The Misses Whatsis, Baron Somebody, and Captain Barclay, who was memorable for the number of ribbons upon his chest and the size of his mutton chops. He had nice eyes, too, and called Maggie "Miss Seacombe," though no one had vouchsafed her last name.

At last her grandparents circled to the couple drinking sherry by the fire. "Sir John Rockland, Lady Char-

lotte, may I introduce our guests—Lady Claire Trevelyan, of Gwynn Place in Roseland. Mr. Andrew Malvern
and Lieutenant Terwilliger. Sir John is our local magistrate. And this is our granddaughter Elizabeth Seacombe, child of our daughter Elaine. And her adopted
sister and companion, Margaret."

Who, evidently, possessed no surname this time, either. Maggie dipped into a curtsey and smiled shyly at
the couple, not allowing the degree to which this bothered her to show in her face. Lady Charlotte smiled
back, but did not extend her hand as she had to Lady
Claire and the gentlemen. Maggie knew something of
the rules of precedence and how low a curtsey was to be
in proportion to the rank of the person to whom one
had been introduced, but she couldn't remember
whether handshakes applied in this situation if one was
not yet eighteen. Or if one had no last name.

Lizzie had no such trouble. She dipped her curtsey
and said, "How do you do? I'm very happy to make
your acquaintance."

"And we yours," Lady Charlotte said. "I understand
you will be with us for a visit of some days?"

"Two weeks, in fact. Then we must return to school
in Munich."

"I don't hold with foreign schooling," Grandfather
said. "Nothing wrong with a good English education."

"I agree," said the Lady, "though it would mean my
being divided from the girls for months at a time, since
I am to begin my career with the Zeppelin Airship
Works there in September. I am afraid I could not bear
it." And she smiled at both girls with such affection
that Maggie's throat closed up.

"Perhaps now that you have been reunited, and the breach in the family circle healed, you might reconsider traveling so far from your grandparents?" Lady Charlotte said to Lizzie. With a smile at Grandmother, she went on, "Demelza and I are confidantes, you see."

"I am afraid it is too late to change our plans for this autumn," the Lady said smoothly, "but if the girls desire it, we may certainly come to some other agreement in the future. But in any case, I believe they would prefer to finish out sixth form in Munich, where the professors know them and they have many friends. When it is time to apply to university, of course, they may make up their own minds."

Grandmother snorted. "Girls of their age do not need to attend university, unless it is to attract the attention of gentlemen, and they had better do that under their own family's roof."

Maggie exchanged a glance with Lizzie, and both waited for the Lady to deal such a setdown that Grandmother would be rendered mute for a week.

But Claire merely smiled. "That would be dreadfully disappointing to the Empress of Prussia, would it not, Maggie? She was so pleased with your achievements when you were presented in June."

In the ensuing ringing silence the butler announced, "Dinner is served."

Tigg offered his arm to Lizzie, and when the Lady turned, she found Mr. Malvern at her elbow, ready to escort her in before someone else beat him to it. Would no one claim her as his partner? Maggie thought with a dreadful pang. Had everyone in the room noticed the lack of salient details in the introductions?

"Do be a dear and save me from Lady Charlotte," came a voice in her ear, and Claude linked his arm with hers, practically waltzing her into the dining room. "She's been Grandmother's best friend since they came out of the Ark, and she terrifies me."

"She didn't seem so terrible," Maggie whispered as he seated her in the middle, a comforting distance from Grandmother at one end and Grandfather at the other. "I thought she was rather nice."

"Don't let looks deceive you. She doesn't believe in cakes for tea. And neither she nor Grandmere are even aware of the existence of mother's helpers—hence the maids. Can you imagine?"

Thank heavens for Claude. Blissfully unaware of the undercurrents in the conversation that pointedly eddied around Maggie and went right over his head, he made sure that their little section of the table was the most entertaining. Tigg and Lizzie opposite joined in, and the Lady and Mr. Malvern, who possessed views so different from the majority at the table that the concealment of them became more and more hilarious, made sure that this dinner at all events, would be remembered for some time to come.

No one would contradict or dare to dress down the Lady, for fear of offending Gwynn Place, and even Mr. Whatsis had heard of Andrew Malvern, the famous engineer. In fact, by the time dinner was over and Grandmother had risen to indicate that it was time to leave the gentlemen to their port and cigars, Maggie was feeling as though her earlier fears must have been the product of an overwrought imagination—or the fish.

"Texican cigarillos," Claude murmured as he pulled out her chair and eyed the boxes on the mantel. "Think I ought to try one?"

"I do not," Maggie whispered back. "They are horrid things. What girl would want to kiss a man who tastes like an ash tray?"

"No danger of that here," he said, his merriment briefly dampened by the thought of the girls of his acquaintance all on the razzle without him in Venice.

"Then consider your own health, and decline when they are offered," she said, before following Lizzie into the drawing room.

Where the ladies, unfettered by the interference of men in their conversation, waited.

8

Grandmother was seated before the baroque silver service, engaged in pouring coffee. Without being asked,
Maggie took cups and saucers and handed them round
to the ladies arranged upon sofas and chairs, beginning
with Lady Charlotte and ending with Lizzie. No one
could say she had learned nothing of civility or the rules
of precedence during her lessons in deportment with
Mademoiselle Dupree. Trays of iced cakes followed,
though it appeared that the enormous trifle taking pride
of place on the sideboard was waiting for the arrival of
the gentlemen.

"Thank you, Maggie," the Lady murmured as she
accepted a small pink cake on a plate. "Do not forget
your own dessert while you are so thoughtfully helping
others to theirs."

"These are delicious, Mrs. Seacombe," one of the three Misses Whatsis said, indicating her glossy round cake with a picture of a steamship in icing on the top. "How very clever of the baker. Is this one of your ships?"

"Indeed it is—the *Demelza*, named by Mr. Seacombe for me, of course. We have them specially made."

"I shall have to tell Mama. In the spirit of being prepared, you know."

"Oh, are you engaged to be married, Miss Penford?" Lady Charlotte asked. "I had not heard."

Miss Penford blushed and her sister explained, "Not exactly, Lady Charlotte. Not yet. But we expect the happy news any day now."

"It is always good to be prepared for any eventuality," Lady Claire said. "I was just a member of my best friend's wedding party on Friday—Emilie Fragonard. You may have read of it in the society pages. She married Lord Selwyn and they are off to the Lakes this week for their wedding tour."

"I did read something of it," Grandmother said. "Was that not awkward for you?"

"Why should it have been?" The Lady sipped her coffee. "Emilie will make a far happier Lady Selwyn than I should have done."

"Our condolences on your loss," Grandmother said in tones that could have wilted the bouquet of flowers on the mantel.

"Thank you, that is very kind. But James and I were not suited, and while his death was a blow of the most shocking sort, it has been five years and we have all rallied. Emilie and Peter will be very happy—and so will we, won't we, girls?"

The Lady smiled at Maggie and Lizzie, while the Misses Penford looked askance at one another. "So are there marriage prospects ahead for you after such a long time, Lady Claire?" the eldest asked. "Or will you go off to Munich with a heart unencumbered and free?"

"I would not say so," the Lady said rather primly from behind the rim of her cup.

Maggie perked up. This was news.

"Lady Claire, you cannot be reconsidering the Prussian prince's offer," Lizzie said with every appearance of sincerity. "What would Count von Zeppelin say if he were to lose you?"

Miss Penford swallowed her coffee the wrong way and snatched up a napkin to cover her mouth. By the time Grandmother had gone to her assistance, the moment for giving answers had passed. Maggie fetched the young lady a glass of water from the sideboard, and the latter took it gratefully.

"Would you be so kind, Margaret?" the second sister said, handing her an empty plate, and before Maggie could do a thing, Lady Charlotte had handed hers over as well.

Since there was no reason she should not clear the plates before the men came and the trifle was served in the crystal dishes arranged upon the sideboard, Maggie did so with a smile. Luckily, when droplets of coffee from someone's saucer fell upon a bit of lace on the front of her dress, they didn't stain the silk. She dipped a napkin in her water glass and scrubbed at it, and nearly all of it came out.

When she looked up, the Lady was gazing at her in a most perplexed manner, and she blushed.

Oh dear. How clumsy she was. Should she have excused herself and gone to her room? But then the coffee would have had time to set, and that would not do.

"This is excellent coffee, is it not, Lizzie?" she asked, sitting next to her sister on the sofa.

"It was, though normally I consider it bitter. Did the company import it, Grandmother?"

"Of course, dear. All coffee is imported. This is from South America, which is why it is gentler and fuller bodied than those you may have tried in London. Your grandfather is very particular about what he serves his guests."

"South America," Maggie marveled. "Does it come all that way by steamship? Would it not be more efficient to send it by air? Or perhaps the company uses airships?"

"Certainly not," Lady Charlotte answered when it appeared Grandmother had a mouth rather more full of coffee than politeness dictated. "The Seacombe Steamship Company is a seagoing concern only. There are some cargoes, you must understand, that cannot be risked in the air."

"There is no risk in airships," Maggie blurted. "They go to the Antipodes and back regularly. And quickly. How long does a seagoing ship take to make that journey?"

Grandmother had recovered her ability to speak. "Are you implying that the Seacombe vessels are not only slow, but outmoded?"

"Of course not, Grand—"

"I suggest you restrict your remarks to that limited number of subjects about which you have some knowledge."

"But I do have—"

"Elizabeth, would you like another cup of this coffee, though it came to us by outmoded methods?"

"I—no, thank you, I've had—"

"Margaret, please pour Miss Seacombe another, if you would."

Crushed, feeling ashamed though she did not understand why she should, Maggie reached for the silver coffee pot. But the Lady got there first.

"Maggie, you have not touched yours. Allow me to refresh the ladies' cups."

Moving gracefully, the Lady proceeded to pour. Once she had finished with the coffee, the men came in and before Maggie's wondering eyes, the Lady not only took over the role of hostess, she became the center of attention, seeing to the comfort of the gentlemen, tucking cushions behind the Baron's back, making jokes with Mr. Malvern and Tigg. In fact, Grandmother was rather put in the shade and had no choice but to retreat to a corner with Lady Charlotte, from whence pointed comments emerged with some regularity and no audience.

When Maggie finished her trifle—which was first rate, being stuffed with plum jam, ladyfingers, fruit, and mounds of whipped cream, and flavored with what tasted like whiskey—she looked around for Lizzie. Perhaps it was just her imagination, but this whole evening seemed to be exceedingly peculiar, and she wanted to talk it over. Lizzie could be relied upon to separate fact from fancy.

But Lizzie was no longer in the room—and neither was Tigg.

Those rascals! Well, if they could make themselves scarce, then so could she. Maggie devoted half a thought to taking Claude's elbow and spiriting him out of the room to join them in a lark, but he was deep in conversation with Mr. So-and-so. Never mind. She would find Lizzie and Tigg and it would be like old times, exploring together and making smart asides about the adults that they would never say to their faces.

A quick search of the upper floor and the gallery proved fruitless. It was a lovely night; chances were good that they had gone out into the garden. Perhaps they were even admiring the moonrise over the sea from the cliff-top.

Why had they not invited her? It was most unfair. If she could not rise to Maggie's defense when Grandmother had snapped at her for asking perfectly reasonable questions, then at the very least Lizzie could include her so that she might be soothed and made cheerful again by their company.

Maggie emerged onto the terrace and closed the French doors behind her. No one was there but the footman, smoking the tail end of somebody's cigarillo in the shadows by the ivy-covered wall. Her steps were light upon the flagged stairs, and then she reached the lawn, her skirts held up in both hands so the hems would not be soaked with dew as she ran for the rose garden.

But Lizzie and Tigg were not in this pretty spot, which, now that she thought about it, should have been obvious from the first. Tigg was not what you might call a rose garden sort of person. Lizzie wasn't, either. No, it was quite certain that they were out on the cliff-top, where he could see the sky and point out the lights of the Royal Aeronautic Corps on St. Michael's Mount.

Fortunately, the moon shed plenty of light, and she remembered the path from Claude's brief tour of the grounds that morning. When she cleared the ornamental trees that formed the border between the order of the garden and the long grass and hillocks of the clifftop, the wind off the sea brushed her face. Beneath her feet, she could swear she felt the boom of the waves breaking against the foot of the cliff below.

And there they were.

A bench had been placed about twenty feet back from the edge, and Lizzie and Tigg were seated upon it. Rather close together. Perhaps Lizzie was cold. Oh, she should have thought to bring one of the lovely soft shawls that Alice had brought them from the Duchy of Venice! But it was too l—

Before Maggie could take another step or announce her presence or do anything but gape, Tigg turned toward Lizzie—Lizzie lifted her gaze to his—and he leaned down and kissed her.

SHELLEY ADINA

9

Maggie clapped both hands to her mouth.

She needn't have—with the wind and the sound of the sea, they could not hear her gasp, and even if it had been as silent as a church, they did not look as though they were aware of very much but their own two selves.

Lizzie and Tigg!

Goodness gracious. It was one thing to suspect that they no longer harbored the feelings of companions at arms. It was quite another to witness a moment that should be completely private and where three was most definitely a crowd.

She must go away before one of them saw her.

A return to the house by the drawing room or front door was out of the question. Her only choice was to go sideways and hope that she might circle around to one of the servants' entrances and slip upstairs to her room. Fleet as a hare, she ran to the west, where the headland upon which the house stood dipped down toward the beach.

The beach. That's where she would go for a few blessed minutes, where there was no one to criticize, no one to look amused behind china cups, where she could enjoy the pleasure of her own company while she gave Lizzie and Tigg enough time to recollect themselves and go back inside before the Lady realized they were gone.

The heath and clumps of thrift on the slope down to the beach seemed to separate rather naturally into a path, though she had to gather up her skirts and crouch on the last bit, where the soil thinned into solid rock and she was forced to pick her way down more carefully. In the daylight, this would be nothing, but at night, the shadows were inky and the footing uncertain.

A sensible person would have climbed back up and gone to bed. But Maggie was not in the mood to be sensible. In fact, she hoped there was a good collection of smooth tumbled rocks on this beach that she could fling into the sea until she wore herself out.

The tide seemed to be on the ebb, which gave her quite a stretch of wet sand to walk upon. Her slippers would be ruined. Perhaps she would go into town and get new ones, and charge them to the Seacombe account. This happy prospect lifted her spirits somewhat. It would not do to spoil her dress, however, so she looped her skirts over one arm and paced closer to the cliff.

Somewhere above sat Lizzie and Tigg. If they ventured closed to the edge and leaned over, would they be able to see her? For it was certain that she could not see very much up there, no matter how she craned her neck.

She would not go far. If she rounded the headland in the opposite direction, she would find herself on the far reaches of the harbor, and that would not do at this time of night. So she skirted farther to the west, in the shadow of the cliff, until at her feet the cliff base tailed off into a nice scree.

And here were her rocks.

For some time she amused herself flinging fist-sized round stones into the water, aiming for the foamy tops of the waves as they peaked and crashed. Then, for good measure, she flung a few at the darkness of the cliff itself.

Clack. Clack. Plonk.

Oh dear. That wasn't right. Could there be something other than solid rock in those shadows? It had not shattered, not with a sound like that, but ... perhaps there was a cave?

At Gwynn Place, not so far up the coast, there were caves in the cliffs, and the Lady had said that as a child, she had found pirate silver in them.

Oh, for a light!

For the moon had not yet traveled enough across the night sky to shed much light on this part of the cliff. She peered into the dark, seeking what had caused that hollow sound.

She bent and tossed another rock. *Plonk.*

Definitely a cave. A deeper darkness seemed to lie on the cliff's face, and as she put a hand on the rock to steady herself, she felt something strange. Her fingers examined ridges and whorls, spaced in a regular pattern. Carving—or chiseling, at the very least, all around the edge of the opening in the stone. How very curious. And then her seeking fingers found a niche—and in the niche were several familiar shapes.

Moonglobes.

She shook one into life and held it up. Its cool light illuminated the carvings in the rock, which resolved themselves into stones—an arch—a door.

A huge door, large enough to admit a landau, or a ketch or other small sailing boat. But who would make a door in the bottom of a cliff? Some long-dead Seacombe, or someone from years before? For the carvings were old—perhaps hundreds of years old, covered with lichen and moss, the lower ones nearly obliterated by the pounding of the sea. At low tide, half the door would be under water, allowing only a shallow arch for a boat to glide in.

If this were not a pirate cave, which tended not to announce themselves with carvings and stone arches, then was it still in use by those above?

Maggie couldn't resist. She'd just have a quick look-see, and then she'd go back to the house.

The floor was sandy, with granite protruding up through it like the caves at Gwynn Place. But to the left was a landing-stair, slick with the green weed of low tide. Carefully, watching where she placed her sodden slippers, Maggie mounted the stair to a wide stone quay.

Holding the moonglobe up high, Maggie surveyed the chamber. It was dry, so the tide did not rise this far, but far from clean. The droppings of sea-birds coated the edges of the landing, as though it made a good place to roost, and the skeletons of long-eaten fish lay toward the end. A pile of empty crates was stacked beyond that, and a tarred rope had been carefully coiled to the height of a person's knee. Mooring hooks protruded from the stones on the edge, so that boats could be tied up. Water dripped in the darkness, and the crash of the surf sounded hollow, as though this cave were being pounded from the outside.

The whole cave smelled of seaweed, rotting fish and old guano, and the damp of centuries gone by.

At the far end of the stone landing, another set of steps chiseled out of the rock itself wound up into darkness. She would bet her week's allowance that it led up into the house.

How very exciting! Had long-dead Seacombes made their fortune by bringing in goods by boat to their home? Or was the presence of the cave simply a coincidence, and had come with the property when the first Seacombe had bought it?

In any case, she now understood the meaning of the arch and wave in the family crest.

The *incoming* wave.

She could not see past the circle of light thrown by the moonglobe. There was nothing wrong with her hearing, however. The sound of the surf had become louder. Either the wind had dropped, or ...

Cautiously, she looked over the side of the stone landing.

Where her footprints had been in the sand, there was now a glassy sheet of water, lapping against the rocks. Cold fear arrowed through her stomach. How was this possible? The tide could not have come in this fast, could it? But then, she had no experience with tides. The closest she had come was the shallow back-and-forth of the Thames, or the beach at Gwynn Place, and there the Lady always made good and sure they were up on the cliff path before it turned.

She could not get out the way she had come in, unless she waded or swam, in which case she would ruin the only evening dress she possessed.

Her only salvation was the evidence before her eyes of the dry stone dock. But still, she didn't much like the prospect of spending the night on it, curled up in the stink, waiting for the tide to go back out again.

Maggie, my girl, you cannot go down. You cannot stay. Therefore, you must go up, and hope there is a door at the top with a lock on this side.

She hoisted her skirts up over her arm more securely, lifted the moonglobe, and began to climb.

The staircase, while not as tight a corkscrew as the tower stairs at Colliford Castle, was still fairly steep. It was wide, though, presumably to accommodate a man carrying a crate like the ones down below. She tried to count the steps, but lost the count somewhere around one hundred twenty. But she had no choice now. It was go on or sleep with soaked feet on a bed of stone.

An eternity of climbing passed, in which the muscles of her legs, though fit, began first to complain and then to wobble. Just when she was convinced that one more step would bring utter collapse, the moonglobe showed her a door.

Thank heaven above.

Gasping, her free hand pressed to her side, Maggie took a moment to recover from the climb, wishing not for the first time that she had not laced her corset so tightly. Henceforth, she would forego fashion in favor of practicality, because it seemed that in her case, there were far more opportunities to succeed at the latter than the former.

Finally, she pushed herself off the rough granite of the wall and examined the door. There was no knob, only a curious configuration of blackened iron that did not look as though it had been used in years. But looks, as anyone could tell you, were deceiving.

In the light of the moonglobe, she studied it. To the unskilled eye, it would be utterly perplexing—a series of gears and clockwork that appeared to have no central focus, no means of triggering entry. Which would make sense—if more than one person were using the dock and stair, keys could easily be lost or stolen. But the key to this lock was in the memory … or in one's powers of observation and past experience with locks.

Maggie leaned in and followed the configuration backward from the latch. Was that it? Could it be that simple—a figure eight, with the trigger point here—?

Maggie pressed what appeared to be a blackened nail head. It gave under her thumb and the mechanism began to move, its parts clicking and creaking and at one point jamming before she gave it a thump with her fist and it lurched into motion once more.

Thunk! The mechanical lock lumbered to a stop in its terminal position.

Maggie pushed on the door and, moonglobe held rather in the manner of a stone ready for throwing, stepped through.

10

Lady Claire Trevelyan allowed Mrs. Seacombe to see the last of her guests off at the door, and found Andrew Malvern out on the terrace, gazing over the gardens and enjoying the scent of the sea mixed with roses and a lingering hint of cigarillo smoke.

"I have never been so glad to see the end of an evening, and considering my mother's fondness for society, that is saying something," she said as she joined him.

"It was quite the performance, I must say. I had not believed you capable of it." Andrew offered her his arm and they paced down the steps and into the garden, where their conversation might be less likely to be overheard.

"It put quite a strain on my ingenuity," she admitted. "But I was so angry that I could not think how else to put a stop to it. How dare she treat Maggie that way? Did you hear her? *Margaret, clear away these cups. Margaret, wipe up your mess. Let me introduce Margaret, Elizabeth's companion.*" Claire's voice rose and cracked in an imitation of Mrs. Seacombe's tones. "She was lucky I merely displaced her shining star and did not up-end the coffee pot over her head."

"You are too well bred for that."

"Sadly, yes." Claire made an effort to rein in the temper that had risen once more in the re-enactment of the offending remarks. "And I would not want Maggie to stoop to such behavior, either. I have grave doubts about the wisdom of our going up to Gwynn Place and leaving the girls here. It cannot be healthy. Maggie must be sensible of the difference her grandparents are making between them."

"If she is, then you must give her credit for being more of a lady than her grandmother, and not showing it."

"Yes, but she cannot be expected to stand there and meekly take the slings and arrows aimed at her. She has not been brought up to accept belittlement or unfairness."

"Perhaps the question we ought to ask is, why are they doing this? Surely they would not hold her parentage against an innocent young girl who is not only lovely, but accomplished as well?"

She squeezed his arm as they walked slowly among the roses, her heart swelling with affection. "Have I told you lately how glad I am that you understand all that goes on between me and the Mopsies?"

With a pat of his hand upon her own gloved one, he said, "Not lately, but I am glad you honor me with your confidence, Claire. Sometimes I forget that there are only seven years between you—and that you are not in fact their older sister. It cannot be easy sometimes to know which is the right course in their upbringing, even now that they are out in society."

"I have had many a white night worrying about them, it is true—especially after the recent events at Colliford Castle. But to return to Maggie, yes, I am certain that the Seacombes are making her pay for what they see as their daughter's shortcomings. Why else make it plain that they view her as merely a companion for Lizzie—a drudge, someone they must put up with for the sake of the legitimate child?"

"Will you speak to them?"

"I fear I must. I cannot let this go on, even if it results in our being turned out of the house before Wednesday."

The sound of low voices at the other end of the garden stopped her, and in the moonlight she recognized a familiar white dress. But who was this at Lizzie's side?

"Lizzie—Tigg—are you enjoying an evening stroll as well?" Andrew said as they met in the middle, by the sundial.

"Yes, we are." Both Lizzie's hands were wrapped around Tigg's arm, and their bodies swayed toward one another in a manner that told Claire that her eyes had not been deceived earlier. Lizzie couldn't keep a smile of womanly pleasure from glimmering in and out like the sun in clouds, and Tigg's gaze only strayed from her face when it was absolutely necessary for the sake of politeness.

Oh my.

She was making assumptions where she had no proof—or any confidence of Lizzie's that would make her think such a thing. But Claire remembered all too well how she herself had felt in the moments after Andrew had first kissed her, that day in his laboratory. She too had been giddy and hardly in control of her faculties.

But at the same time, she was not the sister of the heir to a shipping empire. While Claire might have been expected to make a stunning match at one time, her father's mistake in gambling her inheritance on the combustion engine had put paid to that, and while it had left her penniless, it also freed her to choose her own path. Up until a month ago, Claire had believed Lizzie free to do the same.

But now she wondered. Would the Seacombes welcome Tigg into the bosom of the family in much the way they had welcomed Maggie? Or would his prospects as a lieutenant in the Royal Aeronautics Corps be sufficient to recommend him as a grandson-in-law, if their attachment remained true until Lizzie was of age?

Or was Claire's mind galloping ahead in paths where it had no business, and she was spinning a fancy out of a moonlit night, a white dress, and the scent of roses?

"Is everyone gone?" Lizzie asked. "We slipped away when Miss Penford began at the piano. Is Maggie with you?"

"No," Claire replied. "I thought she might be with you."

Tigg shook his head. "We haven't seen her."

"Then she must have gone up to bed, because she was not in the drawing room when everyone took their leave. Which reminds me, Lizzie—since dinner was in your and Maggie's honor, it was not well done of either of you not to see the guests off at the end of it."

"Oh ... I am sorry, Lady." They had reached the terrace now, and Lizzie's chagrin was illuminated by the wide bars of light falling through the French doors. "I never thought of it. I—we—"

"It's my fault, Lady," Tigg said. "I convinced her to take a walk along the cliff-top, and we lost track of time."

"It happens," Andrew said easily. "But there are bound to be several such occasions over the next two weeks, so bear it in mind. One's obligations to one's guests take precedence over ... moonlit walks upon the cliffs."

And whatever else might have gone on there.

Claire and Lizzie bade the gentlemen good-night on the gallery, and then went their separate ways to their rooms.

But when Claire stepped into the girls' room, expecting to see Maggie, she was surprised to find it empty, the beds neatly turned back, and their nightgowns laid out by Tamsen the maid upon the coverlet.

"That's odd," Lizzie said. "Where could she be?"

"It is not like her to disappear without you," Claire said. "And she is not with Claude."

"Perhaps she has gone into her mother's old room. She found a letter, you know, Lady. Under the floorboard, when we were exploring. We believe it was from a gentleman to her mother, in 1877. I'll just run along there and check, shall I, in case she has gone back for another look?"

"At eleven at night?" But with the Mopsies, one ought not to put limits on what they might do, no matter what time of night it was.

Lizzie was back in five minutes, shaking her head. "I don't understand it."

"Did she seem upset to you this evening?" Claire asked carefully. "Distressed in any way that might have caused her to behave rashly?"

"Maggie? Rash? I don't think so. She seemed perfectly content, and she was laughing at dinner. But then, sitting next to Claude would make anybody laugh. One simply can't help it."

Perhaps Claire had taken offense at something that existed only in her own mind, and Maggie was not in the least upset. But be that as it may, she would not be able to sleep until she knew her girl to be safely in her bed.

"I shall fetch Tigg and Mr. Malvern," Claire said at last, "and we will mount a search—quietly. I do not wish your grandparents or the staff to be alarmed."

Fortunately, neither Tigg nor Andrew had got much further than removing their jackets, and when they assembled in the gallery overlooking the front entry once more, Claire told them what was amiss. "Tigg and I will take the main floor and downstairs—the kitchens and so forth. Andrew, you take Lizzie and search the upper floors. If you can get out onto the roof, do so, since—" She flashed a smile at Lizzie. "—the girls have a particular fondness for them."

"Why should Tigg and I not go together?" Lizzie objected.

There was no time for anything but blunt honesty— which was the only thing that worked with Lizzie in any case. "Because I fear you will become distracted, and I would like a quiet word with him while we are looking."

In the silence of the sleeping house, Claire distinctly heard Tigg gulp.

"Everyone has a moonglobe?" Mr. Malvern whispered. "Right, then. Off we go."

It was almost like old times, if she had not been dressed in dinner clothes and had the Mopsies safely together as scouts. In less than five minutes, Claire and Tigg had determined that Maggie was not in the drawing room, dining room, or any of the parlors. Nor was she in the butler's pantry, the scullery, the larder, or the main kitchen. In fact, the only person awake in the servants' part of the house was the boot boy, whom they frightened practically out of his skin when they loomed up behind him as he was polishing his master's boots.

"Is there anywhere else we might look, then, mate?" Tigg asked him, when it was clear he was too frightened to answer Claire. "We've been all through these rooms and the ones above, with no sign of her."

"There's nowt else down here, sir, but the cellars, and it's not likely the young lady would have found her way there, being the master and mistress's granddaughter and all."

"That, you will find, is faulty logic," Claire said rather grimly. "We have exhausted the likely, so I believe it is time to consider the unlikely. Will you show us the way down, please?"

"To the cellars, milady?" He was so shocked that he spoke to her directly.

"Yes."

"Now, milady?"

"If she is hurt, we will do her no good if we leave her there until morning."

"But, milady—" He scrubbed his hands on a rag. "—it's only Mr. Nancarrow the butler who has the keys to the cellars. Because of the spirits, you see."

Good heavens. Were there ghosts down there? Prior victims of Seacombe pride and heartlessness? "Does he believe they will submit to lock and key?" Claire inquired impatiently.

The boy looked up at her, his face blank with incomprehension.

"I believe he means the sort that comes in bottles, Lady," Tigg murmured.

"Ah, of course," Claire said, ashamed of the relief that swept her. "And Mr. Nancarrow has gone to bed, I suppose?"

"Aye, milady."

From somewhere below, they heard a sound.

"Are you sure you meant only the kind in bottles?" Claire whispered. "What was that?"

Again, the sound—a hollow, muffled sound like the booming of surf ... and a cry.

A cry she would know anywhere on earth—whether above or below ground.

"That's Maggie," Claire said, clutching Tigg's arm. "Where is it coming from? Where is she?"

Tigg dashed down the corridor, following the sound, Claire and the boot boy hot on his heels. At the far end of the corridor, on the other side of the kitchen, was a set of stone steps going down to a door that looked as though it had been there since the Norman conquest.

Someone was pounding on the other side.

Claire pushed the boot boy out of the way and put her mouth close to the blackened iron keyhole. "Maggie? Is that you, darling?"

"Lady!" came a muffled cry. "Oh, thank heavens. I can't get out—and I can't go back. Can you get me out of here?"

"Instantly. We shall get the butler and the keys." She turned to the boot boy. "Go and wake Mr. Nancarrow at once and tell him his keys are needed."

"Oh, milady, I couldn't. I'd be sacked."

"You can and you will," she informed him with the command developed over three centuries of breeding. "Your mistress's granddaughter is locked down there. If you lend her your assistance and be quick about it, not only Mr. Nancarrow but also Mrs. Seacombe will hear of it from me, in the warmest and most complimentary terms possible."

The boy vanished without another word.

Claire turned back to the keyhole. "Maggie, are you hurt?"

"No, Lady," came the muffled reply. "But my feet are soaking wet and I'm cold. The tide came in when I wasn't looking. I had no idea it would turn that fast."

How and why Maggie had been anywhere near the tide were questions for later, over a hot bath and a cup of tea.

"Tigg, while I wait for the keys, do please go and tell Lizzie and Mr. Malvern that we have found her and as far as we can tell, she is safe."

"Of course, Lady. You'll be all right on your own?"

"Certainly. I have no fear of Mr. Nancarrow sacking me. Quickly, now. I would not wish Lizzie worried a moment longer than necessary."

He hesitated on the first step. "Lady—about her—Lizzie—"

"I know I said I wanted a word, but it will have to wait for another time. Just know this, Tigg—"

"Yes, Lady?" In the greenish-white glow of his moonglobe, his brown eyes were worried, and fixed upon her as though she held the keys to his future.

"I have no objections to your forming a deeper attachment than the comradeship you share now. You are just as dear to me as either of the girls, and your happiness has always been my first concern. But she and you may find things more complicated now than they were before."

"I know it, Lady. But we—it just happened—I hardly know how—"

"We will speak of it later, dear one. For now, Maggie's safety must be uppermost."

He nodded, and it seemed to Claire that his face relaxed, as though he had been afraid she would say … what? That she did not approve? That his uncertain parentage mattered more to her than his character, his intelligence, and his prospects? For all he had ever confided in her was that he was the son of a Nubian aeronaut and a Whitechapel seamstress, neither of whom he remembered. One's reputation could not depend upon that of one's parents, as any of them might attest. One was only responsible for one's own, and Tigg had never given a moment's concern in that department.

He took the steps two at a time, and the sound of his boots faded away down the corridor.

"Lady?" came Maggie's voice through the keyhole.

"Yes, darling. I'm here. The keys should be here shortly, too."

"Was that Tigg?"

"Yes. He has gone to tell Lizzie and Mr. Malvern, who are searching the upper floors for you, that we have found you."

After a beat of silence, Maggie's muffled voice came again. "I saw them kissing, Lady. Tigg and Lizzie."

"Yes, I suspected as much. Did you hear what I said to him?"

"Yes. I—I lost my head and went down to the beach so they wouldn't know I'd seen them. There's a cave, Lady, and a stair that leads up here into the cellars."

"Is there, now? Well, I am not surprised. Pirates once used the caves at Gwynn Place."

"This isn't a pirate cave. This one's on purpose, with a quay and a big door in the rock and everything."

"Is it in use?" Claire asked with some surprise. What would the Seacombes be doing with a boat landing in their cellar?

"I don't think so. The bird droppings all over the dock have to be at least as old as Lizzie and me."

"Dear me. I shudder to think of the state of your clothes, dearest." Voices sounded behind her, and a glance confirmed that it was the boot boy and Mr. Nancarrow. "Here are the keys, Maggie. We'll have you out of there in a moment."

The butler, in trousers and shirtsleeves and none too happy about it, turned the huge key in the old lock, and with a well-oiled click, the door swung into the stair well.

And with a gasp of relief, a cold and disheveled Maggie fell into Claire's arms.

11

"I simply cannot believe it of you," Grandmother said at breakfast, for what had to be the third time. "No one but the fishermen's children and sandpickers ever ventures into Seacombe Sawan."

Which neatly relegated Maggie to that happy company—with whom, she thought rebelliously, she would much rather be at this moment.

"I think it was rather splendid of her, to go exploring and to make such a discovery." Claude saluted her with his toast, liberally covered in apple jelly. "I had no idea there was a landing in the ... what is it called?"

"A *sawan* is a cave in the foot of a cliff," Grandmother said. "And we forbid you to go there. It is too dangerous, as Margaret's thoughtless behavior has so amply proven."

"Your family's history began there," Grandfather informed Claude as Maggie concentrated on her food, her cheeks burning from the reproof. "Two hundred years ago, Pendrake Seacombe discovered the *sawan* and the volcanic chute that led upward through the cliff. He modified it and built the house atop it, so that during the Civil Wars, our family not only had a means to freedom, but so did the royal family. King Charles I escaped to France while a guest here, you know, in a Seacombe ship—a fishing ketch."

Grandmother took up the tale. "The *sawan* was also a means by which to import food from France so that the people in the country hereabouts did not starve. This is how our family and company crests came to be."

"My curiosity is piqued with a vengeance." Claude turned to Grandmother. "Please do not forbid us the ... *sawan*. We will be careful, I promise."

"Claude, you heard me the first time, and I do not repeat myself," Grandmother said, though it seemed her tone gentled when she addressed him. "In any case, it is the Lord's Day, and we do not go gallivanting about upon the strand, but attend church at ten o'clock. Dr. Pengallon comes to lunch after the service, and in the afternoon we rest or pursue the more gentle arts."

"What would those be, Mrs. Seacombe?" Lady Claire inquired, cleaning up the last of her sausage and egg pie, which was quite the best thing Maggie had encountered in this house so far, saving only her mother's letter and the sound of the Lady's voice through the heavy door last night.

"I should think you would be well acquainted with them, Lady Claire," was the pointed rejoinder. "I refer to needlework, the writing of letters, or perhaps a sketch in watercolor. One may also visit about the country, but you know so few people here that I fear you must make do with our company."

"I can think of nothing I'd like better," the Lady said smoothly. "Though the Misses Penford did encourage us to call."

"Perhaps another day," Mr. Malvern said quickly. "I do think a walk along the cliff-top would do me good. I have heard tell of a continuous path that stretches from the Lizard all the way to Devonshire. Is it true that such a thing exists, Mr. Seacombe?"

"It does," Grandfather told him. "And you are welcome to take a stroll if you wish. But I should stay clear of the beach until you are more familiar with the tides. We Seacombes can practically feel the pull of them in our blood, but this gift is not given to all."

"I could have used that ability last night," Maggie ventured. "The tide turned and came in so quickly that if it had not been for the stair, I should have been in some danger."

"My point exactly," Grandmother said into her compote. She could have been referring to the tide. In fact, had it not been for that private conversation between her grandparents in the solitude of their room, Maggie might have thought so. But now, she clearly heard, *If you cannot feel the tide, then you are not a Seacombe, are you?*

"I have no idea when the tide goes in or out, do you?" Lizzie said to Claude.

"None," he said cheerfully, apparently quite unconcerned that he did not share the family heritage. "Never needed to know before, and don't much expect to now."

"Do not be so hasty, my boy," Grandfather said, offering him the dish of compote. "When you are steaming over sea on a Seacombe ship, and later, running this company, you will find such knowledge useful."

Claude, for once, was able to keep his thoughts on his future to himself, and in any case, there was no time to hear them if they were to be ready for church.

When they reached the stone church at the top of the high street in town, Dr. Pengallon greeted them at the door and escorted Grandmother to the frontmost pew on the right side, as though she were the first lady in the congregation after his wife, who sat with their children on the left side under the pulpit. Later, during an interminable meal when neither the good reverend nor his wife deigned to speak to her, but made a great fuss of Lizzie and Claude, Maggie was forcibly reminded again of what she had overheard. The wheat, apparently, was already being separated from the chaff.

But her grandparents had not reckoned on the Lady's perspicacity. She, Mr. Malvern, and Tigg stepped bravely into the breach once the roast came in, and the conversation was distributed so equitably around the dining table that her grandparents hardly got a word in edgewise.

It was not until that evening, when they were saying their good-nights, that Grandfather brought up the subject again, saying to Claude, "You'll come in to the offices with me tomorrow, eh? No time like the present to have a look round."

"Tomorrow, sir?" Claude looked all at sea, as well he might, for this was the first they'd heard of it. "We had planned a picnic on the beach, and then a jolly ramble on the cliff-top, if we are not permitted the *sawan*."

"I would have thought you had had enough of picnics and rambles after your friends left in the spring."

"One can never have enough picnics," Lizzie said gaily. "I do hope we are invited."

"You are certainly invited to the Seacombe offices," Grandfather told her, clearly unwilling to let his catch school together and escape the net. "You ought to know from whence your living comes."

"I did not know I had a living." Lizzie went up on tiptoe and kissed him on the cheek. "But I should love to come, and so would Maggie."

"We will talk of that another time," he said gruffly, following Grandmother up the stairs. "Good-night."

"What did he mean?" Maggie said once they were safely in their room. "Talk of me going along another time? Or of livings?"

"Livings, I expect," Lizzie said. "Though I can't imagine what he means, unless he plans to give us an allowance as he does Claude. Fancy that, Mags. An allowance!"

"The Lady gives us pocket money, and we have our investment money every quarter from the Zeppelin Airship Works."

"But this is different."

"I don't see how. Besides, at this rate it's not likely I'll get anything."

Lizzie dropped her shoe and turned, puzzled. "What do you mean? If I'm to get an allowance, then you will, too."

But Maggie could not bring herself to chivvy the facts out into the open, or confide in Lizzie what she had heard her grandparents say. It was too humiliating, too ugly—and she did not want to change Lizzie's view of her family. If she did not see their darker side, then Maggie would not be the one to shine the light upon it. She would just have to rise above it until her grandparents saw her for the lady she was, and welcomed her into the family circle for her own good qualities.

"They will break the bank giving us all an allowance," Maggie said with a smile. "You and I together could not come close to what Claude spends in the course of a month!"

"Isn't that the truth. Wait—you're not putting on your night-clothes, are you? Aren't you coming with us? You must, Mags—you're our guide."

Maggie's fingers halted on the hooks of her corset. "Coming where?"

"Down to the *sawan*. Come on, toss on your boots and raiding rig. Claude is afire to see it, and now that the grands have gone up, the field is open."

"Lizzie! You don't mean to disobey them."

"I do indeed. Oh, we're not going in via the beach, as you did. We'll simply slip down through the cellar and have a proper look."

"But Nancarrow has the keys—how will you explain this to him when he was right there in the room to hear Grandmother forbid our going?" Lizzie smiled that mischievous smile that Maggie had learned to dread. "Lizzie. You didn't."

She reached into her pocket and pulled out a ring from which dangled the heavy iron key. "I did. It was easy as a wink."

"But how—when—"

"When he was serving the coffee, and his hands were full with that big, heavy tray. When I bumped into him at the door, he barely kept it from falling, didn't he?

Oh, don't look like that, Mags. They don't serve spirits on Sundays, so I'll have it back before he notices it's gone."

"Lizzie, your light fingers are going to get you into trouble someday."

"They already have, and I survived, didn't I?"

"I wouldn't push my luck if I were you."

"Oh, stop being a gloomy gumpus. We won't be gone an hour, and if it makes you feel better, I'll slip it under his door when we come back."

Maggie forbore to remind her that this plan would guarantee that Nancarrow would realize it had been pinched, but there was no stopping Lizzie once she had the wind to her rudder. So Maggie pulled on her raiding rig—a practical brown skirt over a black ruffled petticoat and stockings, a wide leather belt with hooks and rings for equipment, and a cream eyelet blouse that was comfortable as well as pretty.

Moonglobes in hand, they crept downstairs and met Claude at the green baize door that led downstairs. His eyebrows rose at the sight of them.

"You look rather like pirates," he whispered in admiration. "Were you thinking the grands would be hosting a fancy-dress ball?"

"Shh!" Lizzie pulled out the key and waved it. "Let's be off!"

They located the stone stairway once again and slipped through the cellar door. Since Maggie was the only one who had been down here, she led the way, winding through stacks of barrels, and shelves constructed of apertures for glossy wine bottles.

Claude gawked about him. "I say, for a pair of old folks, the grands have enough spirits here to intoxicate half Penzance."

"The result of a lifetime of collection?" Maggie hazarded.

"I'd say not. Papa used to keep a rather nice cellar, but the bottles he collected always looked so old and dusty I always wondered how the contents could possibly taste good. And look—this is a recent vintage." He pulled a bottle from its sleeve and showed them a date of two years before.

"Never mind that," Lizzie whispered. "How do we get through this door? Bother it! There must be a second key."

"No, there isn't." Maggie abandoned the stacks of spirits and joined her at the door to the stone stair. "It's a mechanical lock. See if you can pick it as easily as you picked poor Nancarrow's pocket."

"You never did!" Claude breathed in admiration. "Good show."

"It was nothing," Lizzie said modestly, then turned her attention to the locking assembly. "Hm. Well, my goodness. Whoever installed this wasn't very concerned about keeping people out, was he?"

"Are you joking?" Claude frowned at the assembly. "I can't make head or tail of it. And why put a mechanical lock on this door and not the one above?"

"Because the people in the house didn't want whoever came in via the *sawan* to go any farther than the cellar?" This seemed the only practical explanation, in Maggie's mind. "Not unless they were expected, I mean."

"Here it is." Lizzie pressed the old nail head and the assembly clicked into motion, its moving parts clicking and groaning and finally locking into the open position.

"Upon my life, you're a tricky one, Elizabeth," Claude breathed. "How did you figure it out?"

"A lucky guess," she said airily, and leaned on the handle. "Come on, let's go exploring."

This time, Maggie counted one hundred and eighty-four steps down into the *sawan*, and when they emerged at the bottom onto the landing, she surreptitiously massaged her aching legs. Going down didn't affect them quite as much as going up—but then, she'd been so frightened going up that it had probably made it worse.

Lizzie and Claude had ranged over the landing in moments—it was rather bare of interest, unless one enjoyed old packing crates—and jumped down to the damp sand. Maggie followed them to the stone archway and showed them the little shelf where the moonglobes were kept for those coming in from the seaward side.

"Can anyone's blood tell us when the tide will turn?" she asked, gazing out at the waves, which seemed to be a safe distance off. "We don't want to be cut off, and it comes in quickly."

"We're a good hour short of when we found you last night," Lizzie said, "but I wouldn't risk staying out here too long. We have to go up the way we came down or the doors will all be found open in the morning."

"Show us the track up to the cliff-top, then, for future reference," Claude said. "Was it difficult?"

"Not at all," Maggie said. "This way." She passed under the arch and emerged onto the sand of the beach. The boom of the waves sounded much as it had the night before, which some deep instinct inside her took as a warning. They didn't have much time.

She skirted a granite outcrop and pointed up the cliff. "There. Do you see where the black stone turns to soil? The path is more a crack in the rock, but it's wide enough for a person. I came down right here, though the tides have erased my footprints."

Claude approached the rock. "Here?" He began to climb, and Maggie looked over her shoulder anxiously.

"Don't go far, Claude. The sound of the waves is getting louder."

"Nonsense. Look—I'm almost up."

"Maggie?" Lizzie called, and Maggie hesitated, torn between anxiety for Claude—who could not have had much experience in rabbiting about cliffs at night—and the note of puzzlement in Lizzie's voice.

"What is it?"

"What's that, do you suppose?"

Oh, goodness. Claude was a man grown. He could fend for himself, and if he fell off, well, the sand was soft.

"What is what?" She joined her cousin at the water's edge, which was definitely closer than it had been minutes ago.

"That light."

Some thousand yards to the west of the house, a red lamp glowed on the cliff-top, right where a valley cut down to the sea, filled with the dark shapes of trees.

On. Off. On-on-off. On for ten seconds. Off.

"That's the second series," Lizzie said. "The first is what caught my eye. What do you suppose it means?"

"Someone is signaling, that's clear." Maggie looked out to sea, but saw nothing. No answering signal from a boat, no horn, no blast of releasing steam. "But to whom?"

And then her attention focused on the waves. "Lizzie, we have to retrieve Claude and go up. The tide is coming in."

Lizzie dragged her gaze off the red lamp, which was going into its third series of flashes to … no one. "Perhaps someone is practicing. We ought to take a picnic over in that direction in the morning and see what we can see."

"Lizzie! The tide!"

Lizzie finally realized that if she did not move, her boots were going to get wet. They scampered up the sand to find Claude had disappeared completely.

"Oh, that boy," Lizzie said impatiently. "He's probably in the garden by now, congratulating himself on his prowess and planning a mountaineering holiday in Switzerland. Come on—we don't have time to wait for him to come down."

They dashed into the *sawan* and scrambled up onto the landing, heedless of the guano that covered the stone and wood, and ten minutes later emerged into the cellar. They found Claude in the stair well waiting for them, delighted that he had been the first to gain the house—as if it were a race and he had won.

He was so happy over the joke that Maggie just shook her head at him. She noticed, however, that in all the whispering and sliding of keys under doors and sneaking up staircases, neither she nor Lizzie brought up the subject of the red lantern signaling to no one on the cliff-top.

A small thing. A trifle.

But Maggie felt a glow of happiness nonetheless that, despite her cousin's changed circumstances and her own dubious status, there was still something that the Mopsies could share between themselves alone.

12

At ten o'clock the next morning, the girls presented themselves to Grandfather for his inspection. His gaze swept from jaunty straw hats covered in flowers to navy suits to lacy Belgian cutwork blouses to gloves, and with a decided nod, he declared that they would do. He handed them into an open horse-drawn carriage, where Claude was already waiting.

Lady Claire, Mr. Malvern, and Tigg climbed into her steam landau, in which they had come back yesterday afternoon. Maggie had no doubt that all three would thoroughly enjoy the sensation they made as the Lady piloted it through town.

Maggie eyed the rumps of the horses, and leaned over to whisper to Lizzie. "You don't suppose they'll—er—fertilize the road while we're driving, do you?"

"Horses have been pulling carriages for hundreds of years," Lizzie whispered back. "I'm sure someone will have accounted for that. But how very strange not to travel in a landau."

Fortunately, the journey was a short one, taking them down the High Street hill in state. People stopped to gape at the landau, and nodded in greeting when the carriage passed. Some even pulled off their hats, which felt even odder to Maggie than having Tamsen curtsey to her. The procession made its way to the harbor and the carriage driver pulled up in front of the huge, imposing stone building that housed the offices of the Seacombe Steamship Company.

They were ushered into Grandfather's office, which was the size of the drawing room, with a big mahogany desk and shelves and cabinets and all manner of curiosities from foreign parts upon display tables. They were treated to a history of the company from its founding by Pendrake Seacombe, all the way to the enormous map showing the current shipping routes.

Claude rose from the nap he was taking in the upholstered guest chair to trace with his finger the routes painted from Penzance, Southampton, and Portsmouth to the Nordic countries, the Royal Kingdom of Spain, the East and West Indies, and the Fifteen Colonies.

"What an enormous undertaking," he finally said. "I can scarcely wrap my mind round it all."

"That is why I am so anxious for you to begin, my boy," Grandfather said. "While I might wish that your education had taken place here in England, and not France, it is too late to unmake those decisions now. When you graduate from the Sorbonne in the spring, it is my fondest wish that you take a commission and begin serving aboard one of our ships. It is best to begin at the water line, as it were, and work one's way up. That way one understands the entirety of the business."

"To say nothing of the lives of one's employees," Maggie offered. "You will understand how they think and feel if you are doing the same work they are."

Grandfather cleared his throat with a harrumphing sound. "The thoughts and feelings of sailors and long-shoremen are hardly the business of the Seacombes. We have larger concerns, young lady, such as the political and economic states of the countries with which Her Majesty trades."

"But you said—"

"A young lady should not bother her head about it in any case. It is Claude's career of which I speak. Now, Claude, you will notice that there are no shipping routes to Calais or for that matter, any of the French ports."

"The lines appear to have been painted out," Claude said as the Lady whipped her skirts around her and stalked to the window. He tilted closer to the great map on the wall. "Or at least, a darker color has been used."

"That is because the Ministry of Trade has advised us to suspend activity with France until they come up to scratch and stop this nonsense."

"Suspend activity?" Lizzie repeated. "Is there going to be a war?"

Her grandfather beamed at her. "An excellent question, Elizabeth. You see now why some knowledge of global politics is necessary in this very office. France, I am sorry to say, has shrugged off its republican costume and revealed its true colors, putting Bourbons on the throne once more. And you know what they're like."

A LADY OF SPIRIT

"Um. Would that be Louis the Fourteenth and that lot?" Upon her graduation, Lizzie had received firsts in mathematics, German, and the French language, not its history.

"I believe he means that the French kings have always believed themselves entitled to the English throne," Maggie said. "Is that not correct, sir?"

Grandfather harrumphed again at being thus directly addressed. "A tempest in a teapot—or the mind of a crackpot," he said. "Her Majesty and her nephews—the Kaiser and the Tsar—will give that French nincompoop a smack on the side of his schoolboy head and it will all blow over."

But Maggie took courage from the approving look the Lady passed over her rigid shoulder and spoke up once more. "Claude, you go to school in Paris. Have you heard nothing of this?"

"If I did, I made certain I forgot it forthwith," Claude said with a laugh that sounded somewhat strained. "I am afraid horribly dull lectures on history and economics from the professor's podium are as close as I wish to get to that sort of thing."

"You will feel differently when 'that sort of thing' affects your livelihood," his grandfather said. "I must confess I am glad you will only be in that blasted place for a few months more. Come. I will show you the rest of the offices, and then we will proceed to the docks for a tour of *Demelza*, which lies at harbor for the family's use. She is our flagship, you know, named for your grandmother."

Maggie wondered if her lines were as stiff and her temper as uncertain as the woman for whom she was named, but the Lady would never recover if she said such a thing aloud. She didn't know what the others thought of the tour of the offices, but she found it most interesting, particularly on the lower levels, where the goods were stored which had been received and inspected and were waiting to be loaded onto trains for shipping in England. There seemed to be everything from lovely embroidered fabrics to strange hairy nuts and lumber from exotic trees on the warehouse levels, and it fascinated her. Who had woven these fabrics, or picked those nuts? What was the climate like there? And why on earth would one choose to ship goods by sea when it was so dangerous and unpredictable and slow?

But apparently there were as few answers to that last question as there were to the first two.

The warehouse levels bustled with people—clerks, laborers, sailors—and when Maggie turned from her contemplation of a large winch assembly that was loading a cart, she realized that Lizzie and the others were nowhere in sight.

Goodness. She had better catch up, or she'd never find them in this melee. But they had only just been on the viewing platform, so no doubt she'd see them at the top of the wooden staircase.

But she did not.

Instead, she found herself with no prospect but a catwalk strung over the bustle of the warehouse, or a trip back down the steps that would net her nothing more than she had before. In vain she looked for the bobbing froth of Lizzie's hat, or the painfully fashionable yellow-and-black plaid of Claude's jacket.

Why had Lizzie not noticed she was missing? They were close as two peas in a pod—or at least, they had been until they'd come to Penzance. No matter what Maggie did, it seemed Lizzie was far ahead of her—with dazzling prospects, with Tigg, with the family—and Maggie was left behind with nothing but her manners to recommend her.

And a letter to her mother. And the Lady.

In her catalogue of sorrows, she must not forget her blessings, the Lady chief among them. In fact, she would just pull Claire aside and obtain her permission to abandon this whole disastrous excursion. The prospect of laying her hot cheek on the Lady's shoulder and feeling the comfort of her arms around her was immensely appealing.

"I say, are you lost?"

Maggie dashed the moisture from her eyes and turned to see a young man coming across the catwalk as though he were strolling down Pall Mall.

"I am not," she said. "Though my party seems to be."

He took her in from head to foot, and seemed to find the picture more satisfying than had her grandfather. "You would be with Mr. Seacombe's party, then? You are ... Miss Margaret, if I am not mistaken."

Surprise rendered her bereft of speech. She had not seen him before, because if she had, she would have remembered those roguish eyes, that triangular smile, his even teeth white in his tanned face. Then— "I do apologize, sir, but have we met?"

He laughed as if this were a fine joke. "Not ruddy likely, since I'm but a clerk in the receiving office and you're the granddaughter of Howel Seacombe."

"But—how do you know that?"

He made an expansive gesture that encompassed the entire busy operation below. "Everyone knows. We're all on our best behavior while the family visits. I saw you from across the other side, you know—you and your cousin and the young master. Is your cousin as pretty as you close up?"

"Much prettier," Maggie said automatically, and then blushed that she had dignified such a familiar remark with a reply. "I mean—I have become separated from them somehow. Would you be so kind as to help me rejoin them?"

"Oh, now I've offended you. I didn't mean to. Because you are, you know—awfully pretty."

Oh dear, this was dreadful. "I won't trouble you. I'm sure you have work to do. I'll find them myself." Blushing, hot, she stumbled down the staircase, only to hear a *whoosh*—and turned just in time to see him sliding down the rickety banister past her.

"Please forgive me," he said, landing with aplomb and sweeping his tweed cap from his head. "I'm dreadfully prone to personal remarks. People are interesting to me. Come—I saw where they went, and I'll take you up there now."

"I think after that performance you must tell me your name. Not—" she said hastily, as his eyes widened with apprehension, "—to report you for your unsolicited opinions, but so that I may know to whom I am indebted."

He gazed at her. "That was quite a speech. Do you normally use that many syllables?"

She tilted her chin. "Only when they are warranted. I could throw rocks at you instead of words, if you prefer."

"Words can do as much damage, if a person aims them well enough." He offered her his arm and after a second's hesitation, she took it. "Michael Polgarth, at your service."

"Polgarth!" she exclaimed as he opened a door she had not seen at the rear of the viewing platform, and ushered her through it. "I know a Polgarth. He is a poultryman, and I credit him for my interest in the study of genetics."

"Do you, now?"

The corridor was lined with office doors bearing important-looking brass name plates, but he took her past them all to an external door, where she found herself on the street that ran down the side of the building, straight to the sea. In the distance, there were Grandfather, Lizzie and Claude, and the Lady and Mr. Malvern, all engaged in spirited conversation and apparently completely unaware that there was one missing from the party.

Her steps faltered to a halt, and beside her, Michael stopped, too. "Is something the matter, Miss Seacombe?"

"Yes. I mean—no, of course not."

"And yet, you seem unwilling to join your family on *Demelza*. She's a trim little ship, you know, for a steam vessel. You'd probably like her."

"Have you been aboard?" Maybe if she stalled long enough, her party would walk back this way and see her in conversation with this nice young man, as unconcerned for their company as they seemed to be for hers.

"Once or twice, in the course of my duties. She returned from the East Indies one year, and I could swear I smelled cinnamon in her hold when I went down there to deliver the manifests. But it was probably just engine grease. So you know Polgarth the poultryman at Gwynn Place?"

She turned, her eyes wide. "I never said from where I knew him, merely that I did."

He grinned. "There is only one Polgarth in these parts who makes a study of genetics in chickens, and that's my grandfather."

"He never is!" she exclaimed, most inelegantly. "Polgarth—your grandfather!"

Michael dipped her a bow. "Does that make us friends?"

"I should like it to. Have you seen him recently? Lady Claire and Mr. Malvern are to go up to Gwynn Place on Wednesday, but I'm afraid we're stuck here until—I mean—that is to say—"

And he laughed again, the irritating creature. "I'll pretend I didn't hear that. Yes, I go up to see him and my aunt Tressa at least once a month—she keeps house for him, you know, since my grandmother died. He's looking forward to seeing Lady Claire very much. How does she come to be with you?"

"She is our guardian, mine and Lizzie's."

"Well, this bears exploring. Wait here just a moment, will you?" He popped back inside and in less than a minute reappeared. "There, that's settled. I am to be your escort—I've just let my superiors know so that no one thinks you've been kidnapped. When Mr. Seacombe's party comes back, they will be informed."

Somehow she found herself walking at his side, her hand in the crook of his elbow, proceeding up the hill instead of down to the harbor.

He returned to the previous subject with interest. "I'm afraid I don't understand your connection to Gwynn Place. Lady Claire your guardian? I wouldn't think that the granddaughter of Mr. Seacombe would be in need of any such person."

"Well, considering that a month ago, I didn't know Mr. Seacombe existed, much less that I was his granddaughter, you would be incorrect," Maggie said with some asperity. "We have been Lady Claire's wards since we were ten, and we are sixteen and a half now."

He said something in Cornish that might possibly have been the equivalent of "Blimey!" Then he said, "Of course you may depend upon my circumspection. These are facts that are not generally known."

"But surely the folk hereabouts would know of the deaths of our mothers—Elaine and Catherine."

"It is not something that is talked of openly, you understand. Out of respect for the Seacombes."

"But do you know something of it? For you see, I know absolutely nothing of my mother." Except that she liked the scent of lilac, and might have had a May Day beau whose name began with a *K*.

They had reached the top of the hill without Maggie being aware of climbing it.

But all he said was, "I am afraid I cannot say."

Which was most unsatisfying.

"What are we doing up here?" she finally asked. "If you can say that much."

"It is a fine prospect over our fair town," he said. "I thought you might like it, if you did not want to venture down to the harbor."

It was indeed a fine prospect of Penzance in all its busy beauty, its comfortable stone houses and shops tumbling down the hill, stopping just at the harbor's edge. The sun was at its highest peak in the sky, and the sea heaved gently below, the deep blue of the cornflowers that grew in the fields. In the other direction, Maggie could see the airfield, barely half a mile off, and make out the khaki-colored fuselage of *Athena* and the pale silver of *Victory* at rest at their mooring masts.

How long had it been since anyone had gone out to attend to Holly and Ivy? The Lady went every day, but had she been today?

"Thank you for bringing me up here, Mr. Polgarth," she said briskly, extending her gloved hand. "I am going to walk to the airfield. That khaki-colored craft you see there is Lady Claire's airship. I have business aboard that I must attend to."

"Lady Claire has her own airship—as well as that extraordinary vehicle drawn up in front of the office?"

"Yes. The ship is *Athena*, the very first to use the automaton intelligence system for which she and Miss Alice Chalmers are known."

He pushed up his cap to scratch his forehead. "You won't find many in these parts who know what that is, including me," he said, "but it sounds most impressive. You realize, of course, that I cannot permit you to walk out there unescorted."

She raised an eyebrow. "Permit?" The poor chap, he could not be expected to know that she had killed a pair of pirates with a bola gun, flung gaseous capsaicin on the heads of men shooting at her with cannons, and become quite skilled in the Eastern arts of self defense— all before the age of twelve. But neither did one brag about these things to young men one had just met. As the Lady had gone to great pains to teach them, there were certain things a woman simply did not discuss outside her most intimate circle.

Michael looked a little taken aback. "Er—I meant to say, would you permit me to escort you there, Miss Seacombe?"

"Have you no work to do this morning?"

"None as important as being with you. My superiors would think me most remiss if I went back to work and left you wandering about on the moor by yourself—to say nothing of your grandfather's feelings on the subject."

Maggie bit back the first words that sprang to her tongue, and said instead, "It is broad daylight, and in any case, I do not think there is much danger on this moor." It was not, after all, the Texican Territory. Or the diamond fields of the Canadas.

He gave her a sidelong look. "I should not be so hasty as to say that." And then he offered her his arm.

She made up her mind, and took it.

13

Holly and Ivy came running to the door of the aviary when Maggie stepped aboard *Athena* and released them. She knelt just in time for Holly to spring into her lap and dive under her arm, and for Ivy to leap on to her shoulder and cuddle as close to her neck as she could. Maggie crooned and petted the hens, reassuring them that no one had forgotten them in the last day, and neither she nor Lizzie had been eaten by predators in the meanwhile. Finally, she introduced them to Michael Polgarth, which elicited the same reaction of doubtful watchfulness on both sides.

When the hens at last hopped down, satisfied that all was well with the world once more, Maggie led them outside to hunt in the grass under the gondola. The

Lady had built a mechanical device in the aviary in the boarding area that dispensed the mix of cracked corn and grains which Lewis compiled especially for the Wilton Crescent birds. Maggie checked that it was operating as it should, then added water to the bottle that hung inside it and kept a drinking well filled.

When she was satisfied that Holly and Ivy wanted for nothing, she looked up to see Michael Polgarth looking rather befuddled.

"I have never been introduced to a chicken before," he said at last. "I do not know whether to be amused or offended."

"You ought to be neither," Maggie told him, leading the way to the stern. "A bird must recognize that you are not a threat to her, and my including you helps with that aim. It would have been better if you had fed them from your hand. If a creature feeds you, then clearly it does not plan to eat you."

"That is not true," he said. "Many housewives keep hens for just that purpose."

"Not around Lady Claire, they don't."

He appeared to take the warning in the spirit in which it was meant, and changed the subject. "Where are we going?"

"Astern. If a pigeon has come, I'll bring the post back to Seacombe House with me."

"You employ carrier pigeons? I did not think they were in use any longer."

This stopped her at the door to the hold. "Are you serious? Have you never seen a postal pigeon? They are used for non-fixed addresses."

"I don't know any non-fixed addresses. Normal people don't live on airships."

"We do—or rather, we could—and I must inform you that we are perfectly normal, despite the fact that we have been to the Americas and back on airships, to say nothing of numerous voyages to Bavaria, where we go to school."

Now she'd really flummoxed him. Imagine being satisfied to live in such a backward place! Shaking her head, she pushed open the door and crossed the hold to the messenger cage.

Sure enough, three pigeons had come—clearly, the Lady had only visited long enough to care for Holly and Ivy, and had not taken the time to check. Maggie emptied the first two, finding letters from Lewis for her and Lizzie, a missive from the Lady's solicitor, and, in a heavy envelope bearing the Landgraf's wax seal, a letter from Count von Zeppelin.

Delighted, she showed Michael the packet. "We met Count von Zeppelin in the Canadas five years ago, and he became our sponsor during our stay in Germany. He is the inventor of the modern airship, you know."

"I did know, which I am sure surprises you to no end."

"I do not mean to offend you, sir, but goodness—I cannot imagine living in a place, no matter how lovely, that does not use modern technology."

"We get on very well. We do not bother it, and it does not bother us."

"But what if you had to—oh, I don't know—travel to London with urgency? What would you do then?"

"Take the train, of course. The Flying Dutchman is the fastest train in England. We are quite proud that she runs down here, and not to Edinburgh or some other modern city."

Maggie saw that there was no convincing him, so she turned her attention to the last pigeon. Popping open the door in its abdomen, she withdrew a thin envelope with no direction or addressee.

She slit it open with a fingernail and pulled out the single sheet of flimsy post-office paper it contained.

14 08 94 02 00 50L 450KG 6

"What on earth?"

Michael leaned over her shoulder. "What does it mean?"

"It must be a mistake—someone clearly got the magnetic numbers mixed up on the pigeon when they sent it. Though … I might hazard a guess that the first three are a date." August 14, 1894. "But what of the next?"

"A time? Oh-two-hundred hours would be written like that. In which case, it would mean two in the morning, the day after tomorrow."

Misdirected or not, Maggie loved a good puzzle. "All right, then, let us crack this cipher. What do the rest mean? Fifty liters? Four hundred fifty kilos?"

"If you come from Europe, where they use such a system, I suppose they might." Michael took the paper and held it up to the porthole, as if he thought a different message might be encoded there in invisible ink. "And the last? Six?"

Maggie shook her head. "The entire message makes no sense at all—which is only to be expected, since *Athena* is not its intended recipient. I wonder if I should attempt to send it back?"

But the pigeon revealed no clue as to its provenance. Unlike most, which were clearly marked with the names of their base airships, and in the case of the Dunsmuir devices, engraved with the family coat of arms, this one was bare of identifying marks. Rather like those of *Athena*, which went to Wilton Crescent in a manner best not spoken of when there were persons in authority present. Lewis had tinkered with their navigation systems in order for the Lady's correspondence to remain private, and the fact that it was illegal to circumvent the Royal Mail in this manner was simply not mentioned.

Maggie put the slip of paper with the other letters, and stood.

"Are you taking it with you?" Michael rose and held the door open for her.

"Yes. It may be some private correspondence of Lady Claire's, and I would not want to risk displeasing her if that is the case."

"Maybe she'll tell you what 'six' stands for."

"Maybe she will. Come, let us put Holly and Ivy in. I'm very much afraid I shall be late for tea." An idea struck her. "Would you like to come back with me? If you are connected with Gwynn Place, Lady Claire would be delighted to see you."

"I think not. I have not actually met her—or if I did, I was too young to remember it."

"You make her sound ancient. She is only three-and-twenty, you know."

When they reached the offices once more, they found that Mr. Polgarth's message had been given, and the carriage had returned to Seacombe House.

"Surely they have not left her to find her own way home?" Michael said in some surprise to Grandfather's private secretary, a man whose high forehead and myopic eyes led Maggie to believe that it would never occur to him to do as Mr. Polgarth had and take a walk upon the moor.

"Certainly not," the man said. "The party that came in the steam conveyance are enjoying the sights of our fair town until the young lady is ready to leave with them."

So the Lady and Mr. Malvern had remained behind … but … surely Lizzie would not have gone back to Seacombe House without her, especially knowing she was in the company of a young man they did not know. "And Miss Seacombe?" she asked. "Did she return to Seacombe House also?"

"Not to my knowledge. She and young Mr. Seacombe, I believe, are with Lady Claire."

Maggie exhaled in relief. She did not think she could bear it if Lizzie had so forgotten her existence that she would leave without her.

It did not take them long to locate the party. It was past noon and Maggie was certain that if there were a tearoom in the town, she would find Lizzie and the others in it. And so it proved to be.

"Michael Polgarth!" the Lady said with delight, shaking his hand. "You are Myghal's son, then?"

"Yes, your ladyship. My father's brother passed away when I was very small, and my Aunt Tressa is not married. It is up, to me, I suppose, to carry on the family name."

"I am sure you will do it great credit." She smiled at him with warmth, and Maggie was quite certain that if

Mr. Malvern had not been sitting upon the Lady's right hand, Michael would have fallen in love with her then and there.

When they had finished lunch, Lady Claire said, "Perhaps you four would not mind a walk home? I must go out to *Athena* and check on Holly and Ivy."

"Oh, I've done that, Lady," Maggie said, flushing with chagrin that she had utterly forgotten about the post in her pocketbook. "They are well and happy, and had a nice hunt in the grass while I was checking the post." She dug the letters out, and handed Lizzie's to her. "There's a bit of paper in there, too, that I believe has been misdirected. Yes, that one."

Lady Claire pulled out the slender missive and gazed at it, puzzled. "What on earth?"

"Exactly what I said."

"We think it must be a cipher," Michael put in. "Fifty liters and four hundred fifty kilos of something at two in the morning, the day after tomorrow."

"It is a poor cipher, then, if it can be understood so readily. Is it a manifest of some kind?" The Lady handed the sheet to Mr. Malvern. "It is certainly misdirected. I have not ordered fifty liters of anything, I'm afraid."

She rose, and the party prepared to leave. The sheet lay abandoned between her plate and that of Mr. Malvern, so Maggie picked it up and replaced it in her pocketbook. Whatever it was, it was not rubbish, but the private correspondence of someone. It should not be left out in public view.

When they were out on the street once more, Mr. Malvern said, "Mr. Polgarth, Tigg, may I trust you with the girls if Lady Claire and I take a spin in the landau? I have screwed my courage to the sticking point and am ready for my first driving lesson. If I begin on the airfield, there will be no obstacles—and if I run into poor *Athena*, she at least is tough enough to shrug me off without too much damage."

"You will do perfectly well, sir," Tigg told him. "Just remember that she builds up a head of steam while she is stationary, and you must let the acceleration bar out slowly to compensate for it."

"Noted," Andrew said with the air of a man committing a lifesaving fact to memory.

"Mr. Polgarth, if you are escorting the girls home, you must join us for tea at four o'clock," the Lady said.

"Oh, no, your ladyship. I couldn't. I'm just a clerk—Mr. Seacombe probably doesn't even know I exist."

Claire lifted her chin. "Then he will when you arrive and I introduce you. I wish to hear more news of Gwynn Place and you have not nearly satisfied me."

"If you are sure, my lady."

"Oh, goodness. You are only a few years younger than I. Please call me Lady Claire. *Her ladyship* is my mother."

"Yes, your—Lady Claire. If you feel it would be suitable, I would be happy to join you."

"I do. We shan't be long, provided Andrew does not run us into a stationary object."

"Or off a cliff," Mr. Malvern said with his usual self-deprecating humor. "You will not make me pilot it on a road, I hope?"

And reassuring him on that point, the Lady took his arm and they proceeded back along the street in the direction of the harbor, where the landau was no doubt entertaining a crowd.

No sooner did she have her back turned than Lizzie took Tigg's arm in much the same manner, smiling up at him. "This is more like it," she said. "I confess I've had enough chaperonage and proper behavior for one day. How clever of you gentlemen to fix it so that they are alone and so are we."

"What happened to Claude?" Maggie asked. She stood rather awkwardly at Mr. Polgarth's side. It was rather too bad of Lizzie to be so familiar with Tigg when Maggie could do nothing more than take Michael's arm politely. They ought to be on equal ground in public, and people were staring already. "Come. Let us walk round the harbor."

"He went home with your grandparents," Tigg explained, his hand over Lizzie's in a way that, had Maggie not been so embarrassed, might have struck her as touching.

"That's odd—Claude missing out on a—what did he call it? A ramble?"

"I don't think he had much choice in the matter," Lizzie said over her shoulder, the breeze tossing the tendrils of taffy-blond hair at her temples. "Grandfather had not quite finished telling him about the trade routes. My best guess is he might be by teatime."

"Poor boy," Maggie said. "Better he than I."

"Don't you want to learn about the trade routes?" Michael asked, pacing along the harbor promenade beside her.

Maggie ran a hand over the heads of the lion statues as they passed. "I do, very much. But Grandfather has rather firm views on what is suitable knowledge for a young lady. Lizzie, did you see how annoyed Lady Claire became in his office?"

"I did. I must say, I think you or I could do a perfectly capable job of running the company. Poor Claude does not possess what one might call a head for business."

"He may in time," Tigg said. "Give him a chance. He's only just lost his father and come into all this, you know."

"I know, but he has had nearly all his life to come to terms with being the Seacombe heir—and yet he is two and twenty and no closer to accepting it than I am."

Tigg glanced at Michael, who was attempting the impossible—walking directly behind the two of them while pretending not to hear what they said of his employer's family. "What is your opinion of Claude, Mr. Polgarth?"

At being thus directly addressed, Michael swallowed. "I do not think it fair of you to ask me, Lieutenant. I could not express an opinion of those who employ me."

"Of course you can," Lizzie said briskly. "It's only us. Don't you think Maggie and I ought to learn about the business? Wouldn't it be just the thing if the three Seacombes were to run it together? Goodness knows we could all fit in that office with a private secretary for each of us and have room for a string quartet."

"I think there would be entirely too much riotous behavior in there. You would scandalize the captains and no one would get any work done."

Lizzie laughed in delight. "There! I knew you had opinions of your own."

"Ah, but it would not be wise of me to express them. I can be sacked at any moment. You, I suspect, cannot."

"I wouldn't be so sure," came out of Maggie's mouth before she could close her teeth on it.

Lizzie looked at her curiously. "What does that mean?"

But thankfully, they had reached the end of the harbor promenade and Mr. Polgarth handed her down onto the rocks, where a path wound up and around the bluff that would take them up to the house on the promontory. And in the scrambling and pointing out of views and trying to keep their hats on their heads in all the wind, the opportunity for explanations blew away and out to sea.

When the giddy foursome finally gained the top of the bluff and made their way into the garden, Maggie was feeling a distinct glow. The Lady had once told her that her mother had been quite firm on that point: "Horses sweat. Men perspire. Ladies glow."

Maggie was glowing with a vengeance now, and she had the uncomfortable feeling that some of the flowers from her hat might by now be halfway to the Channel Islands. But she felt wonderful, being out of doors again in such amusing company. She and Lizzie had been happy to notice that Tigg and Michael Polgarth had taken a liking to one another—or perhaps it was merely a case of Tigg relaxing his protectiveness of herself and Lizzie enough to appreciate the other young man's honesty and good humor.

The fact that Lizzie allowed their handsome friend to hold her hand on the way up the cliff path when it was not strictly necessary for him to do so in order to assist her may have gone a long way to creating the companionable rapport between the two young men.

Maggie had the presence of mind to drag Lizzie to their room to repair the wind damage before they presented themselves for tea.

"Lizzie Seacombe, how shocking you are," she said, taking down her hair and brushing it vigorously. "Such public displays of affection!"

"To you and the sea birds." Lizzie twisted up her own heavy mane around her head in a French braid and rammed pins into the knot at the back. "And neither of you are going to tell on me." She clasped her hands rapturously. "I still cannot believe that Tigg cares for me."

"I know—his taste in female company is definitely lacking."

Lizzie stuck out her tongue, then the smile returned as if she could not keep it away. "I feel quite dizzy with it—with him, Maggie. It is as if I had never seen him before the pocket watch bomb in Munich—and now I cannot see him in any other way but as that man who called me 'Lizzie-love' when he thought me unconscious."

Maggie's heart seemed to contract with longing. What would it be like to feel this way about someone? To be so happy that it permeated you through and through?

"I am glad you do," she said, squeezing Lizzie's hand and pulling her out the door. "Tigg is a fine, intelligent man, and he has the Lady's permission to treat you as rather more than a companion, doesn't he?"

"Yes, he told me so. Not that it would have mattered if he didn't." She clattered down the stairs, laughing, and was still smiling as they reached the sea parlor, where Tigg and Mr. Polgarth were waiting for them.

The Lady and Mr. Malvern were already in conversation with the Seacombes as Tamsen bobbed a curtsey and ushered them in.

Grandmother glanced at the watch on its pearl brooch at her breast. "Was I not clear that tea was at four o'clock?"

Goodness. They were only ten minutes late. It was Hobson's choice anyway—if they had not taken those minutes, they would have had a lecture on the state of their hair and dress.

"I'm sorry, Grandmother," Lizzie said, when Maggie did not reply. "We climbed the cliff path and it was rather more of a walk than we all expected, having not gone that way before."

"In future you will be more considerate of others and mind the time. Howel, please ring and we will have the tea brought in. Again."

Grandfather did so, and the Lady stepped forward. "Mr. and Mrs. Seacombe, may I present Maggie's escort from the company offices this morning? This is Mr. Michael Polgarth. He—"

Grandmother dropped the plate of cakes, sending petits fours bouncing and rolling about on the low table and scattering crumbs on the carpet.

"Grandmama!" Claude started forward. "Are you ill?"

Breathing deeply, Grandmother bent forward as though she had been struck, her fingers wrinkling her pearl-gray taffeta skirts. Maggie turned in appeal to Grandfather, but he stood near the bell pull, as rigid as the cliff face below the house. What could be the matter? Had they both recognized Michael as a lowly clerk, and were so offended by his presence in their home that they were one step away from an apoplexy? Oh dear, this was dreadful!

The Lady controlled her own surprise and glanced at Tamsen in a manner that made that young lady jump to her duty and begin picking up the little cakes at top speed. The girl brushed the crumbs onto the china platter and hustled it from the room—and still the Seacombes had not spoken.

"Mrs. Seacombe, are you sure you are quite well?" Claire inquired. "Shall I call someone? Send for a doctor?"

Grandmother came out of her fixed stare rather like a swimmer coming up from a great depth. "No," she said hoarsely. "There is no need."

"Perhaps some smelling salts? Or lavender from the garden? Maggie, do run down and pick some. I understand it is most calming to the nerves."

Grandmother, her attention thus directed exactly where Maggie did not want it, said, "I never expected this to happen, but I am not in the least surprised that *you* are the engineer of it."

Maggie's jaw sagged.

"Get out of this house," Grandfather rasped.

"I beg your pardon?" the Lady said, the astonishment in her tone glazed in the thinnest layer of ice. "To whom are you speaking?"

"Him. That bounder there." Grandfather jerked his chin in Michael's direction, and in response, Tigg stepped a little closer to the other young man, as if offering his support. "No one bearing that name shall ever set foot in this house. Take your leave at once."

"Mr. Seacombe," Lady Claire remonstrated in horror, "Mr. Polgarth is here at my invitation. There has been nothing in his conduct that would elicit such a degree of incivility. In fact, he has been kind enough to do you a great service in looking after Maggie when she became separated from our party."

"That's because like attracts like," Grandmother snapped. "You have been deceived, Lady Claire. Your remarks do you credit, but they will have no bearing on my husband's wishes. Mr. Polgarth, Nancarrow will see you out."

But Maggie had had enough. "That's all right, Nancarrow," she said to the butler. "I will do it. I find myself quite in need of some air."

Michael Polgarth's manners did not desert him. He bowed to the Seacombes, and then to Lady Claire and Mr. Malvern, whose jaw was working in a manner that Maggie had only seen a very few times, usually in connection with the underhanded activities of Lord James Selwyn. Then, head held high, he strode from the room, Maggie at his heels.

14

What must he think of me?

Maggie did not have the courage to unlock and open the big front door, used only on formal occasions, so she directed Mr. Polgarth through the empty drawing room and out the French doors onto the terrace.

What must he think of all of us?

"Mr. Polgarth, I am so sorry." Tears of mortification threatened to well up, but she held them back. "I do not know what came over them. I had no idea they were capable of such—"

"You have nothing to apologize for, Miss Margaret."

"Please, I beg you, call me Maggie. *They* call me Margaret and it takes all the pleasure out of knowing my mother had a reason to give me that name, even if I do not know what it was. And I *must* apologize. I have never been so humiliated in all my life—and considering the last day or two, that is saying something."

The length of this speech took them through the rose garden and out onto the lawn and the cliff-top. Just at the place where the order of the mowed grass was disrupted by wildflowers and tussocks of sea-grass and thrift, Mr. Polgarth stopped and turned to her.

"You have been nothing but kind to me, so please do not abase yourself for something you have not done. And if I am to call you Maggie, then you must call me Michael. If you do that, I shall tell you a story."

The dam broke, and a fat tear rolled down Maggie's cheek, to be dried almost instantly by the wind. "Do not patronize me, too. I cannot bear it."

"Patronize you!" In agitation, he took her hand and pulled her along the cliff path, heading west, in the direction from which she and Lizzie had seen the red lamp flashing in the night. "That is the last thing I would do. I have put it badly. I mean only that I have information about my family that may be of interest to you—and give you some little understanding of your grandparents' behavior."

Maggie stopped dragging on his hand like a boat anchor and took a skipping step to catch up.

He released her, and her fingers felt a little chilled in the absence of the warmth of his. "Come," he said over his shoulder. "I cannot speak of these things while the windows of Seacombe House look down on us."

She followed him along the path for nearly a quarter of a mile. The house was lost to sight behind them, and when the way was split by a huge fissure in the cliff face and it meant going inland some distance to continue around it, he clambered down the slope a little way and into a copse of trees that spilled into the gap. At the foot of the cliff, waves lapped on a tiny beach, but he did not walk down the zigzag path.

Instead, he found an outcrop of flat granite, worn smooth by the action of hundreds of years of weather, and folded himself onto a shelf of stone. He patted the warm surface next to him, and Maggie joined him, folding her skirts decorously around her so the wind would not pluck them up and expose her knees.

"I used to come here as a child," he said. "My parents had a cottage there." He pointed to the other side of the gap, where a collection of snug stone cottages spilled down the gentler slope and had access to the sea. Colorful fishing boats bobbed on the water, the ones closer in beached by the outgoing tide.

Was this where the red flashes had come from? Maggie could swear it was—but at the same time, it had been at night and she and Lizzie couldn't see landmarks or judge distance with any accuracy.

However, that was a question for another time. There were more urgent questions to be asked now. "Is that when you became acquainted with my grandparents?"

"No, I have never spoken to them before this afternoon."

"Then how—? Why—? I don't understand."

"When we lived here, my uncle lived with us as well for a few months. We children thought it a great lark—he was home from university and he was our favorite of our various relatives—dashing and funny and always willing to spare a moment to hear a child's confidence. He had a tremendous store of terrible riddles, too, some of which I still remember, after all this time."

"Tell me one."

"Very well—what has a foot but no arms?"

Maggie thought for a moment. "A ruler?"

Michael laughed. "You are much better at it than we ever were. He stumped us every time, and the sillier they were, the more we were stumped. Of course, it didn't help that he was a tremendous mimic, and half the time was telling them in someone else's voice. Part of the joke was to figure out who he was playing, and then what the riddle meant."

A little piece of herself fell into place, and the question uppermost in Maggie's mind began to solidify into certainty. "What was his name?"

"Kevern. Kevern Polgarth—born and raised on the tenant croft at Gwynn Place. When my father and mother married, they came down here to Penzance so Dad could ply his trade as an animal doctor. Uncle Kevern was studying science and engineering at the college in Truro, and he would stay with us on his vacations while he worked on the great steam engines in the mines."

"Wheal Porth," Maggie breathed.

He reared back to stare at her. "How did you know that? That is the mine on the other side of that headland, there." He pointed further down the coast. "You can just see the engine tower above those trees."

"I think I begin to understand." She reached into the pocket of her skirt. "I found this, hidden under a floorboard in my mother's old room, the first day we came."

He read the letter swiftly, then again, more slowly. At last he folded it up and handed it back. "So you do know."

"I know nothing. Only that a young man whose name began with *K* met my mother one May Day and expressed his admiration for her. Nothing else."

"Your grandparents have not told you your mother's story?"

Maggie could not keep the bitterness in her heart from spilling into her tone. "They barely speak to me, and when they do, they speak as they do to the servants—or at best, a companion they have hired to attend my sis—cousin."

He gave her the courtesy of acceptance, and did not try to convince her that she must be imagining things. "Then let me tell you what I know—which is family history according to my aunt Mariah, who by all accounts was great friends with your mother, though your grandparents would have favored that friendship even less than they favor yours with me."

"Who were my mother and aunt to be friends with, then, if they could not choose their own companions?" Maggie wondered aloud. "The daughters of rich folk?"

"I imagine so. The Seacombes are, of course, the first family in these parts, but there are several families of lesser but most respectable consequence in town. They would have encouraged friendships in that quarter. Certainly not with the children of a poultryman down here between terms, no matter how ambitious they were or how successful they became in their respective careers."

"Tell me about your uncle."

"Your letter appears to have been written shortly after they met. All four—Dad, Uncle Kevern, Aunt Mariah, and Aunt Tressa—had gone to the May Day celebrations in town, where your mother was crowned Queen of the May."

"Which had nothing whatever to do with her being a Seacombe."

"I am sure it did not," he said with equal gravity. "But in all fairness, she was reputed to be a great beauty. My aunt Tressa enjoys miniatures, and she painted a portrait of Catherine from memory that day, crowned with flowers."

Maggie resisted the urge to clutch at his arm, but she could not control the urgency in her voice. "I have never seen a single picture of her. Please, does this painting still exist?"

"It does as far as I know. After her husband died, she came back to keep house for my father at Gwynn Place, so it will be there on the farm if it is anywhere."

Maggie resolved on the spot that on Wednesday, no matter what anyone said, she would go with the Lady to Gwynn Place and find that picture. "Go on."

"Following the May Day celebrations—and presumably this meeting on the beach that he writes of—Kevern and Catherine became inseparable."

"How did they manage, if my grandparents did not approve?"

He grinned. "The same way any of us would manage—by stealth and subterfuge. My aunt says they met in the *sawan* at night and would come back to the cottage along the beach at low tide. Sometimes they would go downalong with my father and my aunts, where no one would know them, and laugh and sing until the wee hours of the morning."

"Downalong?"

"That's a Cornish expression for the lower part of town—the docks, the fishing boats, the taverns and inns along the harbor."

Where no one would know them, indeed.

Michael glanced at her. "The next part is not so happy—are you sure you wish to hear it?"

"I have never been more sure of anything in my life."

"Very well, then." He paused a moment, gazing out to sea, where the gulls swooped and mewed. "By the end of July, your mother suspected she might be expecting you, and told my uncle. Aunt Mariah said he told her afterward that he flung himself to one knee and proposed on the spot, and that Catherine accepted."

Maggie could picture the happy scene, and her heart filled with a joy it had never known before. She had been wanted. She had been no more than a suspicion—a twinkle in her father's eye, as Lady Dunsmuir might say—but yet she had been wholeheartedly wanted. Her throat closed up, and tears sprang to her eyes once more.

"Catherine told your grandparents, and you can imagine their reaction."

"Only too well," Maggie whispered.

"They had planned a marriage for her much more grand than to a mere student from a farming family, its connection with Gwynn Place notwithstanding. Catherine was immediately packed off to the Continent, with a story put about that she was visiting her sister, who at that time was living in Paris for several months while her husband attended to his business affairs."

"I take it that was not true?"

"No. She and Aunt Mariah, who had studied to be a nurse, spent the autumn and winter in Cornouaille, which lies opposite us in Brittany, in a tiny seaside village called Baie des Sirenes."

"Bay of the Sirens? No, wait—Mermaids."

"Is that what it means? I have no aptitude for languages—numbers are what speak to me. In any case, in the spring, that is where you were born. We heard later that there had been complications, and she was so debilitated by grief at her family's hardness of heart that she did not have the strength to fight."

The hollow that Maggie had always been conscious of deep inside filled now with an echo of that grief. Grief for what she might have known. Grief for what she did not and could never know. And above all, grief that the two people most intimately connected in this business—her grandparents—had rejected her mother in her moment of greatest need and were continuing that rejection to the second generation.

"Do my grandparents blame me?" she whispered. "For Mother's death? For dashing all their dreams and plans for her because she loved the wrong man?"

"From all accounts, she loved exactly the right man," Michael said gently. "I do not presume to know what is in their hearts, but I do know this … you are all that remains on the earth of a much beloved son and uncle. You know what that means, don't you?"

The pieces that she had not considered before fell into place. "You—are my cousin. My father's brother's son." And there was more. "That means Polgarth the poultryman is—my grandfather!"

From out of nowhere, joy leaped up into the hollow inside her, and expanded and filled it, warming places that had been cold and empty her entire life.

She grasped Michael's hand. "It is true, isn't it? The one person at Gwynn Place besides the Lady with whom I feel truly at ease, truly comfortable—is my own grandfather?"

"It is true. Though I must say, if you have a hidden talent for terrible riddles, I will disown you here and now."

Maggie laughed in delight. "No danger there, though I have been told I have a talent for mimicry, to say nothing of an aptitude for chickens. Do you know that I have been studying genetics, and hope to make it my life's work?"

He smiled at her with something akin to triumph. "There. You see? Even if I were not certain, that would clinch it. I had my suspicions before, because when Elaine and Charles Seacombe returned from Paris, they had two daughters instead of one. But this information gives me certainty. Oh, won't Granddad be amazed and glad!"

And what a change that would be!

"But Michael, you have not told me the end of the story. What happened to my father?"

The smile faded somewhat. "I will end this tale, and then we will talk of happier things. Uncle Kevern, who was not permitted to see you or have anything to do with you once the Charles Seacombes had you, did what many young men do when their prospects seem dim. He joined the Royal Aeronautic Corps, and was killed in an airship crash while on maneuvers—oddly, very close to Baie des Sirenes. My father's practice was in its infancy then and no one in the family could afford to bring Kevern home for burial, but Mariah, who by then was engaged to a French boy, made certain that Kevern was buried in Baie des Sirenes with Catherine, in a single grave."

This time the tears did well up and spill down her cheeks. "I am glad," she cried hoarsely. "I am more glad than I can say that they did not come back here, to be separated in death—for him to be in France, and her to be under my grandparents' disapproving eye in the churchyard every single Sunday until they die."

"Do not be too hard on them, Maggie."

"What else can I be? They separated my parents and if it had not been for Lizzie's mother, I might likely have gone to the workhouse!"

"Maggie, if you only knew what our feelings were when we heard the Seacombe airship had gone down in the Thames, with total loss of life. I don't think my grandfather has ever fully recovered."

"Then I must be the one to tell him the real story of what happened, when we go up on Wednesday."

"May I listen in?"

"If you don't, I will be terribly disappointed. Michael, you do not know how this knowledge has changed me." Maggie's voice wobbled and she swallowed. She must get this out before she broke down altogether. "I have a family that I respected before ever I knew I belonged to it. And now to know that I was truly wanted—that my parents loved one another and intended to make a life together—it is almost too much to take in."

"Would you like some time alone to come to grips with it?" He moved, as if he would push himself to his feet and leave her, but she caught his sleeve.

"I will, but later. Look, the sun is sinking and Lizzie and Lady Claire will be worried about me. I must return to the house, but … do I have your permission to share what you have told me?"

"It is your story," he said. "I am only sorry you had to hear it secondhand."

"If anyone was to tell me, I am glad it was you." She smiled up at him. "Cousin."

"Quite so." He took her hand. "And an older cousin at that, which means you have to do what I say."

Maggie laughed and poked him in his brocade waistcoat. "Not until you tell me this—what gets wetter as it dries?"

With a roar of mock aggravation, he chased her up the cliff path, and couldn't catch her until they were nearly all the way to the top.

15

Claire did not order out the big guns very often, finding it not only embarrassing but in most cases unnecessary. Besides which, doing so made her feel a little too much like her mother, a sensation she preferred to avoid at all costs.

But some circumstances were so extraordinary that the only way to meet them was to call upon all the resources one had at hand. So, upon the departure of Mr. Polgarth and Maggie from the sea parlor, she drew on all the consequence of her title, the heritage of Gwynn Place, and three hundred years of breeding, and looked Howel Seacombe straight in the eye.

"Mr. Seacombe, I must have an explanation for this cavalier treatment of a young man who has done us no harm and nothing but good—and who was here at my invitation."

"I am very much afraid that you do not have the time for a catalogue of his family's sins against this one, so I will spare you," he replied.

"On the contrary, I have nothing but time." Tamsen had come in with a fresh pot of tea, so Claire made herself comfortable upon the sofa and began to pour. "Mr. Seacombe?"

"I mean no offense, Lady Claire, but these are matters best kept within the family."

"I quite agree." She set a cup in front of Mrs. Seacombe, who made no move to take it, and poured for Mr. Malvern, Tigg, and lastly Lizzie, who had remained frozen by the window like a rabbit in a clump of grass watching the hounds ranging back and forth in search of her. "Since I am Lizzie and Maggie's guardian, I am most definitely part of the family. I am quite at leisure to hear the story, I assure you."

She sat back with her cup of tea and raised an eyebrow in expectation.

"Which brings us to a topic that must also be discussed," he said with a glance at his wife. "Since Elizabeth and Margaret have been restored to us, it is perhaps time to decide whether your guardianship is in fact necessary any longer."

"Whether my—" Claire forced down the rising tone of her voice and took a sip of the excellent tea. "I was not aware the subject was under discussion in any quarter. Have you spoken of it with the girls?"

Without my knowledge? The remainder of the sentence hung unsaid in the air between them.

"No," came from the direction of the window with a sound like a squeak.

"Elizabeth, would you take these gentlemen into the park?" Mrs. Seacombe said. "I am sure they do not wish to be burdened with the family's business, and it appears there are topics on which we must enlighten Lady Claire."

The gentlemen did not move. On the contrary, Andrew smiled and said, "I for one am deeply interested in any topic that touches the girls. Lieutenant Terwilliger is of like mind—he has known them since the age of five and in fact was instrumental in saving their lives—he helped to pull them out of the river when the airship went down."

"For which, of course, we are most grateful," Mr. Seacombe said, a muscle working in his jaw under its fringe of beard. "But I must insist that matters which concern my family directly be kept to the smallest of circles. I am afraid I must insist. Elizabeth, obey your grandmother, if you please."

Claire saw at once that either they must concede, or the information she sought would not be provided.

"It is all right, Andrew," she said to him. "I shall not be long, and then I will join you. I have no doubt I shall enjoy the walk."

When they left the room, Claire turned back to the couple who were proving to be such able antagonists. "There," she said pleasantly. "You have my full attention. Especially upon the subject of my guardianship of the girls."

"We will get to that in time. Allow me to put you in possession of all the facts concerning the immediate matter of Mr. Polgarth," Mrs. Seacombe said. "I could not speak of this in front of Elizabeth, for reasons which will become obvious. It is *imperative* that any acquaintance Margaret has formed with that young man be cut off at once."

"You of course have reasons for this?" Claire asked.

"We do. But first, you must know the most salient fact—Margaret is not who you believe her to be."

"Are any of us?" Claire inquired politely.

"By this my wife means that she is—is—Demelza, I find I cannot speak the words."

"She is a bastard," Mrs. Seacombe said crisply. "The illegitimate daughter of that blackguard de Maupassant, gotten upon our innocent girl when he was not satisfied with ruining the life of our eldest."

The blood drained out of Claire's face and she set down the cup and saucer on the low table with the greatest of care, for otherwise they would have fallen from her nerveless fingers and crashed to the floor.

"You have proof of this?"

"One has simply to look at her. The broad forehead, the amber eyes. That uncontrollable will staring out of her face."

"Many people have eyes that color," Claire said. For the life of her, in this moment she could hardly remember what Charles de Maupassant Seacombe looked like other than the final vision she had had of him: a figure below her on a castle roof. A figure who had just fired a pistol at and struck her beloved Maggie and who had been sizzled by a bolt from Claire's lightning rifle in retribution. "And that is not an uncontrollable will you see. It is Maggie's spirit, her sweetness of temper, her insight into and compassion for those around her."

"You favor her, as any woman forced into a mother's position might," Mr. Seacombe said. "But his own admission makes Margaret his child—her conception an act of revenge for our refusal to be blackmailed."

Claire's stomach heaved and bile rose, to be forced down by will alone. How was it possible for any man to be so monstrous?

"It is the only explanation," Mrs. Seacombe went on. "My husband made his decision, and the next thing we knew, our daughter was coming to us with a dreadful secret—that she was expecting an illegitimate child. That devil had threatened us—and then hurt us in a way that would guarantee we never forgot our mistake."

Maggie.

"So this is the reason for the pointed difference you make in your treatment of the girls?" Claire's lips felt stiff, as if her very face were frozen. "Maggie feels it, you know. She feels it most keenly."

"I am sorry," Mrs. Seacombe said just as stiffly. "But we cannot help it. His revenge is written in her features and we cannot help but see him and lose our daughter every time we look at her."

Claire could not bear it. She must speak of something else. "But I still do not understand how Mr. Polgarth fits into this dreadful tale."

"His family were directly involved in the acts in which we refused to participate."

"Criminal acts? I find this hard to believe, since I have known his grandfather all my life."

"You may know the grandfather, but the sons were a different matter," Mr. Seacombe said heavily. "We speak of political and economic acts that in certain circles would be considered treason. But that is in the past. It is the present that concerns us. Suffice it to say that the father and the uncle tried to cover up their involvement by drawing my daughter into their schemes—even going so far as to claim responsibility for the pregnancy when of course that was impossible. They did not even know each other."

"Are you so certain of this?"

Mrs. Seacombe gave Claire a long look. "Can you tell me that when you lived as a dependent in your mother's house that you were permitted to racket about on your own and keep company your parents did not know of?"

"No," Claire was forced to admit. "But I was much younger then. How old was Catherine at this time?"

"Only nineteen. And very protected and innocent of the ways of the world. Which makes it even more distressing to think that her own sister's husb—" Mrs. Seacombe choked and could not continue.

Their distress and grief were palpable, almost another presence in the room. While Claire could not condone their treatment of Maggie for a sin she had not committed—that had been committed a generation ago—at the same time, she could empathize with parents whose child had been abused and then taken from them in such a terrible manner, by someone whom she knew from experience was quite capable of it.

"I appreciate your taking me into your confidence," she said at last, when it was clear they would take her into it no further. "I will counsel Maggie that she must be more careful in her friendships. In return, you must do something for me."

"Must we?" Mrs. Seacombe's spine was beginning to straighten as she recovered.

"Yes. You must not punish Maggie for the sins her father committed. In the end, he did right by her when he adopted her as his own daughter. This does not excuse his behavior on any other front. However, in the matter which concerns me most deeply, I must have this reassurance."

"I am not sure I can," Mr. Seacombe said with surprising honesty. "He is like a ghost standing behind her every time I look at her."

"Then you must look instead for the ghost of your daughter, who most assuredly would entreat you in the same manner as I do."

"Perhaps you are right," was all he said, and Claire realized she would have to be satisfied with that.

Leaving her tea unfinished, she went blindly from the room. Oh, what was she to do now? For Maggie would demand to know what was behind her friend's peremptory dismissal from the house. How was Claire even to begin to tell her?

Or worse, should she step inside the circle of secrecy with the Seacombes and not tell her at all?

16

When one was a young lady old enough to let down her hems and put up her hair, there was nothing quite so maddening as to be told that the adults had been talking about you and you were not allowed to know what they said.

"I still cannot believe they sent you from the room," Maggie said to Lizzie the next morning. The night before, she had confided to her cousin everything that Michael had told her, rejoicing in Lizzie's wet-eyed appreciation of the sad romance and her empathy for her own loss. Now, they were supposed to be acting like young ladies and writing letters, but who could concentrate on that when there were mysteries springing from the sadness that demanded solutions? "And the Lady allowed it—that is the strangest thing of all."

"They must have told her something terrible, Mags," Lizzie said from the window, where the bright day was apparently drawing her like a moth to a lamp. "Did you see her face at dinner? I swear it was positively gray. And then she lost at cards three times in succession— which you must admit is a first."

"It could have been the fish. After three days of fish at dinner, I'm feeling a little gray myself. I shall begin to grow scales soon."

"This is no matter for flippancy. Are you sure Mr. Polgarth had nothing more to say on the matter of your mother and his uncle? For there must be something he is not telling us. It is the only explanation I can think of."

"Nothing more terrible than my parents dying far apart at the hands of ..." Maggie lowered her tone, for the morning-room door was open. "Those two people."

"Please don't be angry with me for bringing it up. I don't mean to imply he is not telling the truth of it ... but I cannot help my feeling."

"I am sure there is more to the story, but I do not wish to hear any more about what the Lady knows or doesn't."

The door opened further to admit ... the Lady, dressed in her nice chestnut houndstooth walking suit with the black soutache trim, and Maggie relaxed. "I am sorry to hear it," Claire said gently, as if she had been part of the conversation all along. "Lizzie, Maggie, would you fetch your hats? I feel in need of a walk, and we must look in on Holly and Ivy. They have not been left alone this long before, and I fear for the contents of the pantry."

Which was nonsense, since the birds were quite content in their aviary in the boarding area, but one never knew who might be listening in the halls of Seacombe House.

Claire twinkled at them. "Billy Bolt," she whispered—their old code for doing a fast scarper to avoid trouble.

Maggie dashed upstairs and fetched their hats, and it was not until they were well down the drive and out of earshot of anyone at an open window that any of them spoke again.

"Will Mr. Malvern come with us?" Maggie asked, despite the fact that their strides were already lengthening with an unladylylike sense of freedom.

"He and Tigg have been invited by Mr. Polgarth to go surf fishing," the Lady replied in her normal voice. "A message came after breakfast, and when Nancarrow showed it to your grandparents, being cognizant of their wishes on that head, they made their feelings plain."

"And they are going anyway?" Lizzie said with a wide smile.

"While I cannot blame the Seacombes for their feelings, it is also true that Mr. Malvern and Tigg are independent gentlemen, unconnected with anyone here, past or present. And it is a lovely day."

"What feelings, Lady?" Maggie was unwilling to let the subject go. "It is too bad of everyone to leave Lizzie and me out of what you are all talking about, when it concerns us most of all."

The Lady walked on for a little without answering, her smile fading into a kind of distressed solemnity, much like the expression she had worn for most of the previous evening. Then she said, "It is only because they do not wish to hurt you, darling. And for the older generation, you know, it is difficult sometimes to speak of the past."

"But Mr. Polgarth has done nothing wrong. All he did was tell me of my parents' love affair—and it was beautiful, Lady. I have proof. Here is the letter I told you about and did not have a chance to show you." She pulled it from her pocket, and the Lady read it swiftly. "They truly loved each other, and I was wanted, Michael says. And there is more. Do you realize that if Kevern—that is the *K* who signed this letter, Michael's uncle—was my father, that makes Michael my cousin, and Polgarth the poultryman my grandfather? Is that not a lovely surprise?"

The Lady's pace faltered. In the distance, past the valley that held Penzance in the cup of its hand, they could see *Athena* and *Victory* tugging longingly at their mooring ropes.

"Lady, what is it? Do you have a pebble in your shoe?"

"No, darling. I have a pebble in my conscience that is causing me much more pain."

"Then you had better have it out." There was something in the Lady's face that made Maggie want to brace herself as soon as the words left her lips.

Claire took the girls' hands in hers and walked between them. "You know I have never concealed the truth about any matter from you, even when it has been difficult to hear."

That was one of the things they loved about her. She did not underestimate either their intelligence or the depth of their bravery and compassion. She simply treated them as she wished to be treated—as a woman who possessed the resources to bear what she must, if she were only prepared with the truth.

Claire's voice gentled as she began to speak in a tone Maggie had heard only once before—when she had told her who Charles de Maupassant Seacombe really was.

Lizzie's father.

Lizzie's.

Not *hers*.

Maggie could not stop the story, much as the Lady did not want to tell it, much as Maggie did not want to hear it.

Oh, no. She could not have come into the world in that terrible way. No, it was a lie and the Seacombes hated her and no no no it wasn't true! None of it was true! Her parents were Kevern Polgarth and Catherine Seacombe, and they had *loved* her and *wanted* her!

"Maggie!" Claire shouted behind her, but Maggie was already fifty yards away, running ... running ... leaping over a stile in the hedgerow and pelting across the field, her goal the flat granite rock in the sun, where only yesterday she had been truly happy to be herself.

Maggie spent the afternoon huddled up on the rock, alternately weeping and thinking and then weeping again. But when clouds began to pile up in the southwest with threatening majesty, and the wind off the sea turned cold with warning, there was nothing for it but to return to the house.

She had two choices.

In the first, she would ask the Lady for permission to spend her last night in Penzance in her own cabin aboard *Athena*, in Holly and Ivy's sympathetic company. In the morning the Lady and Mr. Malvern and Tigg would put this place to their rudder and Maggie would never come here again, leaving Lizzie and Claude to their bright future with her blessing.

In the second, she would stay and ferret out which of the two stories she had been told was the truth, even if that meant going to France somehow to see if that dual grave indeed existed.

The first choice would be by far the easiest one to make. But as the Lady had once said, "There is the easy course—and there is the right one. Sometimes they are the same, but when they are not, that is when we show what we are made of." Maggie had the uncomfortable feeling that if she was ever to know peace in that hollow place inside herself, she would need to choose the right course, as difficult and grievous as it might be.

Then she would quite literally know what she was made of.

Wearily, she climbed through the tall grass and heather and emerged on the cliff-top, her eyes aching and no doubt reddened from wind and crying, her bones stiff from sitting too long on the rock.

Lizzie was perched on a hillock, waiting for her.

"What are you doing here?" The wind pushed Maggie forward, and her hat slid down over her face. She settled it on the mare's nest that had once been a neat French coil, and when she could see again, Lizzie had joined her on the path.

"I followed you, of course," Lizzie said. "If you had flung yourself into the sea you would have needed someone to fish you out. The Lady nearly came, too, but I convinced her to leave you on your own until you got things sorted. I hope you have, because I certainly haven't."

"What do you mean?"

Lizzie glanced at her with an expression that clearly said, *What do you think, you gumpus?* "He was my father, too," she said. "He was a murdering anarchist who tried to kill us both—twice—and it horrifies me every time I am reminded we're related. But I never expected anything as terrible as this. Oh, Maggie." She took Maggie's cold hand in her warm one.

"Being the daughter of such a man is nothing to be proud of, that's certain," Maggie said.

"No wonder my mother attempted to leave him. Plunging to her death in the Thames was better than grieving her sister and living with the shame of being his wife." Lizzie took a breath, clearly trying to shake the bitterness from her tone. "On the bright side, *we* are sisters again. Or half-sisters, at least."

"Lizzie, do not take this the wrong way, but I cannot believe we are. I cannot believe what Grandmother told the Lady when it contradicts what Michael told me in nearly every particular."

"And you would believe him—a man you met yesterday—over our grandparents, who have known us and our mothers both?"

"His story *felt* right, Lizzie. It touched something deep inside me that has been going wanting all these years."

"Because you wanted it to so badly, my dearie," Lizzie said softly.

They were on the lawn now, the house rising up beyond the hedge, its windows perpetually watching for something out beyond the horizon. Behind the glass upstairs in their grandparents' room, a velvet drape twitched and settled back into place.

"I don't know. Perhaps," Maggie said. "All I know is that I must find out whose truth is the real one. When the Lady goes tomorrow, I will stay behind with you and Claude and attempt to get to the bottom of it."

Lizzie squeezed her hand, and together, they passed into the garden, where the roses bobbed restlessly, their petals torn away by the rising wind.

17

A howling gale kept *Athena* on the ground until late
Wednesday. Maggie and Lizzie busied themselves assisting Lady Claire, Mr. Malvern, and Tigg in packing up
and transporting their luggage out to the airship under
protective tarpaulins, where they spent a happy afternoon together preparing for lift.

The pain of not going felt like a weight in Maggie's
stomach, but she did her best not to let it show.

Instead, she and Lizzie helped Tigg tie the steam
landau down in the hold, and then she absented herself
so that the two of them could have a little privacy in
which to say good-bye.

The Lady found her standing in her cabin, gazing
out the porthole at nothing in particular. "You are
quite welcome to come with us to Gwynn Place," Claire

said quietly. "It is entirely possible that you may learn what you need to know there instead of here."

Maggie turned and went wordlessly into Claire's arms. "If I said that I wanted to find out the truth in order to prove them wrong about me, would you think less of me, Lady?"

"I would not," Claire said, hugging her. "But I hope you remember that they are old, and their grief has warped them somehow inside, like a piece of metal that has held one shape for too long. Be gentle in your attempts to change their minds. If they are to be bent in a different direction, I would imagine the process might be quite painful."

Maggie nodded, the well-worn fabric of the Lady's raiding rig soft under her cheek.

"You and Lizzie will come to us in a week," the Lady said, though this had been the plan since they had left Wilton Crescent several days ago. "Mr. Malvern and I will wait for you anxiously, and I hope you will write every day. *Athena* will be moored in the home paddock, since Mama does not keep sheep anymore, so I will be checking the pigeons religiously."

Which reminded her— "We have not checked yet this morning ourselves. I will do that, and then Lizzie and I will man the ropes for you."

To her surprise, there was indeed a pigeon waiting in the messenger cage, though they expected none. And it contained yet another puzzling missive.

DELTA 14 08 94 02 00 100L 1000KG 6

When she showed it to the others, Tigg said, "Whatever they're measuring, it's doubled. The last one said fifty and four-fifty."

"But what is Delta, besides the fifth letter of the Greek alphabet?" Maggie wondered aloud.

"A location?" the Lady guessed. "A river mouth? But there are none in these parts. The cliff faces are too steep to allow for sedimentation."

"In mathematics, delta means *change*," Lizzie said. "That's what this is. A change order, increasing the amounts of liquid and weight, as Tigg says."

"Which still makes no sense at all." Maggie folded up the paper and pushed it into her pocket. "I'm convinced it has been misdirected. There is probably a grocer somewhere, wondering where his potatoes and ale have got to."

"If a grocer ordered things by the ton and possessed a non-fixed address," observed the Lady. "No one but Lewis, Snouts, and ourselves knows *Athena*'s code, and I prefer to keep it that way."

Athena moved restlessly at the sound of her name, and Tigg lifted his head like a pointer sniffing the air. "The wind has changed," he said. "You should be able to lift soon—and I must get myself over to the Mount while the tide is low, or I'll miss my ride to Scotland."

"We cannot have that, though I am mightily tempted to invent some crisis so that I may keep you a little longer," the Lady said with affection.

"The Mopsies are going to be on their own for a week," he said as he hugged her. "Don't tempt Fate."

While the Lady took the helm and Mr. Malvern began the ignition sequence on *Athena*'s great boiler, Lizzie and Maggie gave Holly and Ivy their final cuddles and lifted the birds up on the piping in the navigation gondola, from which they were accustomed to watch the proceedings. Then the girls ran down the steps, Tigg lifted the folding staircase into its closed position, and the three of them took up their positions on the ropes.

"Up ship!" the Lady called through the open viewing port, and they let go. "Good-bye, my darlings—until Tuesday!"

Athena rose gracefully into the sky, shouldered into the wind, and began to make way. The engines changed pitch and she moved off steadily north and east.

When she disappeared into a bank of clouds and the sound of her engines faded, Tigg took Lizzie's hand. "Will you and Maggie walk me to the beach?"

"Try to stop us," Lizzie said, holding his gaze as though memorizing it.

When Tigg boarded the Corps airship that would take him via Bristol to Scotland, where he would rejoin the crew of the *Lady Lucy*, Maggie felt nearly as teary as Lizzie as they walked down through St. Michael's village. By the time they reached the flagged causeway, the great ship was passing overhead, and they waved their handkerchiefs madly until it floated from sight.

Two good-byes, two ships sailing away without them, and now it was just the two of them left. Well, and Claude, but he was being kept practically under lock and key by Grandfather, who was determined he should learn a thing or two about the business before he went back to Paris.

"Are you going to beard the grands in their dens after dinner?" Lizzie wanted to know as they walked along the beach toward Penzance in the distance.

"No," Maggie said. "I have had enough emotional ups and downs for one day. Tomorrow is soon enough. But I am curious about one thing."

"Only one?"

"Only one that I can bear to think about. Do you remember the red lantern flashes we saw the other night?"

"The signal to no one? The ones that seemed to come from the direction of that little valley where I followed you yesterday?"

"We saw the lights ... and then a pigeon came to *Athena*. Do you suppose the two might be connected?"

"I don't see how," Lizzie said flatly. "What connection does someone with a lantern have with us?"

"None at all. But two odd things have happened at the same time. Perhaps we should take naps this afternoon."

Lizzie stopped in her own tracks on the shingle. "What has come over you? We never take naps. Only old people take naps. And what has that to do with pigeons?"

"Old people aren't going to be out on the cliffs at two in the morning to see one hundred liters of something and a thousand kilos of something else landed on the beach."

Lizzie laughed. "Is that what you think will happen? What an imagination you have!"

Maggie hadn't really expected her to go along with it, but nobody liked to be laughed at, either. "You don't have to come, but I'm still going to ramble out in that direction, just in case I'm right and something happens."

"What good will it do you?"

"None ... except the satisfaction of my curiosity."

"I think you're going to meet Michael Polgarth—against the grands' wishes."

Maggie wished that were the truth. "If I did, I should be turned out of the house, and have to walk all the way to Gwynn Place. No, I'm just going to have an adventure. You may stay behind if you like. But even if that message does turn out to be a grocer's list, I'm going to find out what those lights are."

And there would be one mystery she could solve—even if it was the only one.

If Maggie could have invented an illness and taken a tray in her room that evening, she would have. But the possibility of Grandmother inspecting her throat and chest was a consequence too terrifying to contemplate, so she put on her dinner dress, arranged her hair, and presented herself downstairs with Lizzie and Claude as the gong sounded.

The dining table seemed even glossier and much larger without the rest of the London party, unrelieved as it was by so much as a bowl of flowers. But one thing had changed.

"Lady Claire and Mr. Malvern lifted safely?" Grandfather inquired of Maggie, who was so surprised at being thus directly addressed that she nearly inhaled a mouthful of asparagus soup.

"Yes, thank you," she managed as soon as she could speak. "We were a little worried about the force of the wind, but then it changed and they were able to lift without trouble."

A LADY OF SPIRIT

"I do not hold with young people gadding about the skies in these airships," Grandmother said. "When I think of the danger they put themselves in so needlessly, I wonder at their parents allowing it."

"Lady Claire has been independent for some years now," Lizzie said. "And she is to work on airships in Germany, you know, so her familiarity with them will be to her advantage."

"Papa made sure I knew how to fly so that I could travel independently in *Victory*," Claude offered. "And it's not so hard, you know, once you get the hang of wind and steering. When we came down earlier in the summer, even the girls had a go at the tiller."

Grandfather's face flushed. "Claude, you know my feelings about any mention of your father in my house."

"I know, Grandfather, and I apologize. But it is difficult. Up until two months ago, I believed him to be a good man. He was certainly good to me."

But Grandfather was not willing to allow Charles de Maupassant Seacombe any shred of humanity or family feeling, for which Maggie for once was inclined to side with him.

"How did your day go at the office, Claude?" she asked him, since a change of subject was most definitely in order.

Claude heaved a sigh, caught his grandfather's eye, and straightened. "I am finding it a very complicated beast. No wonder so many minds are required to make the company run properly. A single brain cannot hold it all—mine in particular."

"You are not required to know everything, only the important points," Grandfather told him. "Having the right men working for you is one necessary part. A knowledge of politics and economics is another. And a working knowledge of accounts is helpful, too, so that you may understand what others tell you." Grandfather's eye fell on Maggie, and like the clouds massing in the west, she saw a storm coming. "While we are on that subject, Margaret, I feel you ought to know that Mr. Polgarth has been released from his employment with us."

He might as well have turned the pitcher of water at his elbow over her head. "On what grounds?" she blurted. The poor man! How was he to make his living now?

The bushy eyebrows pinched together in a frown. "That is hardly your concern."

"If a man is sacked simply for speaking to me, then it certainly is my concern."

Grandmother laid down her knife with a *clink*. "Margaret, do not be rude to your grandfather or I shall ask you to leave the room."

Maggie could think of nothing she'd like better, but at the same time, antagonizing them would not make them amenable to conversation of a personal nature later on.

"Forgive me, Grandmother—Grandfather," she murmured, ignoring Lizzie's incredulous gaze at her backing down from a fight.

After a few moments, Claude said, "I had the opportunity to spend some time in the accounting department today."

Poor Claude. Truly, the prospect of being cut out of the will was becoming more and more appealing the longer she stayed here.

"And what did you think?" Grandfather accepted a helping of breaded plaice from the footman, and Maggie stifled a sigh. Once they got home, she was never eating fish again.

"Well, I do not think the books they showed me were complete."

"What do you mean, Claude?" Grandmother accepted her own fish, and next to her, Lizzie visibly braced herself.

"From what I could see, it does not look as though the company's receipts are enough to sustain operations throughout the year. Is there more than one set of books?"

Grandfather's eyes narrowed before his gaze fell to his dinner once more. "I am surprised you could make such a pronouncement when you admit yourself that your faculties are as yet not up to the task of understanding the business."

Goodness. That was the closest Grandfather had ever come to a criticism of Claude in all the time they'd been here.

Claude nodded and gave a Gallic half-shrug. "You are quite right. Most of the time I am lucky if I can figure out how to tie my cravat in the morning. The books will take several years to understand, I am sure."

And he subsided into silence while Maggie struggled with the urge to put a hand on his shoulder and tell him he was not as stupid as his grandparents were encouraging him to be. Claude was capable of sensible observation—she'd seen it herself. If he thought the books were unbalanced, then goodness, in all likelihood they probably were.

But bringing that up right now would definitely get her sent to her room. Maggie gazed at the limp plaice as the footman slid it onto her plate. Then again, perhaps she ought to.

"Claude, now that the storm is blowing itself out, do you think tomorrow would be a good day for a picnic?" she asked instead.

"Jolly good idea. I—"

"Claude is to go with me to the warehouse of one of our suppliers in Exeter tomorrow," Grandfather said heavily. "We shall leave on the seven o'clock train."

"In the morning?" Claude said faintly.

"Of course in the morning. Do you think we do business at night?"

"Some men do. Papa used to say more business was accomplished over brandy and cigars than ever got accomplished in offices."

"Claude, I will not remind you again."

"Grandfather, regardless of his crimes, you must admit that Papa was an excellent businessman. In that area of his life, at least, he behaved honorably and with great success."

"I think that, along with your observations of the books, your estimations of your father's honor and success are sadly inaccurate," Grandfather snapped.

Carefully, Maggie put down her fork and instinctively readied herself for … whatever might happen.

"You cannot know that." Maggie had never heard such a tone from her cousin. "I was with him daily on my vacations, accompanying him to meetings and such, and never heard anything from his associates to indicate such a thing."

"That's because they were probably in on it with him."

"In on what?" Lizzie asked.

"Never mind!" Both men turned on her with a simultaneous exclamation.

"Gentlemen, we will change the subject," Grandmother said in quelling tones. "Claude, if you distress your grandfather in this manner again, you will be taking your dinner in your room henceforth."

"I believe I should prefer that in any case." Claude rose and tossed his napkin down on his chair. "Good evening, Grandmother. Thank you for dinner."

"Claude!" Grandmother half rose from her seat.

But he did not stop, and they heard his footsteps cross the hall, then a murmur. When Maggie heard the great front doors thump closed, she realized that he had gone out instead of going to his room.

The breaded plaice waited, untouched, on her plate.

She should have spoken up. She would have been disgraced for a couple of days, but at least she would have had the pleasure of going with Claude to ... wherever he was going.

The Lady was right. Doing the right thing really wasn't easy.

With a sigh, Maggie picked up her fork.

18

Maggie had fallen asleep after the massive clock in the hall had bonged ten times, but by the time it bonged once, she had already awakened and was pulling on her raiding rig.

"Are you really going?" Lizzie murmured sleepily from her side of the bed. "It's cold."

"It won't be once you have your rig on. Are you coming?"

Lizzie groaned and pulled the quilts over her head. After a moment of motionless contemplation, she flung them back and got up, making a big production of shivering until she was buttoned into her black waistcoat and blouse, and had fastened her skirts up for freedom of movement.

Swiftly, the two of them braided back their hair. "It's at moments like this that I wish I'd finished making that lightning pistol," Maggie said. It still lay upon Lewis's work bench at Wilton Crescent, where it was doing no one any good at all.

"Why, if we are only going to watch the cliffs, would you need a lightning pistol?"

"It never hurts to be prepared."

"Prepared for potatoes and ale," Lizzie grumbled, but all the same, she made sure they both had a moon-globe as they slipped downstairs and out the side entrance, where the staff came and went.

"Do you suppose Claude ever came home?" Maggie asked as they ran through the cook's sweet-scented herb garden and out through the garden wall on the west side. It took a little longer to cross the expanse of grass and trees to the cliff-top, but she was not willing to risk going out through the rose garden under the watchful eye of their grandparents' windows, which could be open.

"I never heard him come in—but since the men are in the other wing, we wouldn't have, would we? Don't worry, Mags, he probably went to a tavern to drown his sorrows and then out to *Victory* to sleep it off."

The sea heaved against the foot of the cliff, still restless after the storm. The clouds were being chased inland by the wind, scudding across the face of the moon as though embarrassed to be caught in the light.

"If you were a boatload of potatoes, where would you land?" Maggie asked, not really expecting an answer. It seemed obvious—the tiny harbor formed where the cluster of stone houses tumbled to the sea. Where the red lights had come from someone's window or roof.

"If I were not doing it in daylight, in Penzance harbor like a respectable person, there is really only one safe place on this headland." She pointed in the direction of the granite rock, a quarter mile or so away. "We'd better get on shank's mare. It must be nearly two."

"You know what?" Lizzie said thoughtfully, "If I were bringing in contraband potatoes, I'd land them in the *sawan*. Wouldn't you?"

"The Seacombe *sawan*?" As if there were any other improved caves along here with landings specifically built to accommodate a large cargo—and a rising tide. "I am clearly out of the habit of thinking like a street sparrow or a confidence man. Unlike present company."

"But you have to admit it is a reasonable possibility. However, we can only go and look at one thing—not both, unless we split up. We must choose."

"The tide hasn't turned yet. If it is the *sawan*, the door will be mostly under water—those potatoes could only get in on a raft or a rowboat."

"Maybe they've come and gone," Lizzie said. "Maybe the 'two o'clock' was high tide, and they had to do their business before then. Or maybe—"

She stopped abruptly when Maggie grabbed her sleeve. "Lizzie, what is that?" Maggie pulled her down behind a tumble of weathered rock, and peered over it.

"What? I can't see anything. Ouch, you're pinching my shoulder."

"Lizzie, *the sea is boiling*."

Wide-eyed, the two of them leaned on the rough, lichen-covered rocks, Maggie's breath catching in her throat in sheer amazement. For the sea, which had been breaking in perfectly normal waves on the rocks a moment ago, seemed to be heaving into a dome fifty feet across, coming up out of the deep with such inexorable force that seawater slid down the face of it in crashing waterfalls and torrents, foam leaping back into the air to form a mist above it.

And now it rose and rose and they could see below it an elliptical body made of glass and metal, intricately worked in seams and waves to direct the water past its hull and increase its speed. Facing them, encased in a metal housing worked in the shapes of waves and curves, a huge bubble of glass emerged from the water, which sheeted over its roundness and plummeted straight down into the deep, frothing and hissing.

Inside, lit by an eerie yellowish-green light, several men worked the controls. Others ran to and fro working levers, and standing in the front was a figure with its hands clasped behind its back, as if he were too important to do the job of operating the thing. He merely watched as the whole enormous contraption freed itself of the ocean's grasp, water streaming off its sides in great torrents. Finally, its internal systems seemed to stabilize it and it bobbed on the surface like a duck in a child's bath, the heaviest part of its body still submerged to who knew what depth.

It looked for all the world like an airship, with its parts put on in the wrong places. An airship that traveled under the water.

Where it could not be detected.

Maggie's chest felt tight, and she sucked in a lungful of air with a gasp. She had completely forgotten to breathe.

"What ... is it?" Lizzie managed to whisper.

"I do not know," Maggie whispered back. "What are they doing here?"

"Not landing potatoes, I'll wager."

"Come on. Let's go down the cliff path and see what they're doing."

"Are you mad? They're not exactly the Royal Aeronautics Corps on maneuvers—people with honest intentions don't go swimming about at night in undersea dirigibles!"

"Exactly why we have to know what they're doing. We need to be able to tell Grandfather and the authorities."

"Maggie—"

"Come on!"

Maggie did not know what drove her across to the western side of the headland and down the cliff path. A sense of loyalty to the family that had shown her none? Did she wish to prove herself worthy by putting herself at risk for the Seacombe name? Or was she simply feeling angry and reckless and not one whit concerned about what her grandparents thought? She was going to have an adventure and they could just—just stick their heads in a bucket!

She heard Lizzie slipping and swearing along the path behind her, and waited a moment for her to catch up. "We are going to be in so much trouble," Lizzie panted.

"I'm in trouble anyway. Claude is, too. Why shouldn't you be?"

"Yes, I was feeling a bit left out. Careful—the earth there has fallen away."

Maggie stepped around the notch in the path, and they zigzagged down until the soil thinned and they were clambering over solid rock. She could hear the waves lashing the beach now, the sea still not recovered from the dirigible's intrusion. The noise of it covered any sounds they might have made as they inched around the rocks, their boots sinking into the damp sand where the tide had just begun to turn.

Someone shouted behind them, and Lizzie grabbed Maggie, pulling her back into a crevice. They pressed themselves flat as a rowing boat propelled by a large man dressed in a fisherman's jersey shot across the waves from the direction of the stone houses.

"The last number on the paper that pigeon brought," Maggie whispered. "Six. I wonder if that's the number of men they need to unload whatever it is they're bringing?"

"But they haven't got six," Lizzie whispered back. "There's only him."

"They haven't got the message, either. If that's what it was, none of them know what the other is expecting."

"I still think it was a grocer's order."

"We'll soon see, I hope."

They edged around the cliff face and saw that the dirigible had navigated its way closer to shore. It was not as deep in the draft as she'd thought, Maggie saw now. In fact, if the navigation gondola had been under it instead of on its nose, it would be similar in shape to the Rangers' B-30 ship from which they had escaped in Santa Fe when they were children—slender and fast like a sea creature.

They heard the grinding of machinery, and the dirigible gave a great belch of steam. A hatch opened under the navigation deck, and out of it issued what Maggie could only describe as large glass and metal bubbles— three of them, hooked together like train cars, the lead vessel the only one with an engine and steered by men inside working wheels and levers. They grumbled through the water, wallowing slightly as though weighted down.

The *sawan* gaped black in the cliff face, the head space gradually increasing as the tide went out, and lamps came on in the front of the bubbles to illuminate their way. Through the arch they went, and disappeared within.

Maggie turned to her cous—sis—to Lizzie, her mind struggling to find meaning in a sight so completely new. "What do you make of it?" she said at last.

"That's a lot of engineering for potatoes," Lizzie said in her practical way, her fascinated gaze taking it all in. "What is in those—that—goodness, I don't even know what to call them. The metal coracles. What are they landing on Seacombe property?"

"We aren't going to find out unless we get in there— and we can't do it from here without swimming."

"We shall have to approach from the inside—from the cellar."

"Lizzie, there isn't time for us to climb back up, gain the house, steal the key from poor Nancarrow, and go down that stair."

"Why not? If that message is connected with this landing—and we must believe it is—it will take them some time to unload a thousand kilos of ... whatever."

Before Maggie could reply, the man in the rowboat hailed the *sawan*. "Halloo the boats!" he shouted. "What are you doing here?"

"How many times we got to tell you, these ain't boats?" came a drawl they had only heard on the far side of the Atlantic, in the Americas. "*Neptune's Maid* is a naveer soo-maran and these here are the chaloops, known to regular folks as jolly-boats. Get it right, fer gosh sakes."

Navire sous-marin, Maggie translated automatically. Undersea ship. And *chaloupes*—jolly-boats—smaller boats that ferried people and things between shore and their larger host. Logical, if not very illuminating.

But very French. Why were French ships bringing cargo to the Seacombe beach? To avoid the harbor tariffs? For an operation this size, harbor tariffs would be nothing. What on earth was going on?

"If it's in water, it's a boat," retorted the man at the oars. "What I want to know is, why weren't we told?"

"You signaled. We came. That's all I know. You got a problem, you talk to the boss."

"But we're not prepared!" the oarsman shouted, clearly frustrated. "How much is there?"

"Four hunnert fifty of good Kintuck bourbon and whiskey, and a thousand of china, tinned goods, Texican cigarillos, and cotton cloth."

The air practically blistered as the Cornishman swore, and Maggie could see Lizzie committing a new word or two to memory for later use.

"You fools, if I row back and roust the men, there won't be time for a proper job before the tide goes out!"

"What's tide mean to us?" came the voice. "We're below the tide—and we've worked on the beach before if we had to. Them chaloops got land wheels if we need 'em. Hurry up, then, we haven't got all night. And by the bye, if you'd use a steam-powered craft you wouldn't have to work so hard."

The sound of laughter came out of the *sawan* as, cursing, the oarsman flailed one oar and brought his rowing boat around, then hauled on them both to take him skimming back toward the hamlet.

"We can't go any closer," Lizzie said, "and with more coming, it will only get more dangerous if we are discovered. We must go up to the house and wake Grandfather. At least we know what they're bringing in, so we'll have facts to present to him and the magistrate."

"Lizzie—did you notice something about that conversation?"

"Besides the fact that at least one of those men is from the Americas?"

"Yes, besides that. Did you notice that they made no attempt at secrecy whatever? Once they were in the bay, out of sight of Penzance, the thing surfaced, and neither of those men lowered their voices. Why do they not fear discovery?"

Lizzie stepped out of the concealing darkness of the cliff face and leaned out enough for one eye to take in the proceedings. "Because they have permission to be here?" She turned back. "But surely our grandparents would not give it. They could not."

Maggie's mind was moving so fast that it was an effort to speak. Or maybe it was just that she did not know the effect her words would have on Lizzie. "Let us review the facts. A message comes notifying an unknown party of a certain cargo. A cargo matching weight and content is landed in a place that supposedly has not been used in decades. Claude notices that the books indicate a company much less solvent than is generally believed, and our grandfather flies into a rage. Yet our grandparents live in a style that only a much greater income could support."

"There must be another explanation for that. Grandmother could have an income of her own."

"If so, then why did Grandfather not give it? Why did he turn the argument on poor Claude to the point that he fled—Claude, whom I have never seen with anything but a smile on his face?"

Lizzie was silenced. Then— "The china," she finally said.

Maggie made the connection in a flash. "With a dogwood pattern—a tree that is known to grow only in the Fifteen Colonies. And Grandfather's drink of choice?"

"Kintuck bourbon. One can smell the stuff across the room."

Maggie began to feel distinctly ill. "I am very much afraid that the conclusion is inevitable: Our grandparents are somehow involved in smuggling goods on French ships—goods from the Americas, at that. Which, as everyone knows, are forbidden to enter the country by order of Her Majesty except aboard Count von Zeppelin's cargo airships."

"Oh, Maggie. What are we going to do?"

If only she knew. If only the Lady were here to take charge. If only they'd never come to Cornwall and met these people!

Maggie took several deep breaths to steady her stomach. "Is it our business to do anything? This is obviously well organized—so well that either *no one* or *everyone* in Penzance knows of it—and of long standing. And it must be run at the highest levels, because I have never seen undersea dirigibles like that before. Who even makes them?"

But Lizzie waved this off as irrelevant. "Of course it's our business! It's our future. I don't know about you, but I'm not keen on having to run an international smuggling operation simply to keep the dunner-men from the door."

"Not that you couldn't," Maggie said loyally.

"That is not the point. The point is, this is no kind of legacy to leave one's grandchildren. What if someone puts a foot wrong? Who wants a fleet of nasty *navires sous-marins* turning up every time one steps out of line?"

But Maggie was more concerned with the real dangers of the present than the imagined ones of the future. "We must notify the magistrate—that nice Sir John Rockland. He will know what to do."

"Maggie, listen to yourself. He will arrest Grandfather for disobeying the Crown! Is that what you want?"

"N-no," Maggie said slowly. "But now that we know of it, we are disobeying the Crown ourselves."

"*We* are not landing smuggled goods."

"Neither is Grandfather ... exactly. He may be in the same position as we—knowing of it and allowing it. That does not make it less wrong, but at least he is not down there in the *sawan* in his shirtsleeves, unloading cigarillos. Look, this is getting us nowhere. We must send a pigeon to the Lady from *Victory*. She will know what to do."

As a contrast to an untenable course, the thought of a mile's run over field and stile at three in the morning seemed almost welcome.

And then Lizzie, whose hearing was acute, laid a hand on Maggie's sleeve as she prepared to slip back into the shadows and along the cliff face. "What was that?"

"What?" Maggie could hear nothing but the wash of agitated waves and the subdued chug of the engines of *Neptune's Maid* at idle.

"Can't you hear singing?"

There were legends along this coast of mermaids who swam into coves and bays to sing the sailors into the sea, where they would attempt to take them for husbands—facing eternal disappointment at the sailors' inability to survive under the waves. For one wild moment, Maggie wondered if there were mermen, too, with a penchant for young women.

"They could be singing as they unload those *chaloupes*."

"No, not like that. It sounds like someone is drunk."

Together, they peered around the face of the rock to the outcropping of the cliff on the other side of the little bay. At the foot of it, wavering and stumbling, came a loose-limbed figure from the direction of Penzance, coat and cravat gone, shirt white and flapping in the moonlight.

"O where is my lover dear?
O where now is he-o?
The mermaid's ta'en him by the hand
And led him out to sea-o."

Maggie gasped. "It's Claude! Drunk as a skunk and oh, Lizzie, he's heading for the *sawan*. He'll run right into those men—and then what will they do?"

19

The tide had ebbed enough now to leave a thin strip of wet sand at the foot of the cliffs, the rocks exposed and dangerously wet and slippery with weed. Claude lost his footing more than once, and finally settled for sitting like a child and sliding down the rest of the way, landing with a splash knee-deep in seawater. It was clear his intent was to get into the house unseen through the *sawan*, but equally clear was the fact that he had forgotten the cellar door would be locked. He splashed to the narrow beach and turned to look for the *sawan*'s arched and carved entrance.

At which point he saw the *navire*, its great glass dome rising from the water, the man who must be the captain watching the proceedings from the bridge.

"Halt!" he cried with a tipsy giggle. "Who goes there?"

The train of *chaloupes* issued out of the *sawan*, sitting much higher in the water now that they had been unloaded. "Hey!" cried one of the men in the lead one, which appeared to be the only one with a crew. "Who are you?"

"Might ask you the same question," slurred Claude, "since I belong here and you do not. I say, what an interesh—interst—that is quite the boat."

"Get your arse inside and wait for the next load. When are the rest coming?"

"Dashed if I know. Left most of them sleeping in the tavern."

"Tavern?" The second speaker was the one who had sent the oarsman off to fetch the rest of his companions. "A fine kettle of fish! What are they doing in the tavern when they're needed here?"

"He's not with us," the first man said. "Who are you, boy?"

Don't tell them, Claude, Maggie urged silently. *You're just one of the locals, talking a walk to sober up before going home.*

"Claude. Who're you?"

"None of your business."

By this time the uniformed man in the navigation gondola had issued from the top of the ship onto a kind of platform. The green light of the bridge illuminated him from below in an eerie way that made Claude reel back. "I say, what a fabulous contraption."

"Claude?" the captain said, and Maggie stiffened. The jig was up. "Would that be Claude Seacombe, Howel Seacombe's grandson? Allow me to introduce myself. I am Captain Paul Martin, and this is my crew."

"Pleasure." Claude took off one boot and poured water out of it, then did the same for the other. "Jolly cold water hereabouts, what?"

"Since it appears your grandfather has become reluctant to partner with us for the next stage, despite the profit he derives from our association, I believe some encouragement is in order. Claude, would you like a tour of our ship and something hot to drink?"

"Oh no. Claude, run, if you can!" Maggie moaned.

"Bloody civil of you, old chap." Claude waved cheerfully. "And then I really must go in. Hell to pay if I'm late to breakfast, don't you know."

At a gesture from the captain, the *chaloupe* train reversed direction, ran up on the beach, and one of the bathynauts from the Americas assisted Claude inside the lead vessel with every appearance of hospitality and laughter and camaraderie.

"No, no, no," Lizzie breathed.

It had been a long time since Maggie had felt so helpless, trapped as they were on the far side of the rocks and utterly unable even to shout a warning, much less grab their hapless cousin by the elbows and hustle him to safety. It was abundantly clear that what had been a criminal situation before had now become life-threatening.

She was quite sure they planned to hold him for ransom at least long enough to bring their grandfather back into line. Had Howel Seacombe finally seen the light and realized he was in over his head? But in what? Who were these people, and what did they want from him besides a conduit for colonial goods into England? What was the "next stage"?

The metal maw of *Neptune's Maid* opened once again to admit the train, and when the *chaloupes* sallied forth once more, Claude was no longer inside the lead one with the bathynauts.

"What are we going to do?" Maggie wailed into Lizzie's ear. "Even if we tell the Lady—or Grandfather—or the magistrate—we don't know where that monstrosity is going."

"France?" Lizzie hazarded. "But where? And even if we knew, no one can see it under the water. It could sit on the bottom of the harbor at Calais and no one would ever know it was there."

A shout upon the water signaled the return of the local crew, crowded into the rowing boat and coming much faster with the help of more than one pair of oars. The girls were forced to shrink back into the shadows to avoid being seen, but while the unloading was taking place, at least Maggie got a chance to think.

"We must split up," she said at last, watching the *chaloupes* chug their way back to *Neptune's Maid*. "One of us must tell Grandfather and get a pigeon to the Lady, and the other must stop them from going until help comes."

"What?" Lizzie choked on her own breath. "You can't mean it. We must both run for help. If one goes to Grandfather and the other to *Victory*, it will come much faster."

"And if we don't get back in time, we'll lose Claude somewhere under the sea. No, it must be this way, Liz. And since you're the heiress if something happens to him, I must stall them and you must go for help."

"No! Mags, it's far too dangerous."

"But we cannot leave poor Claude in their hands! What if Grandfather refuses to do what they want and they kill him?"

"What if they kill you, too?" Maggie could not see Lizzie very well in the dark, but there was no mistaking the horror and dismay in her tone. "What will I do then?"

"You will become a great lady, that's what, and erect statues to our memory in the town square. Now, go, and quickly, before they finish."

"But what are you—"

"Lizzie! Go!"

Her cousin was no fool. She could see that they had no choice—they must separate or Claude would be borne away under the water and at best, used as leverage against their grandparents. At worst? Maggie could not bear to think of it.

As the sounds of Lizzie's hasty climb up the cliff path faded, Maggie turned her attention back to the *sawan* and surveyed the situation with all the keenness of a mind focused by fear. She did not care two hoots about this illicit importing business, but she did care deeply about Claude. Under that flippant and fashionable exterior was a kind and merry heart, and she would do everything in her power to save him from his own foolishness.

The tide was halfway out of the little cove now, exposing more rocks and sand. They could not stay much longer—the *navire* was already moving farther out into deeper water, which meant a greater risk of exposure. It would submerge soon. She left her safe hiding place in the dark crevice and crept down onto the beach, hoping against hope that none of the busy figures inside would look out and see that one of the shadows between the rocks was moving.

She reached the arch of the *sawan* and pressed herself against the damp stone, then took a breath and slipped inside. Her boots sank into the wet sand, and the smell of cold seaweed and strong tobacco assaulted her nose. She found half a refuge behind the coping of the arch, and squeezed as far as she could behind it to watch the frantic activity inside.

The *sawan* was lit by the *chaloupes'* running lights and by a series of activated moonglobes set in niches above the landing. Already the stack of crates on the quay was taller than a man, and took up nearly all of the flat space. The *chaloupes* themselves no longer floated; they sat upon the sand on wheels that clearly retracted into their bodies when they weren't needed. They were nearly empty, and as she watched, the fishermen hefted the last of the crates out of the third one, handing it up end over end in a human chain to be added to the larger stack.

Fascinated, Maggie studied them, plans and possibilities flicking through her mind. And then something caught her attention about the hull of the first *chaloupe*, which was closest to her, preparing to tow the others out into deeper water.

Its top half was constructed of thick glass, which divided along a brass seam to retract into the hull so that it could be loaded. An engine grumbled in the stern, where below, a heavy metal connector linked it to the next like a train car.

Something was stamped into the metal, the way pleasure craft had the name of the boat painted on the stern. Maggie squinted.

"That's the lot, boys!" the man from the Americas shouted, and Maggie jumped and hit her head on the coping. Up on the landing, a bag exchanged hands, no doubt payment for an unexpected night's work.

Rubbing her sore noggin, she watched as the Cornishmen ran their rowboat into the water remaining in the *sawan*, and then they shoved the oars in the locks and rowed out of there as fast as they had come in.

Now there were fewer men to see her, and the *chaloupe* lay between them. She crept closer to investigate. What did it say? Could it help them identify who these people were and where they might be going?

She crouched next to the rounded vessel, the ruffles on the bottom of her black petticoat dragging in the wet. Letters were stamped in the brass hull.

M.A.M.W.

Maggie drew in a long breath as memory swept over her in a wave.

A bullet casing from a shot that had nearly cost the life of a dear friend. A mechanical device within that dripped acid, eating through every organic thing it touched—including human flesh. A tiny stamp bearing initials just like these.

Meriwether-Astor Munitions Works.

The man who had tried to kill them all and bring on a world war five years ago had not, it seemed, stayed on his own side of the sea.

20

Panting heavily from her climb up the cliff path, Lizzie ran through the rose garden, heedless of the thorny bushes catching at her skirts. She took the stairs two at a time and dashed down the corridor to her grandparents' room.

"Grandfather!" She pounded on the door with a fist. "Grandfather, wake up!"

No movement came from within.

"Grandfather!"

Were they gone? Were they *dead?*

Lizzie wrenched open the door and flung herself through it, to be brought up like a runaway horse on the thick rug between door and bed.

Her grandparents stood at the window in their dressing-gowns, watching the sea. *Neptune's Maid* was invisible from this angle, but they might have seen her surface earlier.

"Grandfather, you must come quickly! There are smugglers in the cove!"

He did not respond. Grandmother, however, turned toward her and frowned. "Keep your voice down, dear. You will wake the servants, if you have not already."

"But Grandmother—"

"We know."

"But—"

"It is none of your affair. Go to bed, where young ladies who *are* young ladies should be, instead of galloping about in the middle of the night like fishermen's daughters from downalong."

"*Will* you stop interrupting me?" If her grandmother was not inclined to be civil, then that freed Lizzie from any obligation to be the same. "They have taken Claude! You must come at once and do whatever they say so they do not take him away."

This finally made her grandfather turn from his contemplation of the moonlight on the waves. "Claude is there? How can this be? I thought he had come in and gone to bed."

"Well, he didn't. He was drinking in the taverns and—oh, that doesn't matter now. They have taken him aboard. You must come with me. We don't have much time."

"I am afraid that is impossible."

"How on earth can you say that? They know that you will not cooperate with the *next phase*, whatever that is, and to ensure you do, they plan to kidnap him!"

"You have misunderstood," Grandfather said. "These are local men, Elizabeth, whose families have been in the smuggling and wrecking trades along these shores for centuries. They all know my grandson and will not harm him."

"Why should they?" Grandmother put in. "They are not so stupid as to endanger their livelihood."

"Those men did not look like ordinary wreckers and smugglers to me," she said. "They looked organized and well funded—and *Neptune's Maid* is no fishing ketch."

"Are you so familiar with the vessels used in Cornwall?" Grandfather asked. "Perhaps a few among them have the brains to make their trade lucrative."

"As do you." Lizzie could hardly believe her own temerity. At any moment they would toss her from the room—but until they did, and since her urgent message had got no reception at all, she would find out all she could. "How many know you are keeping the Seacombe Steamship Company afloat on smuggled goods?"

"Elizabeth, really," Grandmother sniffed. "Must you use such incendiary language? Seacombes have been importing goods from the Americas since the days of Good Queen Bess. It is hardly likely that an edict from our present queen that has no basis in common sense should get in the way of a tradition of hundreds of years' standing."

"But it is illegal. All imports are to come on Count von Zeppelin's ships."

"Ridiculous."

"We import from France the same way we always have," Grandfather said. "The demand for goods is simply too high to limit its satisfaction to one shipping company—especially one run by a foreigner."

Lizzie ground her molars together and with heroic self-control did not leap to Uncle Ferdinand's defense. "And how do they get to France from the Americas?"

"I do not know, nor do I care," Grandfather said heavily. "I am quite astonished at your quick apprehension of these matters, Elizabeth. I had not supposed you to have the mental acuity for it."

Control your temper and stick to facts. "I took firsts in German, French, and mathematics in school. We studied economics and politics as well. The Bavarian educational system is quite different from the one here. They do not assume that every young lady is going to marry and keep house upon graduation. But enough of that—are you really going to do nothing about Claude?"

Grandfather turned back to the window. "There is no need to worry. Though the pigeon did not come, everything is well in hand as usual, if your report is true."

How could he be so cavalier about the safety of his grandson and heir? Lizzie could not fathom it. But then she fixed on something he'd just said. "A pigeon? Where would it have come? They do not come to fixed addresses." Not unless someone here was as clever as Lewis about tinkering with the pigeons' innards, which wasn't likely. Not in Cornwall, where they still used horses and buggies.

"For heaven's sake, Elizabeth, is there no end to your questions?" Grandmother demanded.

"No," Lizzie said quite honestly.

"Let this be the last one, then, and you will go to bed. When the cargo is ready to ship, the pigeons come to *Demelza*, moored in the harbor. Someone then gets the message to us. Now, are you satisfied?"

But the last one hadn't come to *Demelza*. It had gone to *Athena*. Why? It couldn't have been misdirected, because who here knew the Lady's registry code? How could the pigeon have become confused? What did airship and steamship have in common?

Parts? Magnetic devices? Messenger cages?

"Did you build *Demelza*?" she asked, ignoring Grandmother, who threw up her hands in impatience that Lizzie was still here, still asking questions.

"No," Grandfather said. "I bought her when I was in New York, several years back. She used to run sugar between there, the Louisiana Territory, and the West Indies."

New York. Who else did she know who owned a shipping company and was based in New York? "Was she a Meriwether-Astor ship?"

"In fact, she was. Again you surprise me. That outfit is out of business now, I understand, and no wonder. Terrible management. Meriwether-Astor was selling off his assets, and I picked her up for a song."

That was the connection.

Athena had been a Meriwether-Astor ship, too, before the Lady had stolen her. The pigeon must somehow have responded to her signal, not *Demelza*'s, and brought them the message instead of Grandfather.

If it had not, she and Maggie would be sleeping peacefully and not worrying themselves to death about a danger that no one but they seemed to comprehend.

"Grandfather, the captain of *Neptune's Maid* said something about a 'second phase,' and that was why they took Claude aboard. He said you weren't cooperating with it. What did he mean?"

Both her grandparents stiffened as though turned to stone.

"Elizabeth," Grandmother said to the windowpane in a tone similar to the one the Lady used when she was about to shoot something, "for the last time, go to bed."

And Lizzie's temper, which most of the time she managed to keep under control, boiled over with a vengeance. "I shan't! I do not understand why the two of you are so cavalier about Claude being taken aboard a great bloody undersea dirigible. He's going to be used as leverage for this 'second phase' and there you stand, as cool and uncaring as if he were going to be late to lunch!"

Her grandfather's knees buckled. Grandmother got a shoulder under his armpit just in time.

"What did you say?" someone asked in a ghost of a voice, all color leached out of it by terror.

Lizzie's panic came roaring back in a devastating wave. "For heaven's sake!" she shouted. "It's what I've been saying all this time! *Neptune's Maid* is no fishing ketch, it's a *navire*—an undersea vessel of some kind—and they've taken Claude aboard intending to use him to make you do what they want! Now, would you come before they submerge and we lose them?"

"You did not say—?" Grandmother croaked, since it was clear Grandfather could not speak, though his mouth worked. "But of course it is a fishing ketch. These are our local men."

"Not unless your locals speak with French and Texican accents."

With a cry, Grandfather crumpled. "They would not—he promised—"

"Howel!" Grandmother, trying to hold him up, was borne to the floorboards with him. "Elizabeth, run for Nancarrow. We must have a doctor immediately!"

"But Claude and Maggie—"

"Elizabeth!" her grandmother shrieked, on her knees, her face as gray as moonlight, her eyes wild. "Run!"

Lizzie ran. She got Nancarrow. Who sent the boot-boy for the doctor. Who came.

At least, she assumed he came. Lizzie gave up on a household helpless in its uproar and ran back across the lawn. If anyone was to help Claude and Maggie, it would have to be herself.

She slid halfway down the headland path on her behind, and wound up on all fours in the sand at the bottom. She scrambled up and ran as though the devil himself chased her, into the cove—

—empty—

—into the *sawan*—

—empty—

Empty but for a ton of illegal goods, several crates of fine Kintuck bourbon, and the tracks of something wheeled in the sand, which would be washed away when the tide came in.

She was too late.

Neptune's Maid had gone, taking the only two members of her family she cared about deep under the sea, where she could not follow.

21

It was imperative that Maggie come up with a plan in the next few minutes. But questions flapped and screamed in her mind and, combined with her panic for Claude, took her dangerously close to paralysis.

Catalogue your resources, Maggie, and then apply your imagination.

The Lady's voice in her memory, warm and laced with humor, sounded over the frantic noise in her brain. Resources. Yes. One thing at a time.

The *chaloupes*.

They would be going back empty. She could stow away in one, and once they reached *Neptune's Maid*, she could find Claude and figure out a way to spirit him off the ship when they made landfall.

Wherever that might be.

I don't want to go to France. Not like this. Stowing away was no good. She had told Lizzie she would stall them until help came, but how?

Sabotage.

The men were laughing and relaxing now that their work was done. Someone broke out a flask, and amid joking about not sharing the wealth with the Cornishmen who had gone, they all took a tipple.

Maggie knelt next to the lead *chaloupe* and realized the sky visible through the arch behind her had lightened from black to charcoal. The crew could not risk being seen by an early fisherman, so she had not a moment to lose. She studied the wheel mechanism. If she disabled it, would the proceedings stop? No, they would simply drag the thing into deeper water and start up its engine.

Disable said engine?

A good plan, except that the entire thing appeared to be accessible only from the inside. Reasonable, if you went about underwater, where movable parts could be bent or attacked by roving bands of barnacles. She would certainly be seen if she tried to scale the rounded hull of the thing, which stretched above her head a good five feet.

Blast and bebother it! Think, Maggie!

Her mechanical resources did not seem useful. What others did she possess? She was good with chickens and other creatures. She was good at reading people and understanding what they meant behind what they said. She could mimic just about anyone.

It didn't help that he was a tremendous mimic, and half the time was telling us riddles in someone else's voice. And Michael had laughed as he told her of her father and his talent.

Her *real* father. For it was utterly impossible that the Banbury tale her grandparents had spun was the truth. She possessed none of Charles de Maupassant Seacombe's traits, with the exception of a similar eye color, and if one knew genetics as she did, that was hardly an indication of a direct relationship.

But whom could she mimic that would help in this situation? Oh dear—they were climbing down from the landing now. In a moment they would all load themselves into this *chaloupe* and her only chance would be lost!

M.A.M.W.

Meriwether-Astor had a daughter, did he not? Granted, the languid creature was the same age as the Lady, and Maggie was not yet seventeen, but maybe this lot didn't know that.

Maybe they hadn't met her.

Maggie hadn't seen her in five years, but to give her credit, the girl had helped them out of a very sticky situation. She had a good heart, even if she'd been brought up by a villain. Perhaps she wouldn't mind being generous with her name—if Maggie could only think of it. And her voice. And maybe even her posture.

There was no time. She'd have to go ahead, and hope to heaven the mort's name came to her.

Maggie ducked out of the *sawan*'s arch and shook her skirts out of their clasps so that they fell to cover her ankles, then straightened her collar and wished she were wearing a ballgown or a riding habit or anything more ladylike than her raiding rig.

Then again, she had all kinds of useful devices secreted in its pockets and hems, so in this situation, perhaps raiding rig was the most practical option. Miss Meriwether-Astor would never be caught dead in it, but these men needn't know that.

She dropped her shoulders, thrust out her pelvic bones, and strolled into the *sawan*, crossing in front of the *chaloupe*'s running lights in a way that made them illuminate the ruffles on her cream eyelet blouse and catch the attention of every man Jack on the sand.

Name—name—oh, *what* was the daughter's name?

"Hello, the boat," she greeted them in the flat accents of New York, overlaid with a little British schooling and a generous dollop of *nouveau riche* entitlement. "What are my chances of catching a lift out to *Neptune's Maid* with you?"

The joking and laughter faded into sheer astonishment, then muttering and exclamations. The voice she'd heard first said, "Who in tarnation are you?"

Elmira—no, Sophia—no—

Her eyes widened in impatience. "Didn't you get Papa's pigeon? I've been visiting the Seacombes for a week and I am so *bored* I could scream. I told him I was dying to go to Paris, and he said he'd arrange it with you."

The men looked at one another, then the Texican one said, "I'll ask you again, missy—who are you?"

Gloria—? Gloria! That was it!

She sniffed. "I suppose you can't be expected to know, but believe me, you'll remember next time if you want to keep your job. I am Gloria Meriwether-Astor, of course. Now, are you going to do as I ask, or do I have to go and fetch the Seacombes to vouch for me at four in the morning?"

Someone snickered in the back, and soon two or three were laughing. The Texican grinned at her. "We got us a Seacombe ourselves, and it won't be long before those two snap to it and give your pa what he wants."

How much would Gloria be expected to know about whatever her father was up to? It seemed to Maggie she had known quite a lot, being dragged about from continent to continent. "I should hope so. They'd be quite mad if they didn't. Now, will you hand me into this thing?"

"Where are your *baggages*, mademoiselle?" Another man, who could not be much older than Michael, came to join the Texican, who pulled a lever and lowered the ramp into the lead *chaloupe*. "Surely you do not plan to voyage wiz us just as you are?"

Maggie gave him her best smile and a flutter of her lashes. She knew a thing or two about charming Frenchmen, especially young ones. "Monsieur, you are too kind," she said in flawless Parisian French. "But as to my adventure in the *navire*—from what Papa has said of it, I feel quite sure that the extra weight of trunks and valises would be inappropriate, *non*? To say nothing of the space they would require. It is of no matter in any case—I have clothes enough at the hotel in Paris, and I expect Papa will meet us once he knows I have joined you."

"You are most perspicacious, mademoiselle," he returned in the accents of Arles, in the south, and bowed with the respect of a man who appreciates the young and pretty—and considerate. To his companions, he said, "She brings nothing so as to keep the extra weight in the *navire* to a minimum. She will join her father in Cornaouille."

"The big boss is coming?" someone asked. "Is it really gonna happen?"

"It seems zat it is," the Frenchman returned, offering Maggie his hand. "I predict that Mademoiselle Meriwether-Astor is departing England for more urgent reasons than it is wise to share with just anyone, *non*?" He twinkled at Maggie.

She smiled the kind of smile that holds secrets and the promise of confidences later on. "Monsieur, you are altogether too observant," she told him in a low tone. "I suspect you will go far."

"You are too kind, mademoiselle," he said. "*Alors*, watch this ramp. It is slippery and at the angle so steep. Perhaps a word in your father's ear about these good qualities in your servant Jean-Luc Martin, should you find it convenient …?"

"It will be my pleasure," Maggie told him.

She could not stall any longer. She had no choice but to board the vessel—no one was going to come from the house, and even if someone did, how could an old man like her grandfather hope to stop this rough crowd, who flung crates up on landings as if they weighed nothing? Who did not have the respect for him that would make them stop to listen, much less obey?

They had laughed at the mention of him—her grandfather, who was the first gentleman in all the lands hereabouts. A gentleman who clearly was under the thumb of Mr. Meriwether-Astor, though how that had come about and what it meant for the immediate future she did not know. But she meant to find out.

Riding in the *chaloupe* was rather like being stoppered in a bottle—the kind that sailors on desert islands might throw into the sea with a message inside. There was nowhere to sit but on the floor, so someone threw down a coat and she folded herself upon it, careful to keep her back straight and her skirts covering all possible glimpses of ankle and foot.

The tenders increased the steam pressure, and the *chaloupe*, tugging its train of cars, trundled into the sea. The water closed over its glass dome and Maggie felt the moment when the wheels slid into their housings and the thing began to move through the water under its own power.

"How very extraordinary," she murmured. It was a good thing she did not share Lizzie's fear of water, or the prospect of half the ocean bursting in through the seams above her head would be terrifying.

Jean-Luc, who seemed to have made himself her personal escort, gave her a short course on the control and piloting of it. "But zis is nothing compared to *Neptune's Maid*," he said. "I shall introduce you to her captain personally. He is called Paul Martin and he is one of the premier bathynauts in your father's employ."

"Have you served under Captain Martin long?"

His smile held pride and satisfaction. "I am his youngest brother, so I am in the position particular to say so."

The five hundred yards or so that they had to travel could have been fifty, and far sooner than Maggie would have liked, a shadow loomed over their heads, blocking out the silver light of the moon.

"Monsieur Martin, how are we to be taken aboard?" she asked as innocently as if she had not seen the *chaloupes* embark an hour ago.

Only an hour.

Could it be only an hour since the worst thing she had to worry about was her grandparents' poor opinion of her? She would give nearly anything to be back in that house with Claude and Lizzie safe and sound, and would happily take her grandparents' slings and arrows as long as she knew she and her cousins would all be together.

But that wasn't likely to happen, was it? Even if none of this had happened, the fact still remained that Grandfather was in trouble. Maggie wondered when she would ever feel truly safe again.

And then the great hinged jaw on the underside of the *Maid* opened and sucked them up inside … and there was no more time for looking back.

22

Captain Paul Martin, Maggie saw at once, was not going to be the pushover his younger brother was. When Jean-Luc introduced her, with all the flourishes the daughter of their boss was entitled to, Captain Martin merely regarded her, his eyes shadowed. "And why was I not informed that such an important passenger would be joining us?"

"The pigeon seems to have been misdirected, Paul," his brother said.

"Impossible. M.A.M.W. pigeons fly only to M.A.M.W. ships—or, in this case, to a Seacombe ship under special instruction."

"Must I be included in a discussion of pigeons?" Maggie sighed, practically wilting with boredom. She did, however, finally see why the pigeon had gone to

Athena instead of Grandfather's steamship *Demelza.* Somehow, it had detected the old M.A.M.W. registry code and gone there first, even though Lewis had been careful to reconfigure it so that *Athena* flew practically undetected by anyone except their own pigeons.

"I completely agree," the Captain said. "But you must forgive me for some confusion on this point. Even if I had not been informed regarding your coming aboard this evening, I should certainly have known you were residing at *maison* Seacombe, so that I might have carried messages or extra luggage for you."

"How very kind you are." Maggie gave him a limpid glance from grateful eyes.

Which did absolutely nothing to soften the expression in his.

"Must I present my bona fides, then?" She reached back into her memory—but thanks to Emilie's wedding last week, not as far back as she might have done. "Let's see. I was educated in London at St. Cecilia's Academy for Young Ladies, where I was particular friends with Lady Julia Wellesley—now Mount-Batting—and Lady Catherine Montrose. Excuse me, I mean Mrs. David Haliburton. I returned to the Americas with Papa afterward, and traveled with him to the diamond mines of the Canadas. From there, we—"

"Paul, *mon Dieu*, must we subject the young lady to this so wearisome treatment?" Jean-Luc had flushed with embarrassment. "I think her papa would not appreciate it when he hears of it. May I not show her to a cabin where she may refresh herself?"

The captain stiffened at being thus familiarly addressed in front of the rest of his crew. "I hardly consider questioning an unexpected passenger wearisome.

Might I remind you that the well-being of crew and vessel is my responsibility, not yours?"

"I promise I shall do nothing to affect that well-being," Maggie said in French with a smile. "Except in a positive manner, of course."

Captain Martin's gaze became speculative. "Your French is very good. How long did you study in Paris?"

Oh dear. She would have to fudge, because she had no idea of Gloria's movements in the last five years. The Lady had only heard from her twice, and those were brief scribbles that might have come from anywhere. The girl could have been in the Antipodes studying the dodo bird, for all any of them knew.

She drew herself up, as though the question had been offensive. "We have quite good tutors in the Fifteen Colonies, surprising though that might seem," she said with icy civility. "But with Papa's recent business in France, I have had the opportunity to perfect any ... flaws."

"I did not mean to cause offense, mademoiselle," he said smoothly. "Jean-Luc, please show our guest to my cabin. Our journey will only be of two hours' duration, and we are far enough by now into the Channel that we cannot return her to her hosts the Seacombes in any case."

Maggie allowed herself to gaze out of the glass that allowed the captain a one-hundred-eighty-degree view of their progress under the sea. The running lights pierced the Stygian darkness with a greenish light, touching on submerged rocks and waving forests of weed, on great silvery schools of fish, on the occasional wrecked ship. Perhaps they were sailing over the graveyard of the Spanish Armada itself.

Perhaps they would be sailing over her own, if she did not figure out how to get herself and Claude out of this fix on the double-quick.

She followed Jean-Luc down a passage with rounded walls, much like the barrel of a gun, that branched off in shorter corridors or down ladders to the various areas of the ship—galley, mess, bunks, armory. Jean-Luc pointed them out proudly. Maggie counted her steps and estimated that the *Maid* was roughly a hundred feet long and perhaps a third of that deep.

Was it big enough to hide in, though? And where, among all these chambers and ladders, was Claude?

Jean-Luc showed her into a fairly large room on the uppermost deck, in a location near what might be the pectoral fin on a shark, after politely waiting with his back turned until she had climbed the ladder so that he would not see up her skirts.

And the first thing to meet her gaze was Claude, sound asleep on the bunk in its cupboard, snoring like a locomotive.

"Goodness!" she exclaimed, before lowering her voice. "Are you quite sure it is proper to show me into a room where a gentleman is sleeping?"

"Do you not know this gentleman?"

"Of course. He has been my dinner and dancing partner these last several nights. It is Claude Seacombe, slightly the worse for wear after having a *razzle*, as he calls it, in the taverns of Penzance. But whether I know a gentleman or not has no bearing on the propriety of it, monsieur."

Jean-Luc laughed. "Ah, you colonials. Always so aware of propriety—except when you can get away with having none. I do not think Monsieur Seacombe is in any condition to put your reputation at risk, mademoiselle. Please feel free to wash up—*Neptune's Maid* carries fresh water, as well as that which is produced when the seawater is changed to steam in the boilers."

"She is a lovely ship. I have just decided she is my favorite of all Papa's fleet." She ran a hand over the arch of the door. "Just look at this carving—like the entrance to a treasure cave inhabited by mermaids."

"Ah, but she is small compared to the others. *Neptune's Bride*, for instance, displaces twice as much water, and *Neptune's Messenger* is capable of speeds up to twenty knots. And *Neptune's Fury*, of course—" He stopped with an admiring shake of the head. "Well, the world will soon see what *Neptune's Fury* is capable of."

"What do you mean?" Maggie asked, pretending to bend over Claude's recumbent form to see if he had awakened at the sound of their voices.

"But you test me, mademoiselle, when you are as aware as I that we are not to speak of it." He wagged a finger at her. "I will return in half an hour, to escort you to shore at the Baie des Sirenes."

Maggie straightened so suddenly she banged her head on the upper edge of the sleeping cupboard. Fortunately, the thickness of the French braid encircling her head took most of the impact. "Baie des Sirenes?"

"Yes, that is the deepest anchorage on this part of the coast closest to the Seacombe landing. The town is insignificant, of course, but the bay, while not ideal for surface ships, is made to order for *les navires*. It will become very important to the Bourbon regime, *non,* when your papa's plans are put into motion?"

"But of course," she said. "*Merci,* Jean-Luc. I find myself a little fatigued at the very prospect. I will look for you in half an hour."

He bowed himself out with every appearance of regret, and Maggie heard the key turn in the lock.

Really? He bothered with such a thing when tons of water kept her more a prisoner than any lock ever could? Ah well, no matter. She had no plans to escape now. In thirty minutes of searching, she would know everything the captain's cabin had to tell her, and have time for a face-wash besides.

She knew the two most important things already. Claude was safe and well—though he would likely have a dreadful headache when he woke up—and their destination was the Baie des Sirenes.

The town where Mother had gone to wait for her confinement. The town where Maggie had been born.

Where there was a graveyard that might hold a grave with two coffins in it.

༄

TO: MERIWETHER-ASTOR PRIORITY ONE
FROM: CAPTAIN PAUL MARTIN, *NEPTUNE'S MAID*

Situation Report: Seacombe still unwilling to cooperate. Have secured insurance in form of grandson. Miss Meriwether-Astor is also aboard at her request. This is no place for a lady. Expecting *Fury* by sunset. Request instructions.

༄

SHELLEY ADINA

To: LADY CLAIRE TREVELYAN, *ATHENA*
FROM: ELIZABETH SEACOMBE, *VICTORY*

Maggie and Claude have been taken away by a *navire*—
an underwater dirigible called *Neptune's Maid*—because
our grandparents would not agree to some horrible
smuggling scheme. Mr. Meriwether-Astor is behind it.
That's where the Colonial goods are coming from—the
Americas via France.

Please come, Lady. I don't know where they have been
taken, but I need help.

23

Gwynn Place had first been constructed during the reign of George I, but it had not reached its current size and beauty until the Regency of that witty inventor who subsequently became George IV. The previous evening at dinner, Lady Flora, the second wife of Sir Richard Jermyn, and mother of Lady Claire and the current Viscount St. Ives, had told them the tale.

Since anything connected with Claire was of interest to him, Andrew Malvern had paid more attention than such stories usually warranted.

"My late husband was not terribly clear on the details—but it seems that in her youth, his grandmother was quite the bluestocking, always closeted away tinkering with bits of machinery. Claire, I am quite sure these tendencies must be inherited, for I cannot account for them otherwise. There are certainly no such tendencies on my side of the family."

"I am sure that is true, Mama."

"What was Claire's great-grandmother's name, Lady Flora?" Andrew asked.

"She was called Loveday Trevithick."

"Ah, that explains it," Andrew said with the satisfaction of feeling a puzzle piece slip into place. "That family is known for their genius with mechanics. Richard Trevithick invented the steam engine and put the nation on the path to greatness that it enjoys today."

"Yes, well, at the time, greatness was a long way off, to hear Vivyan tell it," Lady Flora said. He suspected she might have sniffed, but deferred because of his obvious admiration for the Trevithick name. "While she was a gentleman's daughter, and Gavin Trevelyan a gentleman, she had nothing to bring to the match save her talents—and sadly, they did not extend to kitchen and home."

"Unless one needed something fixed, presumably," Claire said into her soup.

Sir Richard and Andrew laughed, and then sobered when Lady Flora did not. "In any case, love seems to have won out, and they had three children—a boy who inherited the estate, and two girls."

"My great-aunts Jenna and Elowen," Claire explained to Andrew. "They married brothers—you will have heard of Admiral Wingate? It was he who first circumnavigated the globe by airship, in eighteen fifty-two."

"I have indeed," Andrew said. "I declare, you have quite the illustrious family."

"We do our part," Lady Flora said, and turned the conversation to other things.

Andrew found it difficult to listen politely to a discussion of local families, and afterward, when Claire and her mother and Sir Richard's unmarried sister passed through into the drawing room, he found himself equally distracted, glancing at the clock and wondering how a man such as his host, who was possessed of both intellect and means, could have so little conversation.

"Sir Richard," he said, interrupting a soliloquy on the merits of two different kinds of grain, "might I ask your advice on a subject requiring some delicacy?"

"Hm? What? Delicacy? What do you mean?"

"I mean Lady Flora's daughter Claire."

"Claire? What about her? Hardly see the girl. About time she left gadding about the world and came to see her family. It's not because she needs money, is it?"

Andrew recovered quickly from his surprise. "No, sir, it is not. I believe her to be quite sound in her management of money, and she would not importune her mother in any case, even if she were not."

Sir Richard harrumphed. "Damned good thing. Gwynn Place is only just getting back on its feet again after that Arabian Bubble business. But what did you want to ask me about?"

Andrew gathered his courage. It was not in his nature to confide in someone he had only just met, but needs must where the devil drives, as his mother used to say. "Some years ago, when she was only eighteen, I asked Claire to marry me." Sir Richard choked on his port, and Andrew handed him a linen napkin. "Are you quite all right, sir?"

"Yes, yes, quite all right. And what was her answer?"

"She—to be honest—she gave none. But her conduct toward me since has given me reason to believe that any indecision was the result of her age and not her inclination. And I have been advised by persons in a position to know that I ought to try again."

"Eighteen. And she's what now? Twenty-five?"

"She will be twenty-four in October, sir."

"Girl's practically on the shelf. No wonder her mother has given up on her. Well, if you're looking for permission to ask for her hand, I'm not the man to give it. Technically you ought to apply to her brother, but since he's only six, Flora is the one. Joy and jubilation in that department, I'll wager." His sandy eyebrows rose as he took Andrew in from head to foot. "Set up well enough to support her, are you?"

"Claire is possessed of an independent competency, but even if she were not, the answer would be yes. I have been quite successful in my field, and with my doctorate in hand, I expect that to continue. I have a standing invitation to take up a professorship at the University of Edinburgh, should I choose, as well as invitations of a similar kind from the University of Bavaria in Prussia."

"Damned cold place to live, Scotland. Never travel north of the Cotswolds if I can help it."

And that had been that. Andrew had risked his sense of propriety and had nothing to show for it, and earlier, when he had applied to Lady Flora in the privacy of the morning room as she wrote out the day's menu for the cook, he had come out not much further ahead.

"Marry Claire?" She had laid down her pen and gazed at him in astonishment. "But I thought you were her—her employer?"

"I was. But on a more personal level, there has been no one for me but your daughter since the moment she turned up at my laboratory five years ago, looking for a job."

Lady Flora passed a hand over her forehead. "Pray do not remind me. But are you certain? I am her mother and I love her dearly, but let us be honest—she does not exactly have the temperament for wifehood."

That depends on the sort of wife one is looking for. "I believe her temperament will suit me exactly. Do I have your permission to ask for her hand, then, Lady Flora?"

She had waved her fingers, as if this idea must be dissuaded from landing in anyone's head. "She has been independent of me for so many years that I am not deluded that my opinion counts for anything … but yes, Mr. Malvern, if you are willing to take her on, you have my blessing. And … I wish you good luck."

Andrew had not been through these proceedings before, but even he suspected that most mothers would not have added that last.

So now all that was left to do was to find the lady herself, and pose the question. But this proved to be more difficult than he might have expected, and the house larger and more confusing than it looked from its serene and Georgian southern prospect, gazing out over Carrick Roads to the sea.

After a series of gabbled directions from a housemaid, he somehow found himself out in the herb garden, and upon blundering through a door, ended up in a neat enclosed yard full of raised beds of vegetables, with a tidy row of small sheds along one wall, where the sun was guaranteed to warm them. *Sheds* was an unkind term; as he approached, he saw they were more like small houses, snugly built and weather-tight.

Houses for the hens.

Ah. He was in the presence of the famous Gwynn Place hens, outside enjoying the day in all their golden splendor, and there, digging joyfully in the grass, were two small red specimens he recognized. "Holly? Ivy? Where is your mistress, ladies?"

Hearing their names and recognizing him as someone who might have cracked corn about his person, they raced across the grass to dance about his feet, looking up in expectation. He knelt to stroke their feathers. "Sorry, girls, I forgot to stock up. Have you seen Claire hereabouts?"

Holly and Ivy did not reply except to express their disappointment in his unreliability, but a voice came across the grass instead.

"If you're looking for the young lady, she was here." A man stepped out from between two of the houses, his hair shining white in the sun, his keen eyes the color of strong tea, wrinkles fanning out from their corners as though he laughed often and made a habit of looking to the horizon.

"But she is not now?"

"No. But she'll be back. I believe she went to that airship of hers that's moored in our paddock."

"Ah. Checking for pigeons, most likely. Do I have the pleasure of addressing Mr. Polgarth?"

"Aye, you do."

"I am Andrew Malvern. I accompanied Claire and the Mop—and her wards down to Cornwall. They were to stay with their grandparents in Penzance, so we left the girls and their cousin in their care and came up here yesterday."

Mr. Polgarth shook his hand with a strength and vigor that belied the white hair and wrinkles. "And did our Mopsies find their grandparents well?"

Andrew dropped the man's hand in surprise, and Polgarth smiled. "Young Maggie has been corresponding with me off and on since she first came down here as a little 'un. She's told me what you call her and her cousin. She has quite an interest in the Gwynn Place hens."

"So I've heard," Andrew agreed. "I believe she plans to study genetics in the future, thanks to your conversations with her during their summer holidays here."

"Does she, now?" Polgarth pushed his tweed cap back with a finger as satisfaction wreathed his face. "That makes me happy. My feathered ladies have much to teach us."

"In answer to your question, though … yes, they found their grandparents well, though I am afraid a period of adjustment might be necessary when it comes to personalities and customs."

"The Seacombes are set in their ways, are they?"

"You could say so."

"Did they treat our girls well?"

Andrew hesitated a moment too long.

"I see you're a gentleman, unwilling to criticize your acquaintance to a stranger. My grandson Michael has told me of the goings-on in that house, and why he lost his position at the Seacombe Steamship Company. Shameful business."

"I quite agree," was all that Andrew would allow himself to say.

"I wish they had come here instead."

"I do, too, but Claire believes them old enough to make their own decisions. And to be fair, it is right that the girls acquaint themselves with their grandparents—the Seacombes are their only family now."

The moment the words were out of his mouth, Andrew realized he had said the wrong thing.

"That is not true, sir." Polgarth's face darkened and Andrew remembered the strength of that grip.

Andrew was not the kind of man who would take a step back in retreat or take one forward in challenge. Instead, he sensed a puzzle and committed himself to ferreting out the truth. "I'm dreadfully sorry. I meant no offense. I am not familiar enough with the girls' parentage to make that kind of pronouncement. I see that you have information that I do not."

"I do, sir. Maggie is my granddaughter, too. My own son Kevern's child. Everyone hereabouts knows it—except them Seacombes, who will deny it to their last breath. They'd rather throw mud upon his good name and call him traitor than admit their girl could fall in love with a poultryman's son."

Andrew's knowledge of the situation at Seacombe House underwent a rapid reassessment. Claire had told him nothing of this—but then, she was protective of the girls and the less said on some subjects, the better. "Then Mr. Michael Polgarth—how does he fit into this?"

"He is Maggie's cousin. My son Myghal's boy, and a more honest, hard-working young man you won't find. But that don't hold water with Seacombe. After turning him out of the house, he found out he was telling our Maggie about her *other* family and gave him the sack as well."

"So he did not know the young man was in his employ—it must be a larger concern than I thought. Well, I understand the situation now, where I did not before," Andrew said slowly. "Where is young Mr. Polgarth?"

"He's hereabouts." Polgarth looked around the enclosed garden, as though Michael might step out of one of the hen houses at any moment. "Spending a few days with his family to get his feet back under him. But tell me this, sir—will the young maids come here after their visit in Penzance is concluded?"

In Polgarth's eyes Andrew could see so much longing that it almost hurt to look. It was with a sense of relief that he was able to say, "Yes, I believe so. We are all flying back to London together in *Athena*—that ship out in your paddock."

"I am glad," Polgarth said on a long breath. "It will be the first Maggie and I will have seen one another since we learned of our connection. I am anxious to know her as my own flesh and blood, not merely the visiting ward of my young lady." His keen eyes flashed as his gaze met Andrew's. "You're the second young man who has come down here with Lady Claire. She's told me much more of you than she ever did of the other one. I understand you're good friends as well as being her employer at one time."

Andrew heard the question under the polite observation. "We are good friends. But with Claire, it's dashed hard to get her attention long enough to become anything more."

Polgarth regarded him for a few seconds, as if making up his mind. "You won't think I'm stepping out of my place if I say a thing or two?"

"I wish you would." The chance for honesty felt like a cup of fresh water to Andrew's spirits. "When I applied to Sir Richard for her hand, he referred me to her mother. Lady Flora essentially wished me luck, by which I inferred I was on my own. To be quite honest, Mr. Polgarth, I never would have suspected proposing to a woman would be this difficult."

Polgarth smiled, his eyes warming with humor. "Is it so difficult to tell a woman you love her?"

"I haven't had much experience along that line, but one would think not. However, Claire is noticeably unlike any other woman I have ever met."

"She is," Polgarth agreed. "But then, perhaps you're unlike any man she has ever met."

"She turned down a baronet's offer a few weeks ago—a fine man, and an excellent match. I hope her mother never hears of it."

"And this doesn't give you hope?"

"It might, if I didn't know about her ambition and her prospects, both of which fly as high as the airships she loves."

"They are not all she loves," Polgarth pointed out. "And when my young lady loves, she's all in—no holding back."

"Don't I know it."

"You strike me as the same, if you'll pardon my saying so. Just tell her, Mr. Malvern. She has not had so much love in her life that she'll turn it down out of hand. She'll see it for the gift that it is—even if she has a difficult time believing the gift is for her."

And with a feeling rather like an explosion in his heart, Andrew realized why Claire held the poultryman in such high esteem.

But before he could speak further, Polgarth pointed toward the gate in the wall. "Speaking of my young lady, here she comes."

But Claire was not strolling back from the paddock, reading her mail and not looking where she was going. Instead, she came flying through the half-gate, slamming it shut and scattering hens right and left as she dashed across the lawn.

A piece of paper fluttered from her fingers, and Andrew's heart constricted in sudden fear.

24

The Baie des Sirenes might as well have been named the Baie des Baleines, so deep it was. In any case, nothing resembled a sounding whale more than these undersea dirigibles, and Maggie could see why sailing- and steamships went elsewhere for their moorage. Cliffs plunged straight into the sea, much as they did across the Channel in Cornwall, but in a notch in the landscape, the pretty town of Baie des Sirenes tumbled from a church at the top to a promenade and long stone quays, where fishing boats were moored on lengthy lines to accommodate the tide.

They had not docked at the stone piers like normal vessels—oh, no. For deep under the water were undersea caverns, where the *navires* could come and go practically undetected by anyone watching from the town or up on the bluffs, where a lighthouse warned of the rocks.

Neptune's Maid surfaced inside one of the caverns that held two other *navires*, and her passengers disembarked on a stone jetty within that led to passages up to the surface, worn smooth by feet and wheels.

Claude was still the next thing to unconscious, and had been removed with his arms flung over the shoulders of two bathynauts, his feet dragging and stumbling as his mind struggled to shake off the haze of drink and resume its functioning once again.

Maggie needed to find a way to stifle him until she had the opportunity to apprise him of her deception. It would be just like him to greet her by her real name and ask a lot of silly questions, which would put them both at risk—herself more than he. For what value did Maggie No-last-name have to these smugglers? None. They'd probably drown her in a weighted sack like a kitten, and with the depth of these waters, no one would ever know.

Her search of the captain's cabin had been as thorough as it was tidy. She had found several sketches of the *navire* called *Neptune's Fury*, which appeared to be a much bigger version of the *Maid*, with a hold that might just be able to contain a whale, if such a thing were necessary. She could only imagine how many crates of Texican cigarillos had voyaged under the Atlantic inside it—and how much money must be possible in the smuggling trade. That rascal Meriwether-Astor was getting his revenge on Her Majesty for her temerity in shutting down his shipping lines, and no mistake.

But why bring the French into it? Or rather, why allow the French to bring him into it, which was what it had sounded like. Maggie could find nothing in desk or bookcase to tell her the answer, except a long and rather dull treatise on the lineage of the current Bourbon and all the countries he was supposed to be king of if his ancestors hadn't had their heads chopped off in the previous century.

They emerged from a carved arch in the rock of the cliff that reminded Maggie strongly of the Seacombe *sawan*, except it was quite a lot larger, and were decanted onto the broad stone quay outside. Their procession along the promenade and into the town would have been rather like the Seacombes' procession through Penzance to Grandfather's offices, if it hadn't been for poor Claude. The burliest of the bathynauts finally slung him over his shoulder and carried him along to the stone inn and tavern that presided over the landward end of the quay.

They deposited him in a comfortable chair in a parlor with a crackling fire in the hearth. Maggie held out her hands to the blaze as Jean-Luc bowed. "You will be comfortable here while a room is prepared for you, Mademoiselle Meriwether-Astor."

"And what of that poor boy?" She nodded over her shoulder.

"We will look after him until his grandparents agree to work with your father."

"To what do they object?" Maggie asked. "I can hardly imagine Papa in partnership with such people at all. They seem rather ... small."

"It is not they but the land they control that interests him. Or should I say the landing—for the beach that runs along their so many acres is perfect for the coming ashore of *Fury*'s cargo."

"Ah, I see," she said, though she did not. "It must be enormous."

"It is indeed," Jean-Luc said in delight. "Have you seen it?"

"No, not yet."

"Then you must permit me to give you a tour while we await the arrival of your esteemed father. My brother had a pigeon sent the moment we surfaced."

How long did it take to fly from Cornouaille to Paris? Not long—perhaps an hour or two? "I shall be so glad to see him. My stay at Seacombe House was only to be a few days, but it seemed like *weeks*."

"Sadly, we do not anticipate his arrival until sunset. The crossing of the Atlantic is no small matter."

Gerald Meriwether-Astor was coming from the Americas, not Paris? On the one hand, whatever they were planning had to be more than a mere smuggling job. On the other, she had a little time to figure out how to get herself and Claude out of this mess.

Maggie didn't give two figs about Texican cigarillos. But her cousin must not be used as leverage against two old people who were probably quite justified in not letting this lot use their beach to illegally import whatever it was. Once she got them away from here, they'd make a brief stop at the cemetery and prove once and for all that it was Michael Polgarth's story that held the truth, and not the horrid tale that the Seacombes believed.... Well, maybe Claude had resources here in France that she didn't know about. She'd welcome even that snobby Arabella de Courcy if the girl came with an airship.

The moment Jean-Luc bowed himself out of the room, Maggie leaped upon Claude and shook him the way a terrier shakes a mole. "Claude! Claude, wake up!"

"Mmph? G'way. 'Smiddle of the night."

"Claude, it's Maggie. We're in desperate trouble and you have to wake up!"

One eye slitted open, then closed again as the light of dawn on the sea outside pierced it painfully. "Maggie? D'you have the key?"

"What key? Honestly, Claude, you have to sit up and listen." She cast around the room, spotted a pitcher and ewer on a side table, and tossed a cupful of the contents in his face.

"Bless me!" He sat up, scrubbing his face with his sleeve. "What'd you do that for?" Then he got a bleary look around. "Didn't I leave the tavern?" With a groan, he fell back. "Be a love and ask the maid for a good strong coffee, would you?"

"There isn't a maid, there's only me. You have to listen. We're in France, Claude. You've been kidnapped."

He snickered. "Bollocks."

A second cupful of water in the face got his full attention. "Steady on, old girl. No need for violence." His right sleeve being soaked, he wiped his face with the left.

"There *is* need. You have to sober up and listen. We are in captivity. Our grandparents have refused to let a lot of French and Colonial smugglers land cargo on their beach, so they have kidnapped you in order to force our grandparents to do it."

He goggled at her. "The devil you say. You, too?"

"No, they think I'm someone else. Their boss's daughter, whose name is Gloria Meriwether-Astor—and don't you dare forget it. My life depends on it."

"Gloria who?"

"Never mind. Just Gloria. We're supposed to be friends. Can you remember that?"

"Righto. Gloria." He squinted at her, the light still obviously paining him. "France, really?"

She filled the cup a third time and ignored the way he flinched as she handed it to him properly this time. He drank it down as she said, "Yes, really. A place directly across the Channel from Penzance, called Baie des Sirenes."

"Never heard of it."

The door opened to admit a young girl bearing a tray with a coffee pot, cups, and a plate of croissants.

"It *is* France," Claude said on a sigh of happiness, and heaved himself out of the chair.

"Can I get you anything else, m—" The girl stopped, and the tray tilted at an alarming angle.

"Watch out!" Maggie dove for it and stopped the coffee pot from taking a header onto the carpet just in time. The girl did not move, only stared at her, so Maggie gently removed the tray from her hands and put it on the table next to the half-empty ewer. "Are you quite all right?"

"Do I know you?" the girl asked in the accented French of Cornouaille.

Just in time, Maggie remembered who she was supposed to be. Would Gloria have gone for the tray, or just let it fall and demanded that the maid clean it up? She would never know.

"I think not," she drawled. "I've never been here before—and if I had, it's unlikely we would have met socially."

"I say," Claude said to the maid between gulps of coffee. "Jolly kind of you. *Café au lait* is excellent."

The girl retreated, never taking her gaze from Maggie's face. "*Pardon, mademoiselle,*" she said. "I must have made a mistake."

When the door closed behind her, Maggie murmured, "That was odd. I hope to goodness Gloria hasn't been here before, or that girl will be haring off to tell the powers that be that I am an impostor."

"Nice bit of acting, step-cousin mine," Claude said, having moved on to the croissants. "Like watching a different person."

He offered her a pastry and she took it. "I *am* a different person. What's my name?"

"Gloria. *In excelsis deo.*"

"And I'm not your cousin, step or otherwise."

Jean-Luc was as good as his word. He returned for them in the company of the two bathynauts who had assisted Claude off the ship, both visibly relieved that their burden had recovered his wits and they would not be required to repeat the performance.

"I've received permission to show you about," he told Maggie, ushering them out the door of the inn and into the sunshine. "Monsieur Seacombe will not be locked in a room in the inn, as I had been led to believe, but he will be in the company of *mes amis* Serge Lavande and Gilles Gilbert at all times."

Maggie's heart sank, but she did not allow it to show in her face. "How considerate of you. I very much appreciate an escort—especially in these exciting times."

"Consider me your *personal* escort, mademoiselle," Jean-Luc said. He would have bowed over Maggie's hand again if she had not wrapped both of them around his elbow in a convincing imitation of a fragile society flower.

"Do show us *Neptune's Fury*," she pleaded. "I wish to be as informed about her as possible when Papa arrives. He would expect no less, as I am sure you can appreciate."

Maggie kept a smile upon her lips and did her best to suppress the uneasiness in her stomach as they proceeded back down to the subterranean caverns. She was not afraid of water, nor of dark, enclosed spaces, but there was something about the aura of hidden power, of a concealed threat, down here in the dark and damp that made her scalp prickle and goose bumps rise on her arms.

Neptune's Fury was easily the size of *Athena*, that former Meriwether-Astor transport which, five years ago, had been used to ship weapons from one end of the Americas to the other in hopes of provoking an international incident and possibly even a war. And from the hints that Jean-Luc had dropped, Meriwether-Astor had not changed his spots despite the severe crimp the Lady of Devices had put in his plans at that time. But unlike *Athena*, the crew's quarters and navigation gondola were of minimal proportions, leaving the vast remainder of her carrying capacity for cargo.

The captain of the *Fury* was pleased to escort them below, and Jean-Luc surrendered her arm with great reluctance. Maggie kept the conversation light and full of admiration, and to her enormous relief, Claude played along, acting the utter flibbet with such success that even the stoic and watchful Serge cracked a smile.

The more their captors underestimated them, the better Maggie would feel. *Wise as serpents and harmless as doves*, the Lady said, and it had become a strategem that had served her well.

The possibility existed that Claude was not in fact acting. He was very convincing, though, and that was all that mattered.

"And here is the heart of *Neptune's Fury*," the captain said, ushering them into an enormous cargo hold—so big that the ceiling was obscured in darkness. It needed to be big. For concealed in the heart of the *Fury* was a machine of such size that Maggie wondered how on earth they had got it in here short of building it on the spot.

It was easily the size of *Neptune's Maid*, with giant circulating treads on iron wheels. Its engines lay in pods to either side, and above that was what Maggie could only describe as a rotating gun fortress, with small glass windows set about it so that gunners could operate the firing mechanisms. Below that was a separate edifice that housed a cannon, its barrel so large that the projectiles must be the size of fishing boats.

It took a lot to silence Maggie, but this massive war machine—for that was what it must be—did it. Horror fought with despair inside her, and if it had not been for the eerie green light in the cargo bay, the captain would have seen instantly that she had been stricken speechless by fear, not admiration.

Claude whistled as he examined one of the circulating wheel assemblies. "Big as a volcano and just as dangerous, what?" he said. "But what's it for?"

The captain smiled. "Can you answer your young friend, Mademoiselle Meriwether-Astor?"

Maggie waved a hand that only trembled a little and struggled to control her emotions. "Why, I assume this is what Papa plans to land on the Seacombe beach, is it not?"

The captain laughed, clearly pleased at her grasp of the situation. "It is indeed."

Claude leaned back to try to see past the wheel assembly, but could not. "What—is he declaring war on Cornwall? For this jolly great thing doesn't strike me as being meant for fishing."

"You are quite correct on both counts, Monsieur, but your scope is much too limited. Your presence here not only guarantees that the beach will remain clear for the landing, but that the Royal Aeronautics Corps will not be mobilized to stop it. With this war machine, France will launch its campaign against both England and Prussia, and reclaim the kingdoms for our King that were stolen in centuries past."

"You mean there is more than one of these?" Maggie finally managed to get past her chattering teeth.

"There is—one on each front. The other launches with the second half of our fleet off the coast of Jutland, where the landing is equally amenable."

"But—how is it to be accomplished? Mechanically, I mean. For it looks too big to get through *Fury*'s hatch." She had seen the drawings in the cabin on the *Maid*, but could not see the corresponding mechanical equipment here. Or was the scale simply so vast that her mind could not take it in?

The captain's black eyes shone with masculine appreciation. "An excellent observation, mademoiselle. In fact, you are standing very near the solution. *Regardez*, if you will, the hinge that runs the length of this deck. And imagine the jaw of a whale, opening to admit the fish upon which she feeds. When we are close enough to our landing, the hinge will tilt down, the Kingmaker will roll to the seabed—while it cannot tolerate submersion, you understand, as long as the engines are clear of the water line, it can proceed up out of the water and onto land. Hence our requirement for a gradual, sloping beach, such as that on the far reaches of the Seacombe lands."

"Goodness," Maggie breathed, her hand tightening involuntarily on his arm as the full horror of the plan became clear. "You have thought of everything. I never dreamed that Papa's tinkering would someday come to this. How utterly thrilling."

"What about the Aeronautics Corps outpost on St. Michael's Mount?" Claude asked. "They might not see you coming, or have any warning, but they'll certainly see this old girl waddling up out of the water."

The captain nodded again, as though pleased his students had learned their lessons so well. "*Neptune's Lady*, which displaces twice the water of the *petite navire* on which you came, is equipped with missiles. The young lady's papa, you will recall, owns a munitions factory that has been very busy lately."

"Too busy," Maggie pouted. "I hardly see him anymore."

Were all Meriwether-Astor's vessels named after Neptune? Is that how he saw himself—as the king of the sea, with his sneaky underwater ships and smuggling and armaments for foreign governments, merrily breaking every possible law? He certainly had enough minions to do his bidding—and from what she knew of the silly young Bourbon presently on the throne, she wouldn't give the latter a worm's chance in a henhouse before he was pushed aside and the real power behind the throne took his place.

"So after the first salvo, the aeronauts will not trouble us," Jean-Luc put in. "I doubt that anyone will trouble us. Local militia cannot stand up to the King-maker, and we will be halfway to London before the other detachments get wind of us."

Maggie could see it now—a swath of destruction miles wide, from Penzance to Exeter to Windsor. A swath that would level the countryside ... and Gwynn Place ... and Polgarth and Michael ... and all Polgarth's prize hens.

Maggie set her teeth. Someone had to stop them. Someone who wasn't mad or blinded by greed or fantasies of lost kingdoms. Someone who had a bit of spirit—who could do the unexpected because no one took her seriously or even believed she had any value.

Someone like herself.

25

By the time the tour concluded, Maggie had educated both herself and Claude as well as could be expected considering that they weren't supposed to know very much. She was not sure of Claude's education at the Sorbonne, but her own had included enough of mechanics and engineering that she now possessed a rough idea not only of how the Kingmaker worked, but how the *Fury* was intended to support its incursion onto English shores.

Two things were painfully, frighteningly clear: One, she could not be present when Meriwether-Astor arrived expecting to see his daughter. And two, she must be on the *Fury* when it departed for Cornwall.

Since those two events were, from what the captain had proudly reported, to happen within hours of each other, it was obvious that solving the first meant accomplishing the second.

Which was going to be the hard part.

They were escorted back to the inn and given separate rooms in the rear, the windows on each side generous in order to catch the greatest amount of light allowed by the escarpment of the cliff behind it. As soon as the door closed behind Jean-Luc and she heard him giving instructions to Serge standing outside, Maggie flew to her windows and opened them, leaning out as far as she dared.

"Claude! Open your window!"

He did so, craning to look up at the sliver of sky between roof and cliff-top, then over at her. "I believe they've locked me in and taken the key, Gloria, old thing. Have they no faith?"

"You're too valuable. Of course, once they've landed in England, you'll be worth about as much as a chamber pot to them. I'm a bit worried about what they plan to do with you then."

"I confess that same thought crossed my mind. I've been considering a daring escape, but the exact logistics of it are defeating me at the moment."

"Whereas I am considering the opposite. I need to get aboard *Fury* unseen and scuttle the Kingmaker."

His elbows slipped off the sill and he practically fell out the window. "Are you mad?" he said hoarsely, tugging at his sleeves and brushing away the lichen from the old stone sill that clung to them.

"If I were, I should be joining this insane enterprise. Claude, what if we were to do both? You engineer a distraction by escaping that will allow me to get aboard that *navire*. Both our ends are then accomplished."

"Delighted, I'm sure, but how? I am locked in, there is a guard upon my door, and we both appear to be on the third floor."

"Let us then catalogue our resources and use our imaginations, shall we?"

She wriggled out onto the sill and, holding on to the frame on either side, leaned out to see what the prospects might be for climbing onto the roof. Sadly, it protruded out too far for her to scale it without falling, though once up there, it would have brought her closer to the cliff, which might be scaled.

She twisted the other way on the sill to examine the cliff. It was granite, and fissured and seamed with weathering, but definitely not climbable.

"Mademoiselle, please be careful." A woman's voice floated up from below. "If you fall, I will not be able to catch you."

A woman's *English* voice.

Maggie slithered back into her room and leaned on the sill to look down. A woman in a flowered dress and a white lace cap pleated and frilled in the French manner gazed up at her, and as she saw Maggie's face in full, her eyes widened and her grip on her basket loosened in surprise. "It's true!" she exclaimed, though no one else was down there to hear her. "I'm glad to know that Katrine wasn't simply spinning one of her fancies."

"What fancies? Who might Katrine be?"

"I know that Mr. Meriwether-Astor's daughter is a guest here. Are you she—or someone else? Her maid, perhaps?"

Here was a conundrum. She had to maintain her false identity until the very last possible moment or risk that burlap sack. But this lady was clearly English—

and from Cornwall, if Maggie's ears didn't deceive her. She was not a guest at the inn—the basket full of what looked like herbs and flowers was proof of that. Would it be safe for Maggie to say who she really was, and seek an ally? Or would the woman simply go straight to Serge or any one of the bathynauts and turn her in for a handful of sous as a reward?

"And who wishes to know?" Questions were easily answered with more questions.

"I am Katrine's mother—Katrine is the maid who waited on you earlier."

"But you are not French?"

"No, though I speak the tongue well enough after nearly twenty years. My name is Marie Lavande."

Hadn't that been Serge's surname? Was this kind lady a relative? "Mary Lavender—that's lovely. Do you work with herbs and simples, then?"

"I do. I came here as a nurse, and stayed because of Henri, the man who became my husband—and because they have no doctor closer than Brest, which is miles away. Can you come down to the garden, miss, while I pick a few herbs? I am getting a crick in my neck from looking up."

"Certainly." Maggie glanced to her left at Claude, who was listening in with the interest of someone who has nothing else to do. "I'll be back shortly."

"I'll be here," he said, his chin on his hand. "Tell Serge to bring a key and another cup of *café au lait*, there's a good girl."

She found Marie Lavande in the sunny garden on one side of the inn next to the kitchen door, her basket at her feet. She offered her hand, and when Maggie shook it, did not release it, but examined her face as though it were a scroll and she a scholar of Hebrew.

"I cannot get over it," she said at last, releasing Maggie to sink onto the stone wall that divided the garden from that of its neighbor. "You are not adopted, are you?"

A tingle ran over Maggie's shoulders and up the back of her neck. She paused in the act of shaping the word No, and changed her mind. "I am, in fact."

"By Mr. Meriwether-Astor? How old were you?"

Maggie regarded her for a moment. "May I ask why you wish to know something so personal about a stranger?"

The woman smiled, self-deprecation in every line, and her lashes fell over speedwell-blue eyes. "You must think me terribly rude, barging in here and asking such intrusive questions. But you look so much like the portrait of a friend that hangs in our hall that it's uncanny. Your mouth, your jaw, even the way your hair waves back from your face—" She stopped, and drew in a breath. "I am sorry. I am reminded of an old grief, that is all. I do beg your pardon, mademoiselle."

"Allow me to ask you a question in return," Maggie said. "Are you a supporter of Mr. Meriwether-Astor's aims here in Baie des Sirenes? Are you even aware of what they are?"

Marie's face clouded, and when she met Maggie's gaze, fury snapped in the depths of her eyes. "And will you turn me over to the royalist bathynauts if I give you the wrong answer?"

Her tone of disdain would seem to indicate she was not related to the guard on Claude's door—or if she was, that family dinners might be rather tense.

"I will not."

"But you must, if you are Monsieur Meriwether-Astor's daughter."

"We have already established that I am not."

"Then who are you?"

Do not be afraid to listen to your heart, Maggie, the Lady said in the back of her memory. *A thimble of your intuition is worth a cup of anyone else's logic.* If she could not trust that compass inside her—what the Lady called her intuition, that had not led her astray yet—then what else could she trust in this strange place with all its danger?

"My name is Maggie," she said, her stomach plunging at the magnitude of the risk. "I am the ward of Lady Claire Trevelyan, of Gwynn Place in Cornwall, and the step-cousin of Claude Seacombe, whom you observed in the other window. We are both here against our will, and I am masquerading as Gloria Meriwether-Astor to keep us both alive."

It took several moments for Marie Lavande to absorb these astonishing facts. And then Maggie saw the moment when she seized upon one in particular.

"You are the cousin of Claude Seacombe? By what connection?"

"His father married my aunt, Elaine Seacombe."

"Your aunt!"

"Yes. My mother was her sister. Claude's father adopted me when—"

"—when Catherine died. Yes, I know. And there was not a blessed thing I could do to stop it."

For the second time that day, Maggie stared, utterly bereft of speech.

"I knew it!" Marie pressed both hands to her cheeks, slipped from her seat on the wall, and took several rapid steps down the nearest row of kitchen herbs. "I knew it!" When she whirled and marched back, tears glistened on her cheeks. "I knew the resemblance was too strong for chance. Oh, Marguerite, I never thought this day would come. Look at you—how grown up and lovely you are! Just as lovely as she was—how can it be possible that you can be here, and against your will at that?"

Maggie had no reply—and couldn't, in any case, as she was pulled against Marie's bosom and enfolded in the kind of motherly hug that she'd only ever experienced from the Lady.

"But—but who are you?" she finally managed when Marie released her a little to look at her again, as if she could not get enough of drinking her in.

"My maiden name is Mariah Polgarth. I was Catherine's nurse, engaged by her parents to see her through her confinement," she said softly. "I came well recommended by Lady Flora at Gwynn Place." A deep dimple of mischief came and went in one smooth cheek. "What they did not know is that I was also Kevern's sister, just back from nursing school and eager to try my wings in the world."

"Sister!"

"Yes. I am your aunt, and Katrine—who is named for your dear mother, my closest friend—is your cousin. Oh, my dear, the sight of you is a gift from God that amply repays any good thing I was ever able to do for Catherine. But you must tell me, how do you come to be alive? We heard the Seacombe airship went into the Thames and all aboard were lost."

"I must save that tale for when we meet again ... Aunt Mariah." Oh, what a strange and wonderful thrill to say those words for the first time! "But I must ask you at once—it is true that I am Kevern's daughter? Because my grandparents are convinced that Charles de Maupassant Seacombe is my father, through such a horrible—I cannot even bear—"

Mariah drew her into her arms again and held her while Maggie wept, her emotions swamping her so that her very ribs ached with sobs of mingled joy and pain.

"Let me reassure you, my dearest one, that you are Kevern and Catherine's daughter, and no one else's. Those Seacombes put that story about when it became clear she did not plan to return to England without you. If she was to be ruined, I suppose, better to be ruined by being taken against her will than because she loved a man who was beneath her."

Maggie could not let go, and Mariah pulled her down again onto the stone wall beside her, one arm holding Maggie tightly against her side.

"It would all have turned out so differently if it had not been for the infection." Mariah sighed, the memory clearly causing her renewed pain. "Six months of grief and stress, and three days of labor exhausted her. She was so slender, and had nothing left to fight with, despite my best efforts and Kevern beside her day and night, pleading for her to hang on until the doctor from Brest could come. Kevern went mad with grief after the funeral—signed up with the Corps and did everything possible to put himself in harm's way. He wanted to join her in death, you see, despite the fact that he had you to live for. But men are different, I suppose."

"He was shot down, Michael says," Maggie whispered.

"He was, and before I could make arrangements to return with you to my father's house, to be brought up at Gwynn Place, Charles de Maupassant arrived and took you away by force at his wife's request. Since I was not your mother, and barely had enough money to pay my passage home, never mind pursue them to Paris, I could do nothing."

"I have nothing good to say about that man, but he did do that one honorable thing," Maggie whispered. "He took in a bastard and gave me a home. And he gave me Lizzie, who is as close to me as any sister could be."

Mariah gaped at her. "Bastard! Why should you think of yourself so?"

"Well ... because I am. My parents were not married."

"Lord, child, who told you that? Your parents were married in this village practically as soon as Kevern found his way over. I think he bribed a fisherman in the dead of night, to tell you the truth. I held her little nosegay of flowers myself, when Kevern put the ring upon Catherine's finger."

"They were married?" Maggie's voice rose in a squeak of disbelief. "Then I am ...?"

"You are their legitimately born daughter, more welcome and wanted than any little baby in the world, and as entitled to the Polgarth name as I am."

Maggie's breath went out of her in a rush, and she burst into fresh tears. But behind the rain, the sunshine of joy was filling her heart, warming and satisfying at last the hollow within that had been waiting all her life.

26

Maggie could have stayed in the sunny garden all day, mining Mariah's memories with the dedication and optimism of a diamond prospector. When she said as much, Mariah gave her one last hug.

"We will have time, my dear one. When all this is over, I will look forward to it—and Father will, too. He misses Kevern sorely, and it will do him a world of good to be reunited with you and the truth revealed once and for all. But for the moment ... if what you say is true and these bathynauts are not, as everyone is being told, merely protecting our shores but actually preparing an invasion, we must inform the resistance, and quickly."

Maggie did her best to put her own need for reassurance and love and family aside in favor of the lives and families of others. According to Mariah, there were those who believed in the republican government left to them by Napoleon only a few generations ago, which had made France a center of education and culture. They were actively resisting the return of the corrupt monarchy that had brought the country to its knees.

Of course, there were always those who enjoyed a country on its knees, and clearly it was now time to stop the slide of public opinion before they got any further in their plans.

"You must send two pigeons for me, Aunt Mariah— one to Lady Claire's airship *Athena*, and one to the Royal Aeronautics Corps detachment on St. Michael's Mount. Theirs is the most immediate danger from *Neptune's Lady* and her projectiles."

In the inn's study, Maggie found paper and ink, and quickly wrote out two missives. When she folded them up and Mariah concealed them under the stems of rosemary and lavender in her basket, she admitted, "It is unlikely that the aeronauts will believe such a fantastical story. I hardly believe it myself. But Lady Claire will. She will inform Count von Zeppelin so that he may act on the Prussian front, and I hope it will not be too late."

"I will be as quick as I can," Mariah said. "While I am gone, here is what you must do." She leaned in close to whisper, "Katrine says the master key to all the rooms is hung in the linen closet. Do not fear Serge—he is one of us and is my husband's nephew. Once you free your cousin, take him to the church. None of the bathynauts ever go there, and the priest is among those who, like my family, do not support the Bourbon restoration. I will meet you in the Lady Chapel in an hour."

Maggie had not used her skills as a scout in quite some time, but as she slipped down the stairs to the innkeeper's rooms and located the linen closet, she found them coming back again. The heightened senses, the alertness, the pumping blood—all stood her in good stead as she quietly lifted the key, slipped it in her pocket, and padded up the servants' stair to Claude's room.

Serge had mysteriously vanished.

He looked up as she came in. "No coffee?"

"Sorry, just the key. Come along, I am spiriting you out of here. Your guard is, apparently, a member of the resistance. Isn't that lucky?"

"I thought he had more of a sense of humor than the usual. Where are we going?"

"The church. My aunt will take you from there."

"Steady on—who? Your aunt, did you say?"

"Yes, that lady in the garden. She is my aunt Mariah, and I will tell you the whole story once we are safely away from here. I must return the key."

She had a bad few minutes when two of the maids came chattering along the passageway, but a chilling look down her nose and a request for directions in Gloria's flat accents got rid of them for long enough to return the key to its hook.

"Mariah said to stay close to the cliff," she told Claude as they went out the back door. "There is a path, apparently, so that we will not be seen on the streets."

And so there was—a damp, dank path made so by the water dripping in rivulets down the cliff face. It was cold, too, but at least it kept them out of sight. The church came into view and Claude finally spoke.

"I say, is that really a church? It looks as though it was carved partly out of the rock."

What would be the transept and altar in any other church was set into the cliff, as though it had begun that way hundreds of years ago with the important part, and the nave extended out from there, built later of blocks of stone quarried elsewhere. The two of them slipped into a door in the back of the transept and found themselves in the cool dimness of the church. A lamp hung over the altar, and while the sun shone through the stained-glass windows of the narrow nave, the light up here had to be provided by the hands of the faithful.

"Where is the Lady Chapel, then?" Claude whispered.

"Let's have a look."

Lady Claire had been in the habit of taking them to church when they'd lived in Vauxhall Gardens, and when they were together at Wilton Crescent, they would go also. She wasn't sure about Lizzie, but Maggie had never quite been able to shake the old belief that if one were to pick a pocket, it was best done on a Sunday, when people were dressed in their best and always had a coin or two for the collection.

She would have had slim pickings in this church, Sunday or no. The nave held a few widows in black, on their knees praying for the souls of those they had lost, but the ladies paid them no attention as they crossed the transept and found the Lady Chapel on the other side.

The Lady, in this case, was illuminated by lamps set high in the ceiling. She was painted on the plaster, her halo and the cross in her hand picked out in gold leaf, her mermaid's tail a grand sweep of Madonna blue, lilac, and deep sea-green. Her hair under its blue mantle swirled behind her as if the currents were moving it, and her eyes, deep set in the Byzantine style, were sea-blue as well.

Staring, awed at the beauty of her, Maggie bumped into a lectern and nearly knocked the book lying on it to the floor.

"Steady on, old girl. Looks like the parish register."

Maggie's attention abruptly left the contemplation of the mother of the One whose symbol had been a fish to a mother much closer to home.

The parish register.

She smoothed the pages into place and rapidly turned them back ... back to the late winter of 1878.

And there they were, the ink faded, the French formal. Maggie translated the words in her mind.

Married 14 February 1878 Kevern Polgarth, age 21, bachelor, steam engineer, and Catherine Seacombe, age 19, spinster, by license and with the consent of those whose consent is required.

"Claude, look," she whispered. "These are my parents. Part of the story I'm going to tell you when we get home."

He scanned the lines, his French as good as hers. "But ... I don't understand, old girl. I thought the pater adopted you along with Lizzie?"

"He did, but that was after my parents died."

"You don't say. So your birth must be in here, too, then. Unless you were born somewhere else?"

She hadn't thought of that. She flipped one page forward, to March.

Baptism 27 March 1878 Marguerite Marie, daughter of Kevern Polgarth, engineer, and his wife Catherine, born 25 March 1878, married in this parish.

"Is that you?" Claude leaned over the page.

"It is," Maggie said. "She called me Marguerite Marie."

"Aren't those the daisies you see everywhere, with the yellow centers and the white petals? The girls at school call them marguerites."

Her mother had loved flowers, and seemed to have spoken the language of them. She scented her letters to Kevern with lilac, for first love. And she had called her only child after the daisy, for innocence.

Marguerite, innocent of the dreadful aspersions her grandparents had cast upon her. Innocent of the pain her parents had gone through for her sake. Innocent of her adoptive father's and her grandparents' crimes.

She pressed her lips together to prevent their trembling, and closed the book softly. The daisy had another quality, too. It was strong and hard to eradicate.

Which she was about to prove.

A whisper of petticoats announced Mariah's arrival. With her was a boy a little younger than Maggie, whose speedwell eyes hinted that this might be her son.

"So you found it," Mariah said with some satisfaction. "I admit to an ulterior motive in sending you here."

"And I am glad you did," Maggie told her with a swift kiss of gratitude.

Mariah introduced her son Guillaume. "There are more ways than by sea to leave Baie des Sirenes," she said. "Guillaume will take you through the caves and over the fields to the next village, where my brother-in-law will arrange passage for you to Paris. We assume that is where you wish to go?"

Claude shook his head. "With all the demonstrations in Paris, my lot have gone to Venice, taking in an exhibition. I think I'll join them—unless you wish me to do something?" He appealed to Maggie.

"No. The sooner you're out of French and Colonial hands, the better, and no one will find you in Venice, with its moving neighborhoods." She hugged him fiercely. "Keep yourself safe—and for goodness sake, Claude, stay out of taverns."

Ruefully, he nodded. "I've learned my lesson well and truly. Strong drink and sea chanties lead to the kinds of adventures for which I am definitely not suited." He released her slowly. "You won't do anything ridiculous like getting yourself killed, will you?"

With a shake of her head, she reassured him, "Certainly not. I have a story to tell you, remember?"

With a smile, she watched the two young men go, and then Mariah took her hand. "Are you determined to do this, Marguerite? Will you not go with Claude? The resistance has plans in motion that do not require a young girl to risk her life."

Maggie did her best not to cry afresh at the fear Mariah could not keep out of her eyes. "But does the resistance have access to that ship and to the King-maker?"

She saw the truth when Mariah bit her lip. So they did not—or if they did, it was not enough to stop the invasion. "All I will say is that your true identity is known where it is most necessary, and you may find one or two allies where you least expect them. Come. I will show you how to get down to the sea caves."

"I know the way," Maggie protested. "It will be tricky, but I can find my way along the quay and inside."

"Good heavens, child." Mariah took a deep, shuddering breath, mastering her emotions as she gazed up at the mermaid Madonna high above their heads. "Not that way. We go the ancient way—the way that legend says the Lady of Heaven first came to the people here."

"But that's a legend." Maggie followed her out of the chapel and around to the back of the altar.

Mariah opened a door and started down the stone steps into darkness. "In Baie des Sirenes, my dearest, you will find that sometimes legends hold more truth than facts."

27

If the French resistance thought it strange that a six-teen-year-old girl had come to their aid, there was no sign of it. There was no sign of anyone, yet in at least two instances it was clear that an invisible helping hand had been extended to her.

The first was in the alarm that went up upon the ar-rival of *Neptune's Throne*, the *navire* from the Americas bearing Gerald Meriwether-Astor, and the subsequent discovery that Claude was not available for either ques-tioning or blackmail, since he was no longer in the room in which he had been locked.

The second was the partially loaded *chaloupes* float-ing next to the jetty, filled with supplies and destined for the *Fury*, which were left unattended while the bathynauts assembled in one of the caves for rousing speeches of encouragement from their leader and the captain of the *Fury*, who was related in some way to the Bourbon pretender that Maggie did not quite catch.

She was busy slipping into the last *chaloupe* and concealing herself behind canvas bags of equipment, and only heard about Claude when the bathynauts returned and were talking several feet away.

A detachment of men had been dispatched to seek him out, but they would be lucky to find so much as a handkerchief. By now, he would be on his way to Venice by steam train or even one of the small *ballons* she had seen floating in the sky over the village, which seemed to be used for transport over short distances.

She felt positively giddy with relief that he was safe, and when the *chaloupe* jerked and rocked in the water as its lead engine towed the vessels out to *Neptune's Fury*, she had quite a time settling herself and concentrating on what she must do next.

From what she had gathered, the invaders were not wasting any time. The fleet of *navires* would launch as soon as ammunition and siege supplies were loaded; they had only been waiting for Meriwether-Astor's arrival to begin.

She did not know what he thought of his daughter's unexpected presence here. Maybe he was convinced she had escaped with Claude. In any case, it was time to shed that disguise and become the person she was meant to be: Marguerite Marie Polgarth, saboteur and English patriot.

The fact that she would probably die in the attempt and no one but Mariah and Claude would ever know about it was beside the point. One had to do the right thing, even when it was not easy. Others had been in-

strumental in saving her life on countless occasions—
Tigg and Snouts, the Lady, and Lizzie. Now it was her
turn to fill her side of the account book, and balance
out that debt.

The Lady would come, and Mariah would tell her
what Maggie had done, and that was a good enough
epitaph for anyone. They would never find her body,
but perhaps they would erect a stone in the graveyard
near the double grave she had not yet seen. Then, at
least, she and her mother and father could be a family
in people's memories.

Maggie remained concealed in the *chaloupe* while the
bathynauts berthed it deep in *Fury's* belly next to the
Kingmaker, amusing herself by running over the mechanical construction of the *navire* in her mind until it
was as clear as a blueprint in her head. The hours crept
by even more slowly than the ebb of the tide. She expected the *chaloupe* to be unloaded every time she
heard voices next to it, and braced herself for discovery.
But evidently this particular train of supply vessels was
to be unloaded once they were ashore on the other side
of the Channel, and no one opened the glass shell.

At last she felt the motion of the sea in her stomach,
and the shudder of powerful engines vibrating through
deck and wheels and metal.

They were under way.

She unfolded her aching legs and cautiously pushed
aside the canvas bags behind which she had curled, like
a dragon in its fortress. After stretching and shaking to
return her circulation to its former efficiency, she risked
a glance over the metal gunwale.

A male voice barked, and she banged her head on the mechanism that opened the glass before dropping to the *chaloupe*'s iron deck.

"Attention all hands," came a disembodied voice from a trumpet in the ceiling high above. "Except for vital positions, report to mess for final briefing and duty assignments."

What were vital positions? Steering, navigation, and the like? Down here in the hold, what might be considered vital?

She only needed a few minutes. Just a few precious minutes, and her duty would be done. But one vital position could scuttle the whole enterprise.

Not until the noise of men vacating their posts and moving off into the central part of the ship slowed to a trickle did she venture to pull the lever that opened the glass top half of the *chaloupe*. She released the door locks and instead of extending the gangway, simply sat in the opening and jumped to the ground, tucking and rolling under the dripping, seaweedy hull and coming up on the other side.

There was the Kingmaker in all its terrifying glory. Her target.

How on earth did one board the ugly thing? Maggie's boots made no sound on the vibrating deck as she circled it, every cell in her body alert for that one man in a vital position who could ruin everything. Ah, here it was. Far above her head she could see a door in the side of the gun fortress, accessible if one used the giant wheels with their circulating treads as a ladder, and from there, stepped from one protruding bolt in its body to another. It looked as if these bolts had been constructed for just this purpose, so there was no need for extra detail such as stairs on the exterior that might slow it down.

"Halt!" came a second disembodied voice that definitely did not proceed from a speaking trumpet.

Maggie's heart leaped practically into her mouth and she froze halfway up the black iron side of the Kingmaker like a fly on a wall.

"Before I shoot, identify yourself." The accent was Texican.

Slowly, Maggie turned her head upward, to see a man on a catwalk holding an aural detonator rifle similar to the ones she had seen aboard *Lady Lucy*. The bell-shaped barrels of aural weapons fired sound waves to incapacitate their targets, and were used on enclosed vessels such as airships, where the incursion of a bullet would be fatal to ship and crew.

And now it was trained on her—a much bigger one than she'd ever seen.

"I—I am Gloria Meriwether-Astor," she said, her mouth dry. "I am seeing the Kingmaker for myself, after Captain Martin gave me a tour of the *Fury* earlier today."

"And why aren't you under escort?"

Maggie rested both feet on the bolt and turned to face her interlocutor in as casual a manner as she could, adding a touch of huffy irritation for good measure. "Because I find it tiresome, being told what to do and observe. I gave my escort the slip when he was called forward for the final briefing. Kindly point that weapon elsewhere, sir."

"Come down from there, miss, before you fall. No one but its pilot and crew are permitted aboard the Kingmaker. I will return you to your father at once."

If she got down, how was she to disarm a man twice her size? If she made a break for the door in the fortress above her head, how would she evade the sound wave?

Frozen between two impossibilities, Maggie could not move.

And then she felt a popping sensation in her ears, and the guard collapsed to the catwalk, his arm twitching where it dangled in the air. The detonator fell from his hand, clanging upon the deck below.

Serge Lavande emerged from behind a stack of crates and despite herself, Maggie tensed, feeling more exposed than she ever had in her life—including that dreadful evening on the roof of Colliford Castle. Whose side was he on, at this moment of crisis? Where did his loyalties lie?

"Mademoiselle Polgarth," he said, and grinned.

Maggie's breath went out of her and her knees turned to rubber. But she was forty feet in the air, so she could not allow herself the luxury of collapsing with relief.

"*Merci, monsieur*," she said.

"I see that we are now compatriots," he said. "I do not expect to survive, but I should like to be sure that you will."

"I do not expect to survive either, monsieur."

"What do you plan to do? My aunt was urgent, but not specific."

"Fire the Kingmaker's cannon and breach the hull. Once the water pressure equalizes in this chamber, the mechanism will lower the ramp, and the Kingmaker will roll out to join the hulks of the Armada below."

"And we?"

"I expect I will go down with it, monsieur, but if you can see your way to saving yourself, then you ought to."

"*Au contraire, mademoiselle.* Democracy will lose too formidable an ally if we do not continue to work together." He smiled and saluted her with his detonator. "I am determined that you shall survive."

Nimbly, he collected the fallen detonator below the catwalk, and when she realized he planned to join her in the gun fortress, she climbed up and opened the door, heaving herself through it and scrambling to her feet. He followed her in and when he stood, he bowed over her hand.

"At your service, mademoiselle. I understand we are cousins by marriage."

"I am honored to make your acquaintance properly, sir. Do you know how to fire this thing?"

"Sadly, no, but it should be fairly straightforward. Let us investigate—and quickly."

Maggie took in the rudimentary controls at a glance. They were not helpfully labeled, but it stood to reason that anything not obviously meant for igniting the boilers, steering, and locomotion must be for armaments.

"No, not that one," she said hastily, as Serge's hand hovered over a lever that, when thrust forward, might send the Kingmaker rolling even without benefit of steam propulsion. "These ones here appear to control the cannon, you see? They are on a separate panel, just below this viewing window."

It took a couple of tries, but she succeeded in making the cannon swing from side to side and nod up and down. So successful was she, in fact, that the massive barrel collided with a lateral catwalk and tore it from the ceiling with a screech of rending iron.

"Oh, dear."

"I should hasten my explorations, Mademoiselle. Of a certainty, someone will come to investigate."

And then she remembered something. On the roof of Colliford Castle, Lizzie's father had installed a giant telescope that was in reality a cannon, meant to shoot the royal princes' airship out of the sky. She and Lizzie had both sat in its cockpit after Maggie had recovered somewhat from his attempt on her life, and Lizzie had shown her how it worked. What if that cannon had also been made by the Meriwether-Astor Munitions Works? What if their cannon design was consistent across all the weapons they made?

And there it was.

Maggie pulled the lever directly below the barrel controls, and in the bowels of the fortress, gears and cogs began to turn. She pulled the lever beside the first, and with a clank, a missile of some kind fell into its slot and was ingested by the mechanism. A lamp came on.

ARMED

She looked to her right, where Serge stood beside her. Though he did not touch her, she could feel his agitation and see his body trembling. Here was the definition of courage—being terrified, and yet doing what must be done.

"Ready?"

"Marguerite, let me tell you what will happen. Once the hull is breached, water will rush in at the same speed as air rushes out. But for the first few moments, the sea will be held back by the greater air pressure within. We have just those few moments to descend from here and enclose ourselves in one of the *chaloupes*, where we will be as protected as possible from the madness that will be unleashed."

Here was a revelation. "You mean we might survive?"

"I do not hold out much hope, but if there is a chance, we must grasp it, yes? For the war will not be over with the destruction of one machine, and we will be needed to fight another day."

She held out a hand. "I shall follow you. We are in this together, come what may."

He took it, his own ice-cold. "Then I leave the honor of firing this monster to you."

28

The explosion rendered Maggie deaf.

Before her terrified eyes, the missile tore through the iron hull of the *Fury* and shot out into the dark depths, leaving a ragged hole the size of a small cottage in its wake.

Serge's mouth opened in a shout, but through the ringing silence in her head, she could not hear it—or her own screams, though the pain in her throat told her she was indeed screaming. He grabbed her hand and they flung themselves out the fortress's door, falling, scraping, bouncing from bolt to bolt until they landed on all fours on the enormous treads. Lights of alarm flashed over their heads, and Maggie felt the vibrations change under her feet. Hesitate. Increase, as though the *Fury* herself had realized what had happened and succumbed to sudden panic.

And then the water leaped through the aperture and into the Kingmaker's nest with the force of a geyser out of control. It spewed the length of the holding bay, soaking the two of them with cold seawater in moments.

Serge yanked on her hand and they sloshed across the floor as fast as the rapidly rising water would allow.

"Halt!" came a shout from above that broke with terror. "Halt!"

Without a word, Serge turned, aimed, and fired the detonator he still held at the men on the catwalk above. He tossed Maggie the second one that had been looped over his shoulder, and she got in a volley, too, before the men in the rear realized that if they did not alert the rest of the crew, the entire ship would be lost.

But Maggie knew in her bones it was already too late for that. The men fled through an iron door and slammed it shut behind them. The clang was dull, as though heard underwater, but her hearing seemed to be recovering from the blow it had taken.

The water was up to her knees now, freezing her feet in her boots, dragging at her skirts, slowing her down.

"Come!" Serge shouted. "In here!"

He pulled a lever on the hull of the lead *chaloupe*, the one that possessed an engine, and she ran to the stern and released the coupling to the train of inert vessels behind it. When she ran back, he had boosted himself up and through the hatch, and reached down to pull her inside. Kicking, pushing on bits of the hull, she hung onto both his hands as he landed her like a great gasping fish.

Within moments, he had the hatch closed and locked, and glanced up at the glass dome over their heads as if imploring it to hold for the next few minutes.

"Now what?" Maggie said breathlessly.

"I will ignite the *chaloupe*'s engine so as to be ready when the landing ramp opens. And then we wait—and hope. If you are on good terms with the Almighty, Marguerite, you might offer a prayer on our behalf."

Since that was the only thing she could do besides glue herself to the glass and watch the water rise, she did.

In a far shorter time than she ever would have believed possible, the sea invaded the chamber to the point that the water toyed with the *chaloupe*, attempting to lift it from the deck. Its level rose more—and yet more—and they were submerged, their view now tinged with green, and blurred with the swirling of the angry current trapped in the landing bay with nowhere else to go. Crates and barrels seemed to attack them from every side as they were swirled and flung willy-nilly in the maelstrom.

And then the sound of metal screeching on metal reverberated through the walls. A horn sounded—or perhaps that was just the agony of the *Fury*, realizing at last the truth of her awful situation.

The deck tipped out from under them.

The massive chains mooring the Kingmaker to the floor snapped as the war machine rolled forward, the whipping motion of their release slowed by the enormous volume of water that now engulfed it.

Slowly, mindlessly obeying the demands of physics, the deck continued to lower, all the contents of the landing bay—Kingmaker, *chaloupes*, landaus, crates, pallets, and machinery, all sliding down the ramp in one huge roiling mass.

The sea's triumph was complete now as it filled the entire bay and began its assault on the rest of the *navire*. Maggie was deafened for a second time from the cacophony of objects striking the hull of the *chaloupe*— so deafened that she could hardly hear Serge's shout.

"We have lost our rudder!" he cried, working the navigation wheel like a madman as they fell slowly into the depths. "That wretched crate of rifles struck us and has bent it—she will not obey the helm!"

When Maggie turned toward the stern with the thought that she might be able to repair it with something, she looked up through the glass.

All the blood seemed to leave her head from sheer horror.

She grabbed Serge's arm and swung him around to look. For the Kingmaker's enormous weight meant that it was the last thing to be disgorged from the *Fury's* sagging jaw. Their *chaloupe* had gone out with the crates and equipment, propelled by the little engine, and with the precipitous angle of the *Fury*, which now pointed at the seabed, the Kingmaker was literally fal- ling—slowly, ponderously—on top of them.

"Move! Move!" she shrieked.

"I cannot! I have no rudder!"

"Goose it—in any direction. Serge, quickly!"

But no matter what he did, the behemoth pushed all before it, their little bubble of glass and brass trapped between its horrific weight on one side and the pressure of the water on the other.

Maggie could do nothing at all but cling to Serge's soaked wool sleeve, watching as the Kingmaker came for them both, as inexorably as death.

29

"This is completely unacceptable," Claire snapped, hanging onto her temper by its last thread.

In the sea parlor at Seacombe House, she, Andrew, Michael Polgarth, and Lizzie faced down the formidable obstinacy of Demelza Seacombe. The woman stood in front of the fire, back ramrod straight, her gaze unyielding. Claire's stomach was hollowed out with fear for Maggie, and she struggled against her rage at the injustice this woman and her husband had dealt to her girl for no better reason than snobbery.

And now Maggie's and Claude's lives were at risk because of it.

"Are you seriously telling me that you have no idea where they could have been taken?"

"We are not in the habit of following smugglers to and fro," Mrs. Seacombe said in quelling tones, but the pallor of her skin suggested she was more affected than she was letting on. "The goods come from America via France. We cannot be responsible for the behavior of criminals in the night."

"No, heaven forbid you should be responsible for anything," Claire said. "You are quite willing to accept the profits of those activities, however, to support the style of living to which you have become accustomed. But that is neither here nor there. I find it very difficult to believe that you have no feeling for Claude and the peril of his situation, even if you cannot spare a drop of compassion for Maggie."

"They will not harm Claude," Mrs. Seacombe repeated, as stubborn as a rock and, Claire suspected, with as little imagination. Her own imagination was working at a furious rate, and it was making her positively ill. "I must believe that is true. Now, if you will excuse me, my husband lies practically at death's door after an apoplexy, and I must return to his bedside."

Lizzie pressed against Claire's side. "It is my fault. I told them about the *navire* and the 'second phase' that the captain was talking about, and Grandfather collapsed."

Claire reached the last reserves of her ability to be civil, and passed an arm about Lizzie's waist. "It is not your fault. If a man will engage in criminal activity, it is his own fault if his conscience catches up with him."

"Claire, we are getting nowhere here," Andrew said in a low tone. "We must apply our minds in a different direction." To Mrs. Seacombe, he said, "We must see a set of charts immediately. If they are crossing the

Channel, they will use the shortest and least dangerous route. Perhaps we can trace some possibilities if we can see the lay of the land."

"Not only the land," Lizzie said. "The seabed, too."

"An excellent point. Marine charts, Mrs. Seacombe, if you please, at once."

If she objected to being spoken to in such peremptory tones, Mrs. Seacombe did not show it. Perhaps she knew that one more sign of reluctance to help would ignite Claire's temper—and Claire had not missed the astonished glance she had bestowed on the lightning rifle in its holster on her back when they'd pushed their way past Nancarrow and demanded an audience.

Wordlessly, Mrs. Seacombe led them downstairs to her husband's study. She deposited the charts on a table and swept from the room. The marine charts showed the floor of the Channel as well as the land masses they knew so well on this side at least. Andrew ran a finger from their location at Penzance to the closest landing in Cornouaille.

"There are miles of possibilities here, but at least it would be a place to start. Perhaps we will be fortunate and see one of the undersea dirigibles surface. From the air, it might be easier to spot them than from land, though since the sun has gone down, that is a slender hope."

Michael Polgarth leaned over the chart and pointed to a tiny dot. "Baie des Sirenes," he said with a sad smile. "That is where Maggie was born."

He had told them the story in the navigation gondola on the way here, its details contradicting in nearly every particular the one that the Seacombes had told her. If Claire had had a moment for regrets, it would be that she had not taken the time to hear the story from Maggie herself. Instead, she had listened to a lie and passed it on believing it to be the truth—and what damage it had caused!

"Baie des Sirenes," Andrew said slowly, tracing the route between that location and theirs. "In the absence of any other information, it is as good a place to start as any. Shall we take it as an omen of good fortune and set our course there?"

Claire made up her mind instantly. "Lizzie says the *navire*—the undersea dirigible—was called *Neptune's Maid*. Neptune's daughters were mermaids. And this translates to Bay of the Mermaids. I believe it is a sign." She let the chart roll itself up with a snap, and scooped it off the table. "Let us lift at once."

Athena was moored rather awkwardly in the orchard, but Claire had not had time to choose a more suitable landing place—or one that would not involve broken branches. But she was in no mood at present to care about the yield of the Seacombes' apple trees. While Michael and Andrew attended to the ropes, Lizzie dashed down to the messenger cage, which she had visited at least twice already, looking for a missive from Maggie.

"Up ship!" Claire called, the men pulled in the ropes, and *Athena* fell into the night sky like a lark leaping for the heavens.

"Lady!" came a shriek from below. "It's Maggie!"

A LADY OF SPIRIT

Lady,

Claude and I are in Baie des Sirenes, France, along with a dozen navires bearing troops of bathynauts set to invade England and Prussia for the Bourbon King. They are armed and led by Gerald Meriwether-Astor, and plan to deploy huge war machines called Kingmakers in Cornwall and Jutland. I intend to scuttle this one on the way across before it lands on Grandfather's beach. You must send a pigeon immediately to Uncle Ferdinand and tell him about the other one. Claude is safe—he is being spirited away to Venice by my family here.

I am so happy to know my real family and my real name: Marguerite Marie Polgarth. But you and Lizzie are the family of my heart. I love you both.

You must marry Mr. Malvern, Lady. He loves you. Name your first daughter after me, and tell Lizzie I expect that statue in the town square.

With all my love,
Maggie

30

Slowly, ponderously, the Kingmaker's enormous weight bore it toward the sea floor, pushing all before it. Maggie clung to Serge, watching unblinkingly as the monster thrust them ahead of it. How many moments of life did they have left before they were crushed? How deep was the Channel here?

A shadow darkened one side of the glass, and Maggie watched in wonder as *Neptune's Fury* spiraled past them, huge air bubbles trailing it like a bridal veil as the water rushed into the *navire*'s decks and crushed the life from the fuselage.

She sent up a quick prayer for the souls of the men aboard, as misguided as they had been, and thought of Jean-Luc Martin, that cheerful flirt who had been so helpful to the young woman he believed to be Gloria

Meriwether-Astor. Where was *Neptune's Maid* at this moment? What would happen to the rest of the undersea fleet when they learned of the fate of their greatest hope, the Kingmaker? Was Gerald Meriwether-Astor even on that ship? And most important of all, had her message reached the Royal Aeronautics Corps outpost in time for them to mount a defense?

Serge's arm tightened about her shoulders and she felt him stiffen, preparing himself for the worst as the Kingmaker began to roll. His lips moved in a soundless prayer—Maggie braced herself likewise—

—Lord have mercy on my soul—

—oh, Lizzie, Lizzie, think of me—

—and a massive bubble issued from the cockpit of the armed fortress, slowly rotating as its heavier weight bore the behemoth to the bottom. The bubble caught them—lifted them—and spat them out to the side.

Maggie and Serge lost their balance as the *chaloupe* rolled. The floor became the ceiling, and Maggie snatched at whatever protruding instruments she could, to no avail. They were flung like dolls from one side to the other until the air within triumphed over the water without, and the *chaloupe* righted itself, glass side up.

Serge dragged himself from the curved wall, blood trickling down the side of his face, one arm held tightly to his body in pain. "We must surface as quickly as possible."

On hands and knees, hardly able to believe she was alive, Maggie gasped, "But we will be discovered!"

"It matters not. If *Fury* did not get off a distress signal to the fleet, they will proceed as planned. If they did, the fleet will be in the disarray absolute. In either case, they will not be surfacing in the middle of the Channel. It is the safest place for us."

Maggie sucked in a breath of pain as she picked herself up from the deck. A quick catalogue of arms and legs proved that all were still operational, though her head hurt and it seemed her leather corselet may have protected her from a possible broken rib. The bruising was going to be ugly, though.

But these hurts were nothing in comparison to the horrific death they had been saved from by a bubble, of all things. Maggie would take the bruises and cuts and be grateful for them.

Serge increased the air pressure just enough to send them shooting to the surface. Seawater sheeted from the glass and cleared, leaving them a view of stars and moon gazing calmly down from far above.

Maggie had never seen anything so lovely in all her life.

"May we open the glass?" If she could only take one breath of fresh air, she would never ask anything of the universe again.

Serge shook his head, pain clearly stripping him of the energy for civilities. "We will be swamped. The pumps will keep us in air until we are rescued, which is all we may hope for without the ability to make way."

"How long will that be?"

He gave a most Gallic shrug of one shoulder. "If we are lucky, sometime tomorrow. But I should prepare myself, *ma petite*. On the French side, all will be focused on the invasion. To the north, England will leap to its own defense. No one will be looking for *une petite chaloupe* bobbing in the middle of the Channel. The tides will take us where they will—and we must pray that it is east and not west." He stopped, out of breath, and folded himself to the deck to recover.

It took a second for Maggie to understand what he meant. The tides could sweep them toward Dover, like a cork in a funnel, where they might make landfall. Or they could be borne westward, out into the Atlantic, where they and their disabled vessel would be lost.

She swallowed, attempting to moisten a mouth gone dry. "Can we repair the rudder? I could go out and attempt to bend it back. I am a very good swimmer."

"It is solid iron, *ma petite*. Even I would not be able to do it without a forge and tools."

"Serge, there must be something we can do to help ourselves."

But he did not answer.

Catalogue your resources, and then use your imagination, Maggie.

Right. They had no rudder, but they had propulsion, and air. Perhaps if they could get the *chaloupe* pointed north and east, they could assist the flow of the tide— or resist it if it went the wrong way.

But which way was east?

She could see no shore—the Channel here was a hundred and fifty miles across. The moon was up, but what time was it? Where was north, exactly?

"Serge, you are a bathynaut—help me!" Rapidly, she outlined what was in her mind.

He did not respond.

"Serge?" Alarmed, she shook his shoulder. "Serge!"

His face had gone pasty white, and he was unconscious. The blows he had taken were obviously more serious than either of them had thought. What if he had gone into shock? There wasn't so much as a blanket in here, and the canvas equipment bags were torn and ruined from having been flung about during their ascent.

Maggie whipped off her practical brown skirt, thankful for the black ruffled petticoat underneath, and covered him with the length of tightly woven gabardine wool. The deck upon which he lay was wet, which would not help the situation, but she tried to tuck as much of the skirt under him as possible. Then she stuffed canvas under his head and heels.

When she had done what she could, she took stock. The undersea fleet would not come for them—unless it was to shoot them out of the water for ruining their plans. The aeronauts on St. Michael's Mount would have their hands full. Mariah and the other members of the resistance were occupied in securing the sea caves and seeing Claude to safety.

If the pigeon had flown true, only one person remained who knew where Maggie was and what she was doing.

Only one person would not give up until she was found.

Maggie tried to imagine the sea from above, with the moon shining down, creating a path of wrinkled silver. The *chaloupe* would be invisible—its glass top as transparent as the bubble from which it took its design.

What did the sea creatures do to be seen? What had been the first thing she had noticed about *Neptune's Maid* when it surfaced?

Its eerie greenish-yellow glow.

Maggie leaped to the *chaloupe*'s simple control panel. Lights. She must have lights. She must create the world's largest moonglobe so that they would be seen from above—a tiny beacon in all this vast ocean.

She flipped levers and pressed buttons—most of which were no longer capable of responding. One of them began to open the glass top, splitting along its brass seam, and Maggie hastily pushed it the other way before the waves sloshed in and swamped them.

Nothing seemed to activate the lights.

Think!

The path of energy was being blocked somehow, after all their acrobatics below. Therefore, she would have to take it from elsewhere. Propulsion was useless without Serge's knowledge of navigation. They did not need it—so she could reroute what power they still had from the engine to the lights.

Maggie snatched a moonglobe from the navigator's station and dove under the control console. Gears and cogs and a small rotating shaft ... move this wheel ... switch the pressure and direction from here to here ... the gears meshed in their new pattern and behind Maggie's shoulder, light glowed.

She increased the power with the propulsion lever and the interior of the *chaloupe* became illuminated with a yellowish-green light. Stronger it grew, until she could see everything inside clearly and in detail.

Including poor Serge's face. He looked dreadful—as though he were not merely unconscious, but dead.

No, she could not think such things. They would be found in time. They had to be.

They had no propulsion at all, and were utterly at the mercy of wind and waves, but Maggie was quite sure that the little *chaloupe* could now be seen from the Lizard to Dover.

That is, if anyone was out there looking.

31

"This is an impossible task," Michael Polgarth murmured in falling tones of despair.

"It is not!" Lizzie snapped. "Our Maggie will have thought of a way to save herself."

"But you said she wrote a letter of farewell," Michael said. He and Lizzie were pressed against the viewing port, watching the sea below as though they expected at any moment to see a swimmer surface and wave her arms.

"She did, but that does not mean anything," Lizzie said stoutly. "She was merely being prudent—most of it was military instructions."

Claire, at the helm, resisted the urge to touch the letter in her pocket. She and Lizzie were the only ones with knowledge of its contents—and for the sake of the last two paragraphs, Claire was not willing to share it with either of the two gentlemen aboard.

The pigeon bearing the news of the invasion was already well on its way to Schloss Schwanenburg. Claire did not have any more information than what Maggie had dashed off in what was clearly a hurry, but details were not necessary. Once the count mobilized the Prussian fleet and they got their first look at the Kingmaker, it would become clear enough what their plan of action must be.

As though Michael's thoughts had taken the same path, he said, "And this Count von Zeppelin will leap into action on the word of a sixteen-year-old girl?"

"We are not talking about just any sixteen-year-old girl, Mr. Polgarth," Claire said with some asperity.

"I know Maggie is a young lady of spirit and talent, but I cannot imagine that—"

"We helped to save his life on more than one occasion, Mr. Polgarth," Lizzie informed him crisply. "If the count receives a message from any one of us saying that immediate action of any kind is necessary, he will not hesitate. He will act, and ask questions later."

Michael Polgarth's astonishment at these revelations about his cousin silenced him, and Andrew, bent over the navigation charts, straightened with a smile. "You will learn, upon further acquaintance with Maggie and our friends, not to underestimate the effect that one woman can have upon the world."

"As might anyone who is a subject of our most glorious Queen," Claire reminded them. "Now, gentlemen, we have reached an altitude above which I dare not go. It is a tricky balance between being high enough to have an effective field of view, and being low enough to see a person signaling for help."

A hundred and fifty miles of water. Oh, Maggie.

Claire fought against despair herself—she must not let it overwhelm her. She needed all her faculties and resources of optimism to face the task at hand—plying the skies above the Channel in hopes of seeing a vessel that might contain her girl. And they did not have much time. If Maggie had somehow managed to escape and was clinging to a piece of flotsam, she would not last long in the cold waters. Even her indomitable spirit might succumb to the forces of nature.

"Lady, we are over Penzance—but what is that?"

Lizzie's eyesight and talent for scouting were gifts for which Claire was grateful, fully employed as they were in the search. "Eight, set the helm at this heading until I return."

The automaton intelligence system responded and Claire felt the wheel steady under her hands as Eight took over its control. Then she rounded the navigation table and joined Lizzie, Andrew, and Michael Polgarth at the viewing window.

For a moment, she could hardly comprehend what she saw. "Good heavens above. Is the sea—boiling?"

As *Athena* drifted further west, far below and to the right came Seacombe House, looking like a pile of child's blocks in its lawns and gardens. And along the beach for at least a mile, the sea roiled and tossed as what appeared to be whales attempted to surface.

"Those are the *navires*," Lizzie said breathlessly. "Undersea dirigibles. Claude was kidnapped in such a vessel. Is it the invasion?"

Claire resisted the pull of scientific inquiry as to how they were powered and what they were capable of. This was no time to be distracted. Maggie's life was at stake.

"If it is, it's a terribly disorganized one," Andrew observed. "Look, they are crashing into one another."

It was like watching a school of fish being beached in a net. No one dirigible seemed to have command, and as for beaching, some had attempted it. Others seemed to be milling about in the deeper water, waiting for some greater authority and seeming unable to form themselves into organized ranks.

"You don't suppose she succeeded?" Michael Polgarth finally said. "What are they waiting for?"

"I believe you are right, Mr. Polgarth," Claire said. It was the only explanation. "The Kingmaker of which Maggie wrote was on the command ship—and its absence has confused them. They cannot proceed. Look, there are more, just surfacing."

"And there is one turning tail and swimming away." Lizzie pointed. "Coward."

"Maybe it is going back to see what's keeping the Kingmaker," Andrew suggested.

"Maggie is what's keeping it, I know it." Claire raised her voice. "Eight, bear six degrees south and follow that dirigible."

There followed thirty of the longest minutes of Claire's life. The dirigible submerged itself so that they could no longer directly follow its course, but Eight held the same heading. *Athena* followed the wide road of the moonlight, bearing south until Lizzie made a sound of surprise.

"What is it, dearest?" Claire scanned the ocean from side to side, hardly daring to hope that a small figure might be visible in the waves.

"Lady—the sea is rising!"

Frozen in astonishment, they could do nothing but watch as an enormous dome of water rose about half a mile ahead. It appeared to be lit from within with the fires of hell—it convulsed—it burst, water sucked up from the gloomy depths below fountaining into the air in an explosion the likes of which Claire had never imagined possible.

It was as though a volcano had erupted in the middle of the English Channel, and a huge wave spread out in concentric circles, traveling at speed in all four directions of the compass.

"The *navires* will be swamped!" Andrew exclaimed. For they were rather closer to the coast of Cornwall than the middle. "And every fishing boat in every cove from here to Truro."

"The coast of France will take a beating," Michael Polgarth breathed.

"They will feel this in the Channel Islands and as far as the Isle of Wight," Claire whispered. "But Maggie? Oh God, where is Maggie?"

"If she is responsible for that, Claire, you may need to brace yourself to learn the worst." Andrew put a hand on her shoulder.

She turned to look up into his warm hazel eyes, her own filling with tears. "I cannot," she whispered. "If there is even the smallest hope, I must believe that Maggie will survive."

"If she has, then she will be waiting for us, and we must not fail her." Gratitude for his unfailing support and faith overwhelmed her, and she swayed against his chest. After a second's hesitation, Andrew slipped his arms around her and hugged her close. "Once the sea recovers from its upheaval, we must go closer."

"Shall I ready the basket, Lady?" Lizzie asked.

Claire took a deep, steadying breath and straightened, Andrew's arms falling away. Lizzie, for once, had greater things to think about, and made no embarrassing remarks.

"Yes, Lizzie. Let Four manage it, though. I need your sharp eyes up here to search the waves for Maggie."

If it took all night and the rest of tomorrow and the following weeks and months, she would search. Neither height, nor depth, nor any other creature would be able to separate her from the girl she loved.

Weeping with pain from a wrist that must be broken, and shivering from shock and cold, Maggie dragged herself up off the deck, grasping at the useless levers and wheels with her uninjured right hand.

What on earth had happened? One moment she was standing under the glass, watching the sky, and the next moment she was being flung about like a blackbird in a windstorm, tossed head over hems as they were engulfed by a wave at least twice as tall as Seacombe House.

And since she had disconnected the propulsion system, she had been unable to steer her way through, but was forced to become a bubble like all the rest, and surface again when the ocean jolly well decided it was time for her to do so.

"Serge?" she croaked.

He lay in a heap against the gunwale, as unresponsive as before. She fetched her gabardine skirt from where it had got wrapped around the hatch lever, wrung the water out of its hems, and laid it over him once more, inadequate to the situation as it was. At least he was breathing, but his color was still ghastly.

She had not much more medical knowledge than a few courses in biology could lend her, but even she could see that if she did not get him to a doctor soon, the family would be down by one. After all he had done for her, she could not bear it. She was just getting used to the idea that she *had* a family. To lose a single member of it was unendurable—and the fact that this particular member had risked his life for her when he did not even know her made the possibility of loss even more terrible.

"Please come," she whispered to the water sheeting off the glass outside, where she imagined the sky must be. Tears and salt water trickled down her face. "Lady, please come."

"There!" Lizzie screamed. "Lady, what is that?"

"Is it another *navire?*" Claire pressed her nose to the glass, as though it would help her see better. Below, bobbing in the wreckage and flotsam that now littered the surface of the ocean in the wake of the monster wave, was an incandescent ball of light.

"No—it's a *chaloupe*." Lizzie's voice squeaked from nerves. "They used them to ferry supplies back and forth from shore to the dirigibles. Oh Lady, what if—"

"Andrew—"

"On my way. Michael! Your assistance, please, in the basket!"

Focus. You must focus on bringing Athena within salvage distance. You cannot go to pieces now.

Claire brought the great airship as low as she could—low enough now to see that there was movement inside the little ball. Someone was jumping up and down inside it, waving their arms.

"Dear heaven, Lizzie, tell me—is it—"

"I can't *see!* The deck is in the way!"

Claire set her teeth. Whether it was Maggie or not, some poor soul needed rescuing. At least she could do that, and continue their voyage afterward. But she could not spend another second here in the navigation gondola, not knowing what the basket would bring up.

"Eight, take the helm. Remain stationary above that lighted vessel until I tell you to proceed. Lizzie, come with me."

They dashed astern, skirts flying. Michael Polgarth manned the winch, his shirt and waistcoat being beaten against his chest and arms by the wind coming in through the hatch.

A cry from below galvanized him into action, winding the rope up as fast as he could turn the crank. The basket came up into its housing and Claire and Lizzie leaped for it.

In the bottom lay a man in the navy-blue wool costume of a bathynaut, soaked to the skin and unconscious.

"She would not come!" Andrew shouted as they hauled the stranger out of the basket, grunting at his weight. "She insisted that he go up first. He needs medical attention immediately."

"Who?" Claire screamed. "Is it Maggie?"

"Yes! Lower me back down before that little vessel is swamped!"

Lizzie burst into tears and would have flung herself into the basket, too, but Claire hauled her back. "Lizzie, if your sister values this man's life at the cost of her own, we must do as she says. Help me carry him to one of the cabins."

He was too heavy for one to take his shoulders and the other his feet, but they could both grasp an armpit and drag him, his boots clunking on the teak decking. Fortunately they had not far to go, and once they got him laid out on a bunk, Claire sent Lizzie astern to watch the basket come up. Though her entire being strained to go with her, she concentrated on the task that Maggie had deemed more important even than her own safety. She stripped the man of his wet clothing, down to his cotton vest and underclothes. Then she chafed him with a wool blanket to dry his feet and attempt to bring some life back into his extremities, and covered him with two more.

There. For the moment, he was as comfortable as it was in her power to make him, and as soon as—oh God, let nothing go wrong—

"Lady!"

At Lizzie's shriek, Claire leaped to her feet and plunged down the corridor.

As Andrew climbed out of the empty basket, a slender figure, pale as a ghost, staggered into the hatchway.

Her hair tumbled around her shoulders, her wet petticoat clung to her legs, and she cradled her wrist in a makeshift sling of what appeared to be a piece of dirty canvas. She could barely stay upright—and Claire had never seen any sight more beautiful.

"I knew you would come," Maggie said through chattering teeth, and Claire swept her into her arms.

32

The Evening Standard
August 27, 1894

INVASION BY BOURBON PRETENDER FOILED

In a daring feat of sabotage, French freedom fighters
have changed the course of world history and saved two
allied nations from falling under the heel of the Bourbon
pretender to the French throne.

Readers will recall the terrifying events of five days ago,
when a tidal wave of unheard-of proportions struck this
nation's shores, causing untold damage to life and property. Scientists could not account for it—there had been

no movement of the earth, and no storms that might have stirred such a wave. The Ministry of Science informed the public this morning that rather than being caused by nature, the wave was the result of an explosion deep under the surface of the English Channel, when a war machine known as the Kingmaker detonated with all the power that was to have been unleashed upon England.

"We owe our lives and freedom to those brave men and women of the French resistance," said Sir Roger Blankenship, of the War Office, in a joint statement to the press today. "In an act of sabotage that will go down in history for its magnitude and sheer pluck, as yet unknown members of the French resistance were able to scuttle the undersea dirigible known as *Neptune's Fury*, which was transporting the Kingmaker to the beaches of Cornwall. The resulting explosion put an end to the pretender's hopes of becoming King of England."

Her Majesty's Royal Aeronautics Corps, having been warned of the invasion scant hours before the landing, engaged with the few troops that succeeded in coming ashore near Penzance. The engagement was short, the Texican mercenaries and French royalist troops being no match for the determination of doughty Englishmen to protect their shores.

A similar invasion of Jutland that attempted to bring war to two fronts has likewise been foiled by the might of the mobilized Prussian fleet. The Kingmaker succeeded in its landing there, but was no match for concerted bombing by Prussian airships, led by the renowned engineer Count Ferdinand von Zeppelin, who has recently been created Minister of Defense by the Emperor.

How the plot was foiled and by what means the Prussian Empire learned of the invasion will, we are quite sure, be revealed in future reports. In the meantime, investigations continue into the provenance of the captured undersea dirigibles, which may have connections with the Fifteen Colonies. Her Majesty is said to be gravely concerned.

♥~♥

"And these, little maid, are the chicks of Seraphina's daughter—you remember Seraphina, whom you met on your first visit to Gwynn Place?"

Three golden chicks nestled in Polgarth's—Grandfather's—cupped palms, and he released them gently into Maggie's lap. She sat cross-legged in the grass, the majestic Buff Orpingtons of the manor's flock strolling about her unafraid, regally ignoring Holly and Ivy, who were bathing in the dirt next to the gate with vigorous abandon.

"I do remember. In fact, I believe I formed the resolution then—at the age of ten—of coming to live here forever." She smiled up at him as he folded his old bones onto a gardening stool next to her, watching the chicks carefully as they ran out of her lap and hopped down to the lawn to forage under their mother's watchful eye.

"Your wrist does not pain you, Maggie?"

"Only a little, if I move too suddenly—and the plaster does not allow much of that. The doctor says I must endure it for two months. What a lucky thing I am not going to finishing school, where young ladies would never dream of indulging in activities that might result in a broken wrist."

"Not every young lady can prevent an invasion of her country by a foreign power." Lizzie strolled up, her hands full of rosebuds from the rambler over the gate. "Have you seen the newspapers this morning? They are full of more questions than answers, it seems to me."

"Let them question," Maggie said. "I shall say nothing of my part in it."

"We'll want to put off any return to Seacombe House, then. Apparently there are more aeronauts and military men and reporters down there than there are sand fleas." Lizzie sat on the grass, too, and began to weave a crown out of the flowers. Maggie had not been allowed out of her sight in six days, as though Lizzie thought she might be spirited away by some vengeful French royalist if she took her eyes off her cousin for a single moment.

The fact that all the French royalists the Royal Aeronautic Corps had been able to capture were cooling their heels in Cornish gaols until Her Majesty decided what to do with them did not seem to weigh much with Lizzie.

"I shall be glad to stay away in any case," Maggie said. She leaned against Grandfather's knee, and his hand came down to stroke her hair. "The Seacombes may be my mother's parents, but I much prefer my father's."

Maggie saw Lizzie's gaze fall to the locket on its ribbon about Maggie's neck. That night they had arrived, and immediately after the doctor had come to see to Serge Lavande and set the bones in her wrist, Maggie had set off for Grandfather's cottage. He had known nothing of the events that had transpired except for the tidal wave that had washed halfway up the cliffs and necessitated a rescue effort for some late-returning fishermen.

They spent until the wee hours of the morning talking, Grandfather reminiscing about her father's childhood, she telling him of her own childhood after the airship had gone down in the Thames, when she and Lizzie had learned to live on the streets of London. Maggie left out nothing—she was determined there would be no secrets standing between herself and her family ever again. In the morning, Grandfather had taken her into Kevern's old room and shown her the miniature of Catherine's sweet face, crowned with flowers and painted when she was only three years older than Maggie was now.

With his blessing, she had threaded the miniature onto a ribbon, silently vowing that her mother's likeness would always lie next to her heart.

"There." Lizzie's clever fingers had finished their work, and Maggie bent so that she could put the crown of roses upon her head. "In the language of flowers, I just gave you your 'reward of virtue.' You look a proper princess. If it were spring, we could call *you* Queen of the May."

Polgarth's face wavered as memory seemed to assail him. "Catherine was the loveliest girl," he said. "You favor her strongly, Maggie. And you have my boy's eyes and spirit. Both of them would have been as proud of you as I am. Somewhere, I believe that they are."

The Lady never failed to give praise where it was due, and Snouts acknowledged a job well done, but Maggie had never received approbation from anyone outside her own intimate circle. The sweetness of her grandfather's loving gaze nearly brought her to tears. Such a contrast to Demelza Seacombe's stony face! No wonder Catherine had run away to be with Kevern. Despite the brevity of their acquaintance, his family had welcomed her and loved her, and had likely filled her heart in just the way Maggie's was filling now.

"Oh, I mustn't forget," Polgarth said in an obvious attempt to regain control of his emotions. "A package come for us. Mariah has sent us both some sachets of lavender for the linen closet, and a packet of letters written by your parents."

"Letters?" Maggie sat up.

"Aye, old and scented with lilac. I took the liberty of glancing through them. Seems Catherine kept every letter she and Kevern sent to one another—and after her death, Mariah kept them safe, tied up in a ribbon. When we go back to the cottage for tea, I will give them to you."

"We could go now," Lizzie suggested. "Maggie will be anxious to read them, won't you, Mags?"

"I am," she said softly. The scent of the roses in her crown wafted around her. "But I am happy here, too, in the sun with you both. Mama and Papa have waited for me for seventeen years—they won't mind waiting a little while longer."

Across the lawn, Michael emerged from the kitchen door, Serge Lavande leaning upon his arm.

"Mariah's Henri will be glad of news of his nephew," Maggie said. "I'm so relieved we were able to get him to a doctor in time."

"He needs to be careful," Grandfather said, watching closely the progress of the pair across the grass. "Pneumonia could still set in, after the beating and chill his body took. But never fear, he is young and strong and we will care for him well here at Gwynn Place." His hand lay warm on Maggie's shoulder. "I confess I'm not sure I can let you go next week to your school in Bavaria. What if something happens to you?"

"Lady Claire will be with us, Grandfather. We are a flock."

He laughed, delighted. "Aye, you are, and a more loyal one I never saw. My young lady may not be married yet, but she is as good a mother as any and better than most."

Holly finished her bath and shook out her feathers, a cloud of dust surrounding her like a nimbus. Then, her neck stretched out in anxious anticipation, she ran across the lawn to climb into Maggie's lap, where she occupied as much space as she could in case her sister should have the same idea.

Stroking the little hen with loving fingers, Maggie exchanged a glance with Lizzie as Serge and Michael joined them to complete their family circle on the grass. Since Maggie was in safe hands with her grandfather, the Lady and Mr. Malvern had been prevailed upon to leave them for long enough to take a refreshing walk along the cliff path this afternoon.

A refreshing walk *alone*.

ร้อง

A LADY OF SPIRIT

"So Maggie still plans to return to Bavaria with you, despite her injuries?" Andrew strolled next to Claire, the tweed of his jacket warm from the sun and the pressure of her hand. The breeze off the ocean teased at the brim of her hat, making the blue and green ribbons that trimmed it bob and flutter. But despite the cool and playful breeze, the sun felt glorious.

Or perhaps it was the peace that filled her that was so glorious. Peace and relief and gratitude that nearly all the people she loved most in all the world were right here with her, safe as houses.

If only Alice and the occupants of Wilton Crescent could be with them, she would be perfectly happy. But then, Lady Flora would be aghast at such an invasion, so perhaps it was just as well that she believed there were only four in her party. Of Serge Lavande and the events of a week past, her mother and Sir Richard Jermyn had no knowledge whatsoever. Claire was quite happy that they should continue to believe that her abrupt departure in *Athena* had been upon receiving the report of Maggie's broken wrist, nothing more.

"She has not confided in me plans of a different nature," Claire replied in answer to Andrew's question. "In fact, she may be more set on it than ever—she comes by her taste for genetics quite honestly, you know, and she is anxious to add her own contributions to that field of study. I believe she wishes to honor Polgarth's work, which is quite unknown outside Cornwall."

"And the count's most recent letter? Will you tell her of that?"

Claire hesitated. "Of course."

"But?"

"Oh, Andrew. You know how she is. None but we know of her bravery, and she is quite content that it should remain that way. How will she feel to know the Emperor wishes to bestow the double eagle upon her?"

"I understand that is quite an honor."

"Yes. The highest the Prussian Empire can give a civilian. It comes with an annual stipend as well as the medal—and I am quite sure her Uncle Ferdinand had something to do with it."

"Whether he did or not, Maggie deserves it, and you must tell her before you land there."

"I know. Of course I will. We have no secrets from one another."

You must marry Mr. Malvern, Lady. He loves you.

No secrets, indeed. It was a sad state of affairs when one must be told of a gentleman's regard by one's ward. Of course, Claire had known practically from the beginning of Andrew's feelings toward her. She had shared those feelings. But her experience of men had tarnished her expectations a little.

Why did she attract men who seemed to appreciate a woman of strength and intellect, but when it came right down to it, still expected her to abandon her dreams and be content presiding over home and hearth once the ring was on her finger?

Not that these were dishonorable things. She possessed a home, and enjoyed the security and warmth of her own hearth very much, thank you. Why, then, did gentlemen not see the matter as she did—that managing a home and enjoying a career were not incompatible?

With a sigh, she bent her attention to the path in front of her, winding its way through yellow clumps of gorse in which tiny gold finches twittered and flitted.

"What is the matter, Claire? On such a lovely day, what can there be to sigh over?"

She smiled up at him. "Nothing, Andrew."

But his eyes did not hold an answering smile. "You have no secrets from the girls, but after all we have been through, you cannot share the honor of your confidence with me?"

Oh, dear. How was it possible to hurt a man without saying a single word?

"You are quite right," she said softly. If she could hurt him by her silence, surely speaking could not inflict any more damage. "I was just thinking of James Selwyn and Ian Hollys, and my abysmal luck with men."

She did not know what he had been expecting, but with his bark of startled laughter, she knew it had not been this.

"I don't know how you can call it abysmal," he said, chuckling. "If my information is correct, they both cared enough for you to propose."

"Yes, but the terms of the proposals were not acceptable."

"And what were they? I know James's terms, but it has been a mystery to me why you should have turned down Captain Hollys. He is handsome, honorable, cousin to Earl Dunsmuir, and a baronet in his own right. What more could a woman wish for?"

"I do not expect you to understand. If my mother knew of it, she certainly would not." She gave him a quick glance from under her hat brim. "On no account are you to tell her."

"You have my word. Help me to understand, Claire."

"Ian is all the things you say, and more. And he cared for me, as I did for him. But he wanted to leave the Corps and settle to the life of a landed gentleman. He wanted a chatelaine for Hollys Park and a mother for the future baronet."

"And you could not be that woman? I should think you uniquely fitted for the role."

"I could ... but when I asked him to wait until I had tasted the world as he had, until I had known for myself the accomplishments that men take for granted, he was not willing. And so ... we parted."

"And it was a final parting?"

"Oh, yes. Do you not read the society pages? He is as focused upon securing the next Lady Hollys as any debutante's mama could be. He will make quite the sensation when the Season begins."

"And the thought causes you no pangs of regret?"

His tone was light, but Claire wondered at the direction of these questions. Surely he was not ... but no. He could not be. He was her best friend, and after all these years, she could not expect ... could she?

You must marry Mr. Malvern, Lady. He loves you.

"No," she said. "He proposed a number of times, you know. If I had any regrets after the first time, he gave me the chance to change my mind. And yet, I did not."

"That is one thing I value about you, Claire. When you make up your mind to a thing, it is made. No shilly-shallying and dithering about."

"Only one thing?" she teased, thankful for a chance to lighten the mood.

Somehow they had stopped walking, and the gorse had closed around them to form a barrier against the breeze. She could even hear the bees buzzing in the yellow flowers, the sweet scent hanging heavy in the air.

"There are many things I value about you, but enumerating them would take all afternoon." He smiled, then patted her hand upon his arm. "How would you envision an ideal marriage, if you were given *carte blanche* to arrange it?"

He released her hands to give her a moment to think, and broke off a sprig of gorse to tuck it into his lapel.

"When I suggested to Ian that a laboratory at Hollys Park would be a fine idea, provided the children were taught not to knock over the Bunsen burners, he did not seem to agree," she said slowly. "When I suggested that while our journeys might be quite extensive—I testing airships for the Zeppelin Airship Works and he flying for the Dunsmuirs—he did not appreciate the thought of coming home to one another in the same way I did. So you see, even if a woman has ideas about the ideal marriage state, a man's ideas do not necessarily coincide."

"I have always thought that working among the scientists in other cities would be beneficial," he mused. "The Imperial Board of Scientific Exploration has invited me repeatedly, you know, to set up a laboratory in Munich, with weekly salons inviting the leading minds of our day to discuss our research."

Claire stared at him in astonishment. "They have not! Why did you never tell me?"

"It is difficult to catch up with you, Claire. In fact, these few days here at Gwynn Place are the longest I have seen you in once place in quite some time."

"I am in Munich for months at a time, Andrew."

"My point exactly."

What was he saying? What meaning was she to glean from these revelations, this warm gaze bent now upon her?

"Claire, I wrote you a letter once expressing the feelings of my heart, and you never answered it."

"You did not bring up the subject again."

"When a lady who makes up her mind as firmly as you do declines to reply, that sends a message a man can hardly ignore. Especially when she proceeds to entertain proposals from other men."

"The Kaiser's nephew does not count."

"But Ian Hollys does."

"Not any longer. Andrew—"

"Yes, dear?"

"Maggie wrote something to me in the letter she sent warning us of the invasion. She wrote it because she believed she was about to die, and that the truth must be spoken at all costs."

"And what was it?"

"She said, *You must marry Mr. Malvern, Lady. He loves you.*"

"Ah," Andrew said. "She has a fine sense of intuition, does our Maggie."

"And is it true?"

"Yes, very much so, on both counts. There has never been anyone else for me but you since the day I frightened you half to death in my helmet and breathing apparatus."

He took her hands in his—her cold hands. She trembled—she, who had faced down death in several awful incarnations with hardly time for a quiver.

"So here are my terms. While you are employed by the Zeppelin Airship Works, I will come to Bavaria and open that laboratory and salon. In our home, the greatest minds of the age will be welcome. Conversation will flow as freely as our excellent wine, and new ideas will be as welcome as our friends and family. Should there be children, they will grow up among the finest people I know—for among young men like Tigg and Snouts and Lewis, and young women like Maggie and Lizzie, how could any child help but grow up strong and intelligent and brave? And with a mother like you, my darling, those children may very well change the world—as you have already done."

Claire could not speak. Her throat had closed and her eyes welled up with tears that spilled over and trickled down her cheeks.

"I am not worthy of you, Claire. But if you will give me your heart, I will do everything in my power to make you happy."

She swallowed, her lips trembling. "It is I who am unworthy of you," she whispered. "You have been the truest friend a woman could ask for. You have stood by me when I have been afraid, comforted me when I was hurt, and loved me when—" She choked. "When I thought I loved another. But all the time ... it was not the terms of the proposals, was it?" At last she saw the truth, and from the quiet joy in his gaze, so did he. "It was simply that the wrong man was making them."

"And now?" Andrew kissed her knuckles.

And now ... the right man had spoken so eloquently that she could practically see the future forming before her eyes. A wonderful future. A future that the two of them would create for each other, and for the people they loved.

"And now I think you must kiss me again. For there has been no other man for me since the moment of our first one."

He gazed at her over their clasped hands. "Does this mean that we are engaged?"

"I think it had better," Claire said softly. "If we go back to the house and the Mopsies learn we ignored Maggie's dying wish, we will be in dreadful trouble."

"Nothing we haven't faced before." Smiling, Andrew lowered his head and kissed her.

Soundly.

Very soundly indeed.

Epilogue

Dear Claire,

It has been quite a while since I've written, but I have all your and the Mopsies' letters and think of you often, so I hope that counts for something. Most of the time we're outside of the pigeons' range, which is why my correspondence has been spotty in the last year or so.

I'm in a bit of a tight spot and wonder if I could ask for your help. See, I had a couple of jobs running cargo (diamonds, furs, and such) into the Duchy of Venice for the Dunsmuirs and it seems some folks took exception to it. I've applied to them for help but they are back at the Firstwater Mine and help could be a long time coming.

Count von Zeppelin is giving me sanctuary for the moment, but I can't see it lasting long. I figure if we put our heads together we can come up with a plan. I hope so. I don't much hanker to end my days in one of them underwater torture chambers they got.

Please advise.

Your friend,
Alice Chalmers

P.S. Please give my regards to Mr. Malvern. His recent paper on powering locomotives using sun cells was inspired. Peony Churchill says it caused quite a sensation in the Royal Kingdom of Spain and the Californias, being as trains powered by something God created is right up their alley.

P.P.S. Jake is well and sends his regards. He says he's had a price on his head before, so it don't much bother him, but this is a new one on me. Please write soonest.

A.C.

THE END

Neptune's Maid
A Cornish Steampunk Sea Shanty

Sailors, will you gather round
And hear my own sad tale-o
Of men who hear the siren's call
O'er steam and sea and sail-o.
O'er steam and sea and sail-o.

There was a young man, braw and hale
And to the Lord so dear-o
With a voice so strong and true
The birds would come to hear-o.
The birds would come to hear-o.

One day she heard him, Neptune's maid,
As waves she rode to land-o
She changed her shape and came ashore
And met him on the strand-o.
And met him on the strand-o.

He forgot he trothéd was
To church and lady fair-o
He took the mermaid to his wife
With seashells in her hair-o.
With seashells in her hair-o.

O where is her lover dear?
O where now is he-o?
The mermaid's ta'en him by the hand
And led him out to sea-o.
And led him out to sea-o.

Come the nights of stormy gales
When wives fear for their kin-o
Some say they hear him singing still
Beneath the waves and wind-o.
Beneath the waves and wind-o.

Sailors, will you gather round
And hear my own sad tale-o
Of men who hear the siren's call
O'er steam and sea and sail-o.
O'er steam and sea and sail-o.

A NOTE FROM SHELLEY

Dear reader,

I hope you enjoy reading the adventures of Lady Claire and the gang in the Magnificent Devices world as much as I enjoy writing them. It is your support and enthusiasm that is like the steam in an airship's boiler, keeping the entire enterprise afloat and ready for the next adventure.

You might leave a review on your favorite retailer's site to tell others about the books. And you can find the electronic editions of the entire series online, as well as audiobooks. I'll see you over at www.shelleyadina.com, where you can sign up for my newsletter and be the first to know of new releases and special promotions.

And now, I hope you'll enjoy a live performance of "Neptune's Maid" by JR Shanty Co., on YouTube:

http://www.youtube.com/watch?v=1jfWglM32_E

About the Author

The official version
RITA Award® winning author and Christy finalist Shelley Adina wrote her first novel when she was 13. It was rejected by the literary publisher to whom she sent it, but he did say she knew how to tell a story. That was enough to keep her going through the rest of her adolescence, a career, a move to another country, a B.A. in Literature, an M.F.A. in Writing Popular Fiction, and countless manuscript pages.

Shelley is a world traveler who loves to imagine what might have been. Between books, she loves playing the piano and Celtic harp, making period costumes, and spoiling her flock of rescued chickens.

The unofficial version
I like Edwardian cutwork blouses and velvet and old quilts. I like bustle drapery and waltzes and new sheet music and the OED. I like steam billowing out from the wheels of a locomotive and autumn colors and chickens. I like flower crowns and little beaded purses and jeweled hatpins. Small birds delight me and Roman ruins awe me. I like old books and comic books and new technology ... and new books and shelves and old technology.

A LADY OF SPIRIT

I'm feminine and literary and practical, but if there's a beach, I'm going to comb it. I listen to shells and talk to hens and ignore the phone. I believe in thank-you notes and kindness, in commas and friendship, and in dreaming big dreams. You write your own life. Go on. Pick up a pen.

AVAILABLE NOW

The Magnificent Devices series:
Lady of Devices
Her Own Devices
Magnificent Devices
Brilliant Devices
A Lady of Resources
A Lady of Spirit

Caught You Looking (contemporary romance, Moonshell Bay #1)
Immortal Faith (paranormal YA)
Peep, the Hundred-Decibel Hummer (early reader)

To learn about my Amish women's fiction written as Adina Senft, visit www.adinasenft.com.
The Wounded Heart
The Hidden Life
The Tempted Soul
And in 2014, the Healing Grace series:
Herb of Grace
Keys of Heaven
Balm of Gilead

COMING SOON

A Lady of Integrity, Magnificent Devices #7
A Gentleman of Means, Magnificent Devices #8
Emily, the Easter Chick (early reader)
Caught You Listening, Moonshell Bay #2
Caught You Hiding, Moonshell Bay #3
Everlasting Chains, Immortal Faith #2
Twice Dead, Immortal Faith #3

CPSIA information can be obtained at www.ICGtesting.com
Printed in the USA
LVOW08s1630060516

487046LV00007B/516/P